Magical Misfire

Book I of
The Moonstone Chronicles

Carol R. Ward

Magical Misfire
ISBN 978-1-937477-31-8
Magical Misfire Copyright © 2013 Carol R. Ward
Published by Brazen Snake Books
All rights reserved.

Cover art by Jamie DeBree

Dedication

The first twelve chapters are for R.F. Cairns, English teacher extraordinaire, in keeping with a promise I once made. The rest is for Karen Bridgman, who was there when this story was conceived.

Acknowledgments

A special thank you to Jamie DeBree for her continued support and encouragement, and for pulling my fat out of the fire when it came to getting my thee's and thou's straight. Thank you as well to Dolly Garland for her insightful comments that were indispensable during the editing process.

Prologue

The room had a dark and cold feel to it, despite the fire blazing in the stone fireplace. A tray of food sat untouched on a small wooden table, beside which lay several empty wine bottles. Paranithel paused just inside the doorway.

"It would please Anakaron greatly to see you in your present state, Kiranthus."

There was no response from the man who sat in the enormous wing chair facing the fire. Paranithel heaved a sigh and then motioned to the servants waiting in the doorway.

Lancer entered carrying a cradle, which he placed close enough to the fire for warmth but far enough away that it was safe from stray sparks. He was followed by the housekeeper, who was carrying a baby. With a disapproving look at Paranithel, she placed the baby in the cradle. Paranithel gestured and the servants followed him out of the room.

* * * * *

For a long while the only sound was the snap and crackle of the fire. Soon, a faint snuffling was heard from the cradle, building into a strong, wailing cry.

As the sound crept into his awareness, Kiranthus was at first merely annoyed but then anger began to build. Why did someone not come and remove the child? Stubbornly, he ignored it.

When a note of real distress crept into the baby's cries he could stand it no longer.

"Paranithel, send for the child's nursemaid. Paran!" Kiranthus pushed himself up out of his chair and strode to the door. "Paran? Lancer? Someone come and see to this child!"

There was no answer. Kiranthus stalked over to the cradle and stared down at the baby. What was the matter with it? There was no way of telling without picking it up and his fists clenched to stop himself for reaching out.

He paced back to the door, but the corridor was empty. The wailing from the cradle continued. Kiranthus went back to the cradle and finally reached down and picked the baby up.

His hold was awkward, his hands trembled. As he nestled the baby snugly in the crook of his arm its cries dwindled. It looked up at him and the crying ceased.

Kiranthus was mesmerized. "You have her eyes," he whispered.

* * * * *

When Paranithel looked in much later, he was relieved to see Kiranthus asleep in the chair, the baby tucked safely in his arms. He hated to disturb them, but already too much time had passed.

"Kiran," he said gently. "You must wake and make plans."

Kiranthus stirred and looked up. "Plans?"

"Do you really believe Anakaron will rest with only Farena's death?"

A shadow of grief touched Kiranthus' face. "Anakaron must be stopped."

"He must first be found. Meanwhile, there is the babe to be considered."

Kiranthus looked down at the sleeping baby. "Without Farena . . . Paran, what am I to do?"

"She must go to a safe haven."

"Is there such a place?"

"I believe I have found one. Come with me."

Kiranthus laid the sleeping baby back in the cradle and followed as Paranithel led the way down into the lower levels of the Keep. With a wave of his hand and a muttered incantation, Paran lowered the wards set on the heavy oak door of his workroom, raising the wards again as they passed through.

There was a scrying pool set in the center of the room, a circular hollow lined with black tile. It was bordered by polished crystalline stones that reflected back the light from the flickering torches ensconced on the walls.

They knelt at its edge. Paranithel chanted under his breath and passed his hands over the water. It stirred, it boiled, and when the surface settled again they both leaned forward to take a better look at the image that appeared.

The scene in the pool had little colour to it. Tall grey buildings lined impossibly straight roads made of some kind of black substance. People hurried along the sides of these roads while strange metal vehicles, with no obvious means of propulsion, raced to unknown destinations.

"It is a world of little magic," Paranithel said. "There is no reason for Anakaron to seek it out."

They watched in silence for several minutes as Paranithel caused the image to pan to a less busy section of the city.

"It seems a most cold and inhospitable place," Kiranthus said finally.

"There is much good to be found as well. There, that woman," Paranithel pointed to a woman carrying what seemed to be foodstuffs, judging by the blunt end of a narrow loaf of bread and the green leafy top of some vegetable sticking up from her bag. "She has suffered the loss of both husband and child. She would be an ideal foster-mother."

"I must think on this," Kiranthus said, standing upright.

"There is no time!" Paranithel said fiercely. "You have wallowed in your grief for weeks. Farenalyssia may have been your wife, but she was my daughter. I will not let Anakaron take her child as well!"

Kiranthus sagged against the wall, "What must I do?"

"Leave. Tonight, if possible. It will distract Anakaron long enough for me to take the child to safety."

"But. . ."

"Head for the port and take the first ship you find. It doesn't matter where it's headed. Anakaron will not be able to resist following. Once you're at sea you'll be almost impossible to track. He was never as skilled at water magic as he believed himself to be."

"And what of you and my daughter?"

"I will take her to this other world. Anakaron know a world-walking spell has been activated, but when he sees only my power signature and not yours he will think no more than I'm an old man in fear of his life, not worth retrieving."

He griped the younger man's shoulder. "Son of my heart, I understand your pain, but it is the only way. When I return I will journey to the southern continent. There are many ways for a man to become lost there. Who knows, perhaps I may even open a school for those southerners with the Gift."

"Gift," Kiranthus said bitterly. "It is no gift when it brings such destruction."

"When you are able, journey southward to me. Together we will find a way to defeat Anakaron and bring your daughter home."

Kiranthus removed a thin gold chain from around his neck. At its end dangled a milky white disk, carved with a magical symbol of good fortune.

"This was Farena's first gift to me," he said. "I leave it in your keeping for our child."

Paranithel took it from him. There were tears in his eyes as he watched Kiranthus turn and leave.

Chapter One

J essica whimpered in her sleep, a helpless sound of fear. The sheets and blankets twisted beneath her hands as she sought escape. There was noise and death all around her. The creatures attacked without warning and without mercy. There was a glimpse of furred bodies, the flash of knives and fangs, and then screaming started.

Twisting, turning corridors sped past her. There was sunlight on her face, the sound of a fountain. Suddenly, there was darkness again, a long, terrifying blackness. A light – a milky white disk suspended by a chain. She reached for it. Just as it was within her grasp she felt an awful wrenching sensation as though she was being pulled away.

Jessica sat bolt upright in her bed, gasping for breath, one hand still raised as though reaching for the pendant. Her heart was hammering wildly. She stared without recognition at the darkened room, the shadows on the walls, the ghostly shapes of furniture.

Her breathing slowed, her heart slowed. A light in the hallway snapped on, making her jump.

"Are you okay, Jess?"

She locked eyes with the young woman in the doorway. Dimly her brain registered the presence as "Ellen"– long time friend and roommate. Jessica shivered and took a deep breath, letting it out slowly.

"I heard you crying out in your sleep." Ellen came over and sat down on the bed. "Are you okay?"

"God, Ellen. It was so real, like I was really there." Jessica reached over and turned on her bedside light. The soft amber glow chased the last of the shadows away.

"Do you want to talk about it?"

"No, it was That Dream again. It's just . . . it was just really bad this time, that's all."

Ellen frowned. "You haven't had it in so long, I thought you were over it."

"Me too." Jessica pulled her knees to her chest and sat with her arms wrapped around them.

"Look at you," Ellen said gently. "You're shaking like a leaf. Can I get you a glass of water or something?"

"No thanks. El. I think I'll be okay now. You go back to bed."

"Jess . . ." Ellen bit her lip and then forged bravely ahead. "Don't you think it's time you saw someone about this?"

"Like who, a shrink? I don't think so."

"But there's got to be some sort of subconscious reason for it," Ellen persisted. "This isn't normal."

"Lots of people have nightmares. Haven't you ever had one?"

Ellen shook her head, "Not the same one over and over."

"Go back to bed," Jessica told her. She gave a half-hearted shove with her foot. "I'm going to get a cup of tea."

"Jessica Jane O'Conner, you're the most stubborn person I know." Shaking her head, Ellen got up from the bed.

Jessica grinned at her, "And you're too easy going. That's why we make such good friends."

Ellen snorted and went back to her own room.

Jessica dug under the bed for her slippers and then padded out to the tiny kitchen to make tea. She chose chamomile from the selection of jars lining the counter, adding just a touch of sugar to the oversized ceramic mug. With a sigh she sat down at the table and wrapped her hands around the mug.

The nightmare started just after she turned three years old. In the beginning it had been nothing more than a formless fear that kept waking her up. She would crawl into bed with her mother and the fear would go away.

She had the dream when she was five, and again

when she was seven, just after her mother died. Her aunt and uncle believed she was just being difficult and took away her nightlight as a punishment.

The nightmare didn't return again until she was twelve, but by this time she knew enough to keep it to herself. As with the other times, she had it every night for a couple of weeks and then it just disappeared on its own.

Throughout her teenage years the nightmare plagued her off and on, always for two weeks and then it would disappear for months at a time. She hadn't had it since she left her aunt and uncle's house, six years ago.

Jessica seldom talked about it, partly because of her aunt and uncle's reaction and partly because talking about the dream made it seem too real. Ellen had known about it since high school, but only because Jessica had been at Ellen's for a sleepover once when the nightmare struck. Ellen nagged her until she told her everything.

What Jessica hadn't told Ellen was that the nightmare was getting progressively more vivid. The creatures were taking on definite form, as were the corridors and the garden, and the feelings of fear and loss were much stronger.

Despite the remnants of the nightmare still plaguing her, Jessica finished her tea and went back to bed to read until she fell asleep - a restful, dreamless sleep that she woke from when Ellen's alarm clock went off. Five minutes later her own sounded, an arrangement they'd devised to keep them from going back to sleep, especially useful for mornings following a late night.

"Rise and shine, Ellen," Jessica called.

There was a muffled reply from Ellen's room.

Jessica stretched and surveyed her wardrobe.

"Hey, Ellen," she called.

"What?" Slightly less muffled, but definitely grumpy.

"Can I borrow your black belt?"

"Only if I can borrow your jade earrings."

"Deal."

"Woven, leather, metal or plastic?" Ellen asked.

"It's Wednesday," replied Jessica, delivering the earrings, "so I'd better go with woven."

"What's Wednesday got to do with it?" Ellen yawned hugely and handed over a black belt made of woven hemp.

"Our stock of vases is delivered on Wednesdays. Mr. Pressman always likes to supervise the unloading to make sure the supplier isn't trying to rip us off." Mr. Pressman was the owner of the florist shop Jessica worked in.

"I still don't get it."

"I like to dress a little earthier when Mr. P. is around, that's all," said Jessica. She headed down the hall to the kitchen.

"If your wardrobe were any earthier it would be

covered in dirt," came the muttered reply.

"I heard that!" Jessica said, but with a grin on her face.

She put a pot of coffee on and by the time she was showered and dressed it was ready. Pouring herself a cup she sat down at the tiny table tucked under the kitchen window. Absently, she began checking the plants that choked the window sill to see if they needed watering.

Plants were one of the few interests in life Jessica stuck with. Aunt Sandra, who raised her after her mother died, hated plants. They were dirty and attracted bugs, and Sandra was allergic to most of them. But the neighborhood they lived in held plenty of gardening enthusiasts who welcomed the young Jessica's questions and help.

She became interested in herbs in high school when a substitute history teacher gave a lecture on how the pioneers coped with illness. The idea of using bark tea and poultices fascinated Jessica. She acquired a book on plants and their uses that same day and shortly afterward started her first window sill herb garden, hidden behind the blind on her bedroom window.

Eventually she started a notebook to keep track of loose bits of information she gained from research and from talking to some of the residents of the nursing home she volunteered at after school. The first thing she bought when she moved away from her aunt and uncle was a plant. It was a spindly Boston fern, but she nursed it back to health and now it held the place of honour, a brass plant stand, in the living room.

Jessica glanced at her watch. It was eight o'clock, time to go. She finished her coffee just as there was a knock at the door to the apartment.

Whoever was at the door was persistent, knocking twice more before she got there and got the three locks undone.

"Howard!"

Surprise warred with admiration at his early morning appearance. Admiration won out. His dark, shoulder length hair was tied back in a tail with one elegant wave falling in front of his blue eyes. He wore a white button-down shirt, tucked into black jeans. Though not heavily muscled, Howard still managed to exude an aura of wiry strength.

"Morning Jess. I heard the shower going and figured you must be up." He handed her an envelope. "This was delivered for you yesterday and I promised I'd pass it along."

"Thanks, Howard. You want some coffee?"

"No thanks," he was already starting down the stairs. "I'm just on my way out."

Jessica stared after him. On his way out? This, from the man who once explained in great detail why mornings should be prohibited by law?

"Was that the door I heard?" Ellen asked from

behind her.

"Howard dropped this off for me," Jessica replied, waving the envelope at her.

"Howard from upstairs Howard?" Ellen asked. "What's he doing up this early?"

"I don't know," Jessica replied absently. "He said he was on his way out."

"Darn! Remind me to leave a note on his door, could you please? The faucet in the bathroom needs to be fixed."

Jessica sat down, still looking at the courier envelope. "I wonder what this could be?"

"Well, open it!"

She glanced at her watch. "No time, we've got to go."

There was the usual mad rush for coats, shoes and purses and a promise to meet at the mall for lunch. The mystery of the envelope would just have to wait.

Chapter Two

❝ You know what I'd like for my birthday this year?"

Ellen tore her gaze away from the Cultures menu board and glanced at her friend.

"An adventure," Jessica continued before Ellen could answer.

"A what?"

"An adventure."

They paid for their salads and carried their trays to their favourite table under a pair anemic-looking trees under the skylight in the centre of the food court.

"Look at my life," Jessica continued once they were sitting down. "It's like tofu -no flavour. All I want is a little excitement, one tiny adventure. That's not too much to ask for, is it?"

Ellen eyed her friend doubtfully. In her opinion adventure was the last thing Jessica needed. A sense of direction, some purpose in life, would be a better idea. Five jobs in as many years, and each one Jessica's true calling.

"I'd watch it if I were you," she said at last. "You know the old saying, be careful what you wish for, you might get it."

"That's the whole idea," Jessica said, waving a forkful of bean sprouts for emphasis. "I'm tired of hum drum existence. Boring job, boring life."

"I thought you liked working for the florist?"

"I do like it," Jessica sighed. "It's just. . .it's just not enough, you know what I mean?"

Ellen nodded. "Maybe," she suggested, "what you really need is a new man in your life."

"I swear, Ellen, you think the world's problems could be solved by a new outfit or a new man!"

"And what's wrong with that?"

"I can't afford your kind of clothes and I already have a man - Howard."

Ellen choked on a piece of lettuce. "Are you kidding? Howard is, is . . ."

"Sweet?" Jessica suggested. "Kind?"

"He's gay!"

"There is that," Jessica agreed with a giggle. "But you've got to admit he is kind of cute."

"Very cute," Ellen agreed. "And very weird."

"You're being hard on poor Howie," Jessica said,

spearing a carrot curl with her fork.

"The guy thinks he's the next Merlin!"

"Well it was certainly magical the way he fixes our plumbing."

"He's our landlord, he's supposed to do things like that." Ellen directed a hard stare at her friend. "Don't try and make me believe you've been harbouring a secret passion for Howard all these years, 'cause I don't buy it. You're just trying to distract me."

Jessica grinned, unrepentant. "Nice try, wasn't it?"

"Humph!"

"We've gotten off our original topic - my birthday." She snapped a breadstick in two and offered Ellen half.

Ellen shook her head. "What about a trip?"

"I don't have enough vacation time for a trip to anywhere really interesting."

"How about a weekend? You could go for one of those mystery weekends. You know, dinner and a murder."

"I don't know El . . ."

"We'll work on it," Ellen promised. "Now, I gotta dash. Lunch was over about ten minutes ago for me."

"Don't forget to pick up your dry cleaning," Jessica reminded her.

"Right. And I'll make a list of ideas for celebrating your birthday," Ellen called back over her shoulder. "If you change your mind about a new outfit come to the store and use my discount."

* * * * *

Jessica watched as Ellen wove her way skilfully through the crowd. Shimmied was more like it. Ellen was without a doubt the trendiest thing in the mall and she worked damned hard to keep it that way. She claimed it was good advertising for the boutique she worked in.

Must be something to that, Jessica thought ruefully. Ellen was promoted to assistant manager after only one month at the new store. She was a far cry from the badly dressed, nervous fourteen year old she'd been when they first met in high school.

Howard said they were a study in contrasts and Jessica guessed he was right. Ellen was small and exotic with blue black hair that hung straight to her hips while was Jessica taller, more rounded with rich coppery hair that fell past her shoulders in natural waves. Ellen was buoyant and energetic; Jessica was quiet and thoughtful.

They'd met their first day of high school. The kids tended to be cliquish and the fact that Ellen was so shy didn't help. They shared several classes and lunch that first day and had been best friends ever since.

When Jessica broached the idea of sharing an apartment, Ellen jumped at the chance. Sharing living space with parents, grandparents and five brothers left Ellen longing for her own place.

For Jessica it meant being able to move out of the depressing boarding house she'd moved into after her aunt and uncle were "born again" and moved to a religious colony. Things had become increasingly strained at home during her last year of high school. It had been a relief to be out on her own.

She sighed as she looked at her watch. Time for her to go as well. Just as well, serious thinking could be habit forming.

* * * * *

Ellen arrived home from work and smiled at the sound of loud Celtic music coming from the apartment. A Celtic band meant a gourmet dinner. Ellen blessed the memory of David, the boyfriend of Jessica's who wanted to be a chef. Jessica spent hours with him in the kitchen, helping him study for his exams. Who said nothing good ever came from a bad relationship?

She followed a tantalizing smell into the tiny kitchen.

"I swear you're psychic when it comes to food," Jessica told her. "I just finished draining the noodles to go with the beef stroganoff."

Ellen laughed. "Comes from having five older brothers who eat like horses. You've got to be fast in my family, or starve."

"I've always wondered how you stayed so

skinny."

Jessica dished up supper with a flourish. They ate slowly, savouring an all too rare home cooked meal. Mostly they just took turns buying take-out. Ellen, more often than not, just brought food from her family's diner.

"So, what was in that mysterious envelope Howard gave you this morning?" Ellen asked. She almost laughed at the chagrined look on Jessica's face.

"You know, I forgot all about it. I did notice it was from Aunt Sandra though."

"That old tight wad sent you something through the courier? Maybe it's a birthday cheque," Ellen suggested. "I mean, why else would she use a courier?"

Jessica snorted. "I doubt it, El. Aunt Sandra's always been suspicious of the postal system. She claims they have secret ways of snooping through private mail."

"That's nuts!"

"Tell me about it."

They left their dishes to soak in the sink and went into the living room. Jessica pulled the battered envelope out of her bag and broke the seal.

"Well?" Ellen demanded impatiently.

"They're relocating to Arizona. She's shipping me a box of old stuff that belonged to my mother."

"Jessica, that's great!" Ellen was genuinely happy for her friend. From what she could gather, Jessica knew very little about her parents. Maybe this would help fill in the gaps.

"What's the matter?" she asked as Jessica continued to frown at the envelope.

"I can't help feeling there's something strange about this. Why now, when for so many years she's told me she didn't save anything of my mother's?"

"I don't know, Jess. Maybe her conscience is finally kicking in."

"Somehow I doubt that very much."

"Well, you'll just have to figure it out when the box arrives."

* * * * *

Two days later the bus station called to tell Jessica the box had arrived and she needed to pick it up within seven days. Since she and Ellen both had the morning off there was no putting it off. While Ellen went grocery shopping, Jessica went to the bus depot. She was still having mixed feelings when she picked the box up and brought it home.

The box was just large enough to be awkward, and it was heavy. She left it on the floor of the living room and went into the kitchen for a diet soda.

"That's funny," she said, frowning at the table. "I don't remember leaving a plant there." A purple African violet in full bloom rested dead center on the vinyl tablecloth. "I must be more tired than I thought. Good thing this is Friday."

She took her soda into the living room, but before she could settle in her favorite chair there was a clatter on the stairs and the door burst open.

"Howard, didn't we have a discussion about barging in without knocking?"

When she first moved here Howard had the bad habit of dropping in whenever he felt like it. Sometimes his presence was welcome, sometimes it was not. After Ellen moved in she finally took him aside and explained that although he may be a good friend, as well as landlord, he couldn't just come in without being invited first. Although in this case it was her fault for leaving the door unlocked.

"Jessica, did you see it? Is it here?" Howard was flushed with excitement. He stared wildly around the room. "I don't see it, where is it?"

"Howard," said Jessica patiently, "It'd help if you told me what you were talking about."

"Have you seen a . . . uh . . . an African violet?"

"You mean the one in the kitchen? Did you leave it there?"

"Kitchen!" Howard darted out of the room and reappeared carrying the violet. "I did it, I really did it!"

"Howard, look," Jessica led him over to the couch and pushed him down. She'd never seen him so worked up before. "Now, take a deep breath and relax. You're going to make yourself sick."

"But—"

"Not a word," Jessica said sternly. "Not until you

calm down."

Howard opened his mouth and shut it again. He took several deep breaths, trying to pull himself together.

There was a loud thump from outside the door.

"Hey, you wanna lend a hand with these groceries?"

Jessica hurried to help Ellen.

"I picked up the mail too," Ellen said. "Oh, hi Howard. How's it going?"

"I—I—it—"

"Breathe, Howard," Jessica told him. She hurried Ellen into the kitchen.

"What's with Howard?" Ellen whispered.

"I don't know, I think he's having some sort of breakdown."

"It's all that weird magic stuff he's always messing around in. Sometimes he really gives me the creeps."

"Howard's completely harmless."

"Well, he's your friend, you deal with him," Ellen told her. "I'll put away the goodies."

"Thanks a lot," Jessica made a face at her and took a soda out to Howard.

"Jessica, you've got to listen to me," said Howard a little desperately.

"Okay, Howard. Take it easy," Jessica sat down beside him on the couch. "Start from the beginning and tell me all about it."

"You know I've always had a thing for magic," he

began. He looked at her anxiously and was reassured when she nodded.

"You're the only one that's ever taken me seriously, even if you don't really believe in magic." He held up a hand as she opened her mouth. "It's okay, I know how farfetched some of my ideas sound, but everything's changed now!"

He leaned forward and stared at her earnestly. "I did it, Jess. I cast a real magical spell!"

"Howard—"

"The violet, don't you see?"

"Howard—"

"You've got to believe me, Jess. I cast a spell and sent the violet to your coffee table."

"Howard, the violet was in the kitchen."

"So my aim is a little off, but the spell worked!"

"I'm sure you believe it worked," said Jessica carefully.

"It did work! Just watch, I'll do it again."

Jessica inched away from Howard as he set the violet on the coffee table in front of them. He waggled his fingers over top of the plant, chanting in a sing song voice. After several minutes, he stopped.

"Nothing's happening, Howard."

"I know nothing's happening! I just don't know why. I'm sure I'm doing everything right." He jumped up and walked around the living room, nose in the air like a dog trying to catch a scent.

"I can't sense any interference, but that doesn't

mean anything," he muttered.

"Maybe you just need some rest," Jessica suggested, following him around the room. She took him
gently by the arm and steered him towards the door.
"You've been working awfully hard lately, Howard.
You've been up late every night this week - I've heard
you pacing above me. Maybe you've just depleted
your magical energies."

"You might be right," Howard said. "As soon as
I've re-energized myself I'll come back and show you.
You won't believe your eyes."

"I'm sure I won't," Jessica said as she closed the
door behind him.

"Honestly, Jess. I don't know why you encourage
him," said Ellen.

"Howard's pretty harmless, Ellen. Even when we
were kids he was obsessed with magic - the Merlin
kind, not the Houdini kind."

"Still. . ." Ellen shook her head. "Just be careful,
that's all."

Ellen just didn't understand. Jessica had grown up
with Howard. They'd played together, built forts together, shared secrets - he'd been a combination of
brother and best friend. They'd both been devastated
when Jessica's aunt and uncle moved her to a different part of the city, right before she started high
school.

Four years ago Jessica answered a "For Rent" ad
and was elated to find that Howard owned the house,

an inheritance from his mother. Like most of the old, Victorian style houses in the neighborhood, each floor was converted into a separate apartment. Howard lived on the top floor, Ellen and Jessica on the second floor, and a group of four art students shared the ground floor.

"I'm ready to go," Ellen announced. "Do you need a ride?"

Jessica shook her head. "It's too nice out and I've got just enough time to walk if I leave right now."

"What about your box?"

It lay forgotten on the floor. "Well, it's waited who knows how many years. I guess it'll just have to wait a little longer."

"You're the most frustrating person I know! I would have torn into it right there in the bus station."

Jessica shrugged, "I'm not so sure I want to know what's in it."

"Maybe it's furs, jewels, savings bonds . . ."

"With my luck it'll be full of bills and old income tax returns."

"Don't forget, we're going out tonight after work," Ellen reminded her, doing one last check in the mirror before leaving.

"I did promise, didn't I?" Jessica sighed.

"You'll have fun. Trust me."

To Jessica, that almost sounded like a threat.

Chapter Three

J essica stared at herself in the full length mirror and made another vain attempt at stretching the bottom of her dress downwards. Trust me, Ellen had said. Granted emerald green was her colour, but the dress was altogether too tight, too short and much too expensive.

"You want me to send the Navy in after you?" Ellen called.

Jessica grimaced one last time into the mirror and opened the bathroom door. "That won't be necessary."

"You look great," Ellen pronounced. "Should I wear boots or shoes with this outfit?"

Jessica eyed her critically. Ellen was wearing a black leather mini skirt and a gauzy white silk blouse with a black leather vest over top to cover all the strategic places.

"I have a feeling I'm going to regret this," Jessica said.

"Come on," Ellen took her arm and pulled her towards the door. "I told Ben we'd meet him at Barney's at eight."

Ellen went on ahead as Jessica locked the door behind them. Unused the height of the heels she'd been loaned, Jessica was a little more careful going down the stairs and Ellen was already waiting in the car by the time she reached the porch.

"Let me guess," Jessica said, as Ellen wove her Honda Civic through the Friday night traffic. "Ben just happens to have a friend that's in town for the weekend and wouldn't have time for you at all unless you could come up with a friend for his friend."

"It's a cousin, actually," Ellen admitted. "And it's not as if Ben didn't want to see me, he just has a strong sense of family obligation."

"For this I went into debt over a new dress?"

"The dress wasn't for Ben's cousin, it was for you. I thought having a few heads turn your way might cheer you up."

"Who says I need cheering up?"

"I do. You've been down in the dumps for weeks now. And the message from Sandra didn't help any."

"I know," Jessica sighed. "I guess some old memories are just harder to shake than others. I'll open the box tomorrow."

Ellen glanced at Jessica. "Hey, no long faces.

We're the party girls tonight and we're going to have fun even if it kills us."

"It just might," Jessica muttered.

* * * * *

This was, Jessica decided later, just what she needed. Either that or the five Barney Specials she'd had.

Ben's cousin, Kevin, was good looking in a book-ish sort of way and he was a great dancer, which made up for the fact that he spent most of the night talking about his girlfriend.

There was a country trio playing on the little stage to one side of the dance floor. Not Jessica's favorite type of music, but it seemed to fit her mood tonight.

She watched Ellen and Ben dancing a slow dance and wondered if things were getting serious. Ellen changed boyfriends as often as she changed her taste in clothes, but Ben had been around for weeks now.

"Well, well, well. If it isn't Jessica O'Connell."

Jessica stiffened at the sound of the voice. She thought she'd gotten rid of Daniel Paxson months ago.

They'd met at the florist shop when he'd come to do some minor repair work. The big attraction for her had been his movie star good looks, but it became obvious, all too soon, that his looks were all he had going for him. After a couple of dates, Jessica told him she didn't think it was going to work, they were too different. She thought she'd let him down easy, but he had other ideas.

He began showing up at her place after work, usually drunk. He phoned at all hours until she and Ellen had their phone number changed, twice. It wasn't until she threatened him with a restraining order that he finally left her alone.

"You're drunk, Daniel."

"Yeah? Well I wanna know what you're doing here with pencil neck, when you coulda been with me."

Jessica swiveled around to face him. "I think you'd better leave before you cause a scene."

"Oh, you do, do you?" He grabbed her arm and pulled her out of the chair. "Well I want a dance first."

Jessica grabbed the almost full pitcher of beer Ben and Kevin had been sharing and dumped it over Daniel's head. He roared with anger and pulled back his fist to hit her. Fortunately, Jimmy the bouncer intercepted it.

"Trouble?" he asked Jessica. Jimmy was six four and built like a truck. He was also a friend.

"I think he was just leaving," Jessica said.

Daniel mumbled under his breath, but left without any further trouble. It as obvious to Jessica he'd tangled with Jimmy before and didn't care to again.

* * * * *

"I'm sorry I ruined the evening," Jessica said when she and Ellen got home.

"Are you kidding? You didn't ruin anything. You should have seen Daniel's face."

"God, I hope this doesn't mean he's going to start up again."

"If he does," Ellen said grimly, "I'll just have my brothers have a talk with him."

Jessica grinned, "How many of them?"

"At least three out of five. How did you and Kevin get along?" She looked at Jessica expectantly.

"We got along just fine. Did you know he's going for some kind of degree in Agriculture?"

"Really?" Ellen fluffed a pillow with feigned indifference.

Jessica nodded, a devilish gleam in her eye. "So's his girlfriend."

"Girlfriend! You're kidding!"

"Oh, Ellen. The look on your face." She laughed as Ellen threw the pillow at her. "Did you really expect love at first sight?"

"It had crossed my mind," Ellen admitted, flopping down on the couch. She kicked off her shoes and began massaging her feet.

"Wishful thinking. Brought on, I suspect, by present circumstances. Just how serious are things between you and Ben?"

Ellen snorted, "Too serious. But don't worry, it's mostly one sided."

"Well, just handle him like you do all the others and everything will work out fine. I think it's admirable how you stay friends with all the guys you dump."

"Well I've got a news flash for you. It isn't Ben who's serious, it's me."

"What?" Jessica plunked herself down in a chair.

"You heard me," Ellen admitted glumly. "I finally get serious about a guy and he wants to keep things easy going."

"Tell you what," Jessica said. "To take your mind off your troubles you can help me with my mystery box tomorrow."

Ellen brightened. "Why don't we do it right now?"

Jessica yawned. "You're just like a kid."

"One of my more endearing qualities, so I've been told. Aren't you the least bit excited about it? I can't believe you still haven't opened it. Just think of the possibilities."

"I have thought about the possibilities," Jessica said slowly. "And a shiver goes down my spine every time I do."

* * * * *

It was a rare Saturday morning that found both Ellen and Jessica off work and it was a rule that when this happened alarm clocks were never used. Despite this, and the lateness of the night before, Ellen was up, dressed and waiting when Jessica finally put in an appearance.

Ellen had moved the box onto the coffee table so they could get at it easier. It was all she could do to wait until Jessica got dressed before pulling her into the living room where she had a coffee and Danish waiting for her.

"You're impossible!" Jessica laughed as Ellen dragged the coffee table, box and all, closer to them.

"So open it already!"

Ellen watched impatiently as Jessica slowly pulled the brown paper wrapping from the mysterious box.

"This is worse than Christmas," Ellen muttered.

"It's just," Jessica paused and glanced at her friend. "This is going to sound really stupid, but I can't help feeling that whatever's in this box is going to have a drastic effect on my life."

Ellen shivered, "I don't like premonitions."

"Sorry," Jessica took a deep breath and opened the box. Inside was another box, also wrapped in brown paper, with a sheet of buff coloured stationery attached to it.

"This is really ridiculous!"

She pulled the note free and handed it to Ellen. "You read, I'll keep unwrapping."

"It says," said Ellen after a few moments, "that the woman who owned the house you lived in with your mother in Guelph found this box in her attic. She sent it to Sandra who sent it along to you. She believes it's a box of your mother's old clothes."

By this time Jessica had the second box free of its wrappings. She looked up. "That's weird that she doesn't know for certain. I would have thought she'd check it out before sending it along."

"I think she did," Ellen said. "Look at this tape, it's not that old. And the paper is the same as the stuff from the outer box."

Jessica hesitated, and then opened the box

"Whoa!" They both leaned backwards from the musty smell that wafted up from a layer of newspaper.

"I guess now we know why Sandra didn't just keep it. She has a fear of mould. I wonder how long this thing was in that woman's attic?"

Ellen got up to open a window. "Your aunt didn't say. But from the smell I'd say a long time, and that the old lady's roof leaks."

"Look at this!" Jessica was bravely exploring the contents. She'd set aside the layer of newspaper and pulled back a layer of thin plastic, like the kind dry cleaners used. "Baby clothes!"

"They're probably yours," Ellen sat beside her for a better look. "Look at this stitching, they're made by hand."

"I can't believe this," Jessica said. "Can you imagine the work that went into these?"

Each tiny garment was sewn by hand and heavily decorated. Some of them were embroidered with thread that had lost only a little of its colour, some were trimmed with handmade lace and ribbons. There was no sign of moth damage or mildew, but there was no doubt it would take a great deal of effort to get rid of the smell.

Sandwiched carefully between layers of delicate baby clothes were a glass unicorn and a pair of crystal candlesticks.

"I've never seen these before," Jessica said, holding the candlesticks up for a closer look. "And I'll bet Aunt Sandra didn't know about them either."

"How so?"

"If she'd known about them, she would have sold them."

Next to come out was a once white sheet, separating the baby clothes from another layer of mildewed newspapers. The next layer was sealed in a bright green plastic bag, like the kind used for picnicking in the 60s or 70s . Jessica gingerly lifted it out and Ellen swept the boxes and wrappings onto the floor.

"We're making a real mess," Jessica told her.

"So, we'll clean it up later. What's in the bag?"

It had a zipper, which they couldn't get to work. Ellen fetched the scissors from the kitchen. The plastic was tougher than it looked, but Jessica was persistent, cutting carefully around the edge.

Sitting right at the top was an old photo album. Jessica turned the pages carefully but it seemed to be in pretty good shape.

"I don't recognize any of these people," she said after a few pages. "Wait, here's one . . ."

Her voice trailed off as she gazed at a picture of a dark haired young woman in a wedding gown. "That's my mother," she said.

The next picture was a wedding portrait. The bride was holding her bouquet, standing next to the groom, a handsome young man in a police uniform.

"My parents," Jessica whispered. "I've never seen my father before. He was a policeman, shot in the line of duty before I was born. They weren't married very long." She bit her lip to keep from getting too misty eyed and set the photo album aside. She could look at it later.

Next was a layer of neatly folded clothing, maternity clothes by the look of them, two dresses and a pantsuit. Wrapped up in one of the dresses was another book. This one was smaller, with a lock on it. Jessica looked up at Ellen.

"It's got to be my mother's diary. I didn't know she ever kept one." Jessica set it aside.

The last item in the bag was a small, ornately carved wooden box. "This is beautiful," she said, admiring it as she turned it around in her hands. "I wonder where it came from."

"It looks hand carved," Ellen said. "I wonder if — Jessica, are you all right?"

The blood drained from Jessica's face as she opened the box. Wordlessly, she handed the box to Ellen. There, nestled in a velvet lining, was the milky white disk from her nightmare.

"Is this what I think it is?" Ellen asked.

Jessica nodded.

"My God, Jessica. Do you realize what this means?"

Jessica stared at her mutely.

"That dream of yours, it must have something to do with your mother. Maybe even something that happened when you were a baby."

"I don't know, El . . ."

"I know you won't see a shrink, but Mom knows this woman who interprets dreams. I've been meaning to mention it to you. You really should go see her."

"I — I'll think about it."

Ellen glanced at her watch. "Damn! I promised I'd see the folks for lunch. Are you okay? You want to come with me? They'd love to see you too."

Jessica shook her head. "Another time maybe. I've got too much to think about."

Ellen rummaged around in her purse and pulled out a slip of paper. "Here's that woman's number, just in case."

Jessica nodded. Ellen hesitated, then shook her

head and left.

Jessica sat the wooden box on the coffee table and picked up the diary. Maybe the answers to her questions would be found within its pages.

An hour later had her pausing to get a tissue. There was no doubt her parents had loved each other. Her mother sounded so young, so happy. They'd only been married three months before she learned she was pregnant. And then to have her husband taken from her before their baby could be born - it was all so tragic.

She couldn't help but wonder how different her life might have been if that gunman's bullet hadn't struck her father in the head, if she hadn't lost her mother to an aneurism. Would her parents still be in love? Would they even be together?

And then Jessica had to wonder if they would have liked the person she'd become. Although the person she was now was shaped largely by the fact she'd grown up without them. It was enough to give her a headache.

As she rose to go find an aspirin, another thought struck her. Would she still have suffered from nightmares if one, or both, of her parents had lived?

Chapter Four

J essica was frowning at a very puzzling entry in her
mother's diary when there was a knock on her
door. She was still frowning as she let Howard in.

"I'm glad you're home, Jess. I—" he stopped
suddenly. "What's that awful smell?"

"Oh, just that," Jessica waved vaguely at the box,
contents strewn over the couch, wrappings still litter-
ing the floor.

"That," Howard repeated. He eyed her with con-
cern. "Are you okay?"

"I don't know," Jessica replied, sitting back on
the couch.

Howard went into the kitchen and returned in a
few minutes with a cup of tea.

"Drink up," he said, when she didn't seem to take
any notice of it.

Jessica obediently took a sip. "Yuck! It's Valerian,
isn't it?"

Howard grinned at her, "You look like you needed it. You want to talk about it?"

"I guess, maybe."

Slowly, hesitantly at first, Jessica told Howard about the letter, the box, and the box's contents.

"And now," she said, finishing tea and story together. "I've been reading my mother's diary, and there's something that just doesn't make sense."

She showed him the entry. Howard read it and then turned a puzzled look on her. "I don't understand. She talks like your father's death caused her to miscarry. Right here: 'I've lost Andrew, and now I've lost our baby. I've nothing more to live for.'"

Jessica nodded. "There are a few blank pages, then it starts again the day she brought me home."

She sighed and set the diary aside. Picking up the wooden box she showed it to Howard.

"This is another piece of the puzzle." She told him about her nightmare, and its connection to the pendant. Lifting it out of the box, she passed it to him.

Howard reached out, then jerked his hand back before actually touching it.

"What is it? What's the matter?"

He tried again, taking the pendant gingerly by the chain. "This is very powerful, Jess."

"I don't understand. What do you mean powerful? What kind of power?"

"It has . . ." he hesitated. "It has a great deal of

energy. I think it might be some kind of amulet." He held it up to the light. "Look at the symbol on the back."

The symbol was like a letter, but from no alphabet either of them had ever seen before. Howard peered closer at the top of the disk. He turned the whole thing around then slid a fingernail into an indentation at the top. They both jumped as it fell apart like a locket with no hinge.

"Sorry, Jess. I don't think it's broken though, I think it was supposed to do that."

"What's this?" Jessica bent down to retrieve a scrap of paper that had been wedged in between the disks.

Howard squinted at it. "It looks like . . . Jesseminathus, I think."

"What does it mean?"

"I have no idea."

Jessica sighed again. "And so the mystery deepens."

"Can I borrow this?" Howard asked. "Maybe I can figure out its meaning."

"Please do," said Jessica. "If we know what it means, maybe we can figure out why it keeps giving me nightmares."

Howard put the pendant back in its box and rose to leave. "I'll see what I can find out about it."

"Thanks, Howard." Jessica walked him to the door.

"Oh, before I forget, the reason I came over here in the first place was to ask a favour."

"Sure, Howard."

"Wait until you hear what it is before you agree. It has to do with what I was telling you before about my magic."

"Maybe we should sit down," Jessica said, shutting the door again

Howard nodded. They went back into the living room where he perched on the arm of a chair, turning the box around and around in his hands.

"Sometimes it's really hard to be different, you know?" He looked at her.

"You're not just talking about being gay, are you?"

"No, I'm not. It's the magic thing. It makes me feel more apart than being gay. Lots of people are gay, but the magic thing, that's something else altogether."

"Magic is for fairy tales and the movies," Jessica said softly.

He sighed and slid down into the chair. "Do you remember when we were kids and we used to play swords and sorcery games?"

Jessica nodded, smiling. "You were going to be the King's High Wizard and I was going to be a Lady Knight."

"But we grew up, and you put aside your sword . . ."

"Not entirely," Jessica said slowly. "I still keep up with the fencing I took in high school, and I've practically memorized every swashbuckler that's ever been filmed. In fact, that's how I got the lead in the Little Theatre production that's in rehearsals right now."

"I forgot about that," Howard admitted. "Something about the Three Musketeers, isn't it?"

She nodded. "I took the part more because it lets me practice with the sword than for any great love of the role."

"Then maybe you might understand. I never gave up my dream of becoming a wizard, a real magic worker. I've got books, done years, a lifetime, of research, taken reams of notes . . . I went to Europe three summers in a row to look for proof that magic really exists." He sighed. "I've made just enough progress to keep hope alive."

Jessica opened her mouth, then shut it again. When he paused she motioned for him to continue.

"Anyway, I came across an ancient manuscript— trust me, you don't want to know what I went through to get my hands on it. Jess, this thing is amazing. It's so old it's written on animal skins, that's how it survived.

"It took me almost three years to translate even a small part of it. You just can't imagine the world of possibilities it's opened for me."

Unable to sit still any longer, Howard jumped up and began to pace.

"It confirms everything I've always believed in. Magic exists, Jess, real magic. After all these years of studying and sweating and keeping the faith, I'm able to work an actual magical spell."

"What kind of spell?" Jessica asked, intrigued more by Howard's intensity than what he was actually saying.

"It's a transferral spell."

"Transferral?"

"It allows you to move an object from one place to another."

"You mean like telekinesis?"

"Telekinesis is moving objects with your mind, this is done using pure magic. I know how all this sounds, Jess but—"

"I remember some of the stuff you used to be able to do as a kid," she said slowly. "Those weren't just magic tricks to you, were they?"

"No, they weren't."

"Is that what the deal with the violet was all about? You really did teleport it into my kitchen?"

He nodded and sat down beside her.

"I have only a small amount of magical energy so I was only able to move a small object. It's not enough, Jess. I want more."

Jessica reached over and put her hand over his. "I'm listening."

"I've been in touch with a local coven . . . covens are great at raising magical energy, but they just release it. I want to try and channel it into the transferral spell. I want to try and move a person."

"You mean me, don't you? You want to use magic to transport me from one place to another."

"That's pretty much it in a nutshell, Jess," Howard said in a small voice. "I know how all this sounds, but you're the only one I could think of that would even come close to understanding, and—"

"Okay, Howard."

"What?"

"I said okay, I'll do it."

"You will?"

"Howard, we've been friends for a long time and maybe I don't buy into all this magic stuff, but any fool can see how important this is to you."

"Oh, thank you, Jess, thank you," he jumped up and hugged her. "I'm right, you'll see. This is going to be great!"

"Just so long as it doesn't involve sacrificing chickens or anything like that."

Howard was not amused. "You know me better than that. All you have to do is stand in one spot."

"That I can do," Jessica assured him. "When is it?"

"The Saturday after next."

"I have a rehearsal until 11 p.m."

"That works out great, I won't need you until after that."

"Okay, Howard, you've got yourself a guinea

pig."

"Great! I can't tell you what this means to me. I'll let you know about the pendant." With that he was gone.

* * * * *

Howard and his magical aspirations, Jessica tried to tell herself, were nothing to be worried about. In the week since their conversation she'd seen him twice, once when he needed to know her height and weight and once when he stopped by to fix their leaky faucet. Both times he seemed like the same old Howard she'd always known.

As Saturday approached, though, Jessica couldn't help becoming just a little jittery.

"If you're that worried about helping Howard, why don't you phone one of the people who are helping him?" Ellen suggested. "They can tell you better than anyone what's going on."

"I suppose you're right," Jessica said. "But then it would seem like I don't have any faith in him."

"Do you?"

"It's not so much a question of faith in his abilities, it's more a question of his sanity. He said he's going to cast a spell to teleport me."

"There you go, then. Nothing to worry about." Ellen picked up her purse and headed for the door. "You want anything while I'm out?"

Jessica shook her head and Ellen left.

She sighed and sipped her tea, and remembered the incident with the plant. Maybe just to be on the safe side she should check on Howard's so-called powers. But who to call? She scrolled through the contacts on her phone, looking for inspiration.

"Here we go. Sam Russell and Howard go way back, and he's pretty open about being Wiccan. I bet he's part of Howard's group."

Jessica was grateful Sam was the kind of guy who left forwarding numbers. The woman who answered the phone at his place gave her another number to call, and the man who answered that yet another number. Even then, she had to wait for several minutes before the girl who answered could ferret Sam out of his room.

They chatted for a few minutes before Jessica got to the point. "Listen, Sam, the reason I'm calling is Howard."

"Howard? Great guy, real talented too."

She jumped on the word. "Talented, that's it exactly. Just how talented is Howard?"

"I don't know what you mean."

"Sam, you know exactly what I mean. He's set up some kind of magical experiment and I'm sure you and your coven are part of it too. I just want to know if it's, you know, dangerous."

"Dangerous," he squawked, "Us?"

"Howard got me to agree to participate and I'd

like to know what I'm in for."

"Oh, that. Listen, Jess, you've got nothing to worry about. Howard couldn't magic his way out of a wet paper bag, trust me."

"But he did do something pretty extraordinary with a violet . . ."

"Look, I've seen people do a lot of weird stuff like moving objects or bending spoons. It's psychic energy, not magic. The energy the coven raises is totally different. We agreed to this experiment of his to get him off our backs."

"I gotta say, that sounds kind of cold Sam."

"He's drawn up solar charts and moon charts and mapped out ley lines - all to work a magic spell. He thinks that under the right conditions the group can raise enough power to feed to him so he can work a bonefide, pure magical spell."

"What if he can?" Jessica asked, in spite of herself.

"Hey, don't get me wrong. If it works it would be totally awesome. But don't you think if it was possible someone would have done it already? Nah, Howard's a dreamer, just like the rest of us."

"Poor Howard."

"Wicca's a religion, a way of life really. We gather at the Sabbats, observe the three-fold law and generally just try to make the world a better place to live in."

"Sounds harmless enough."

"Then along comes Howard with his spells and cones of power. The sooner we get this over with, the better."

"Well, thanks, Sam. If nothing else, you've put my mind at ease."

"I'll let you know when we're ready to take over the world."

"You do that," she grinned. "I can see it now, Howard, King of the World."

Sam made a noise between a snort and a laugh and hung up.

Jessica stared thoughtfully at the phone. She almost felt sorry for Howard. Maybe it was for the best though. He was spending an awful lot of time on his "magic" lately and it was starting to worry her. He was investing so much of himself in this . . . what was he going to do when his spell failed?

She remembered his ninth birthday when his mother hired a magician for his party and his acute disappointment when he learned it was just tricks.

No, she was definitely going to be there when he cast his spell. He was going to need a friend.

Chapter Five

It had been a slow day for flowers. Jessica leaned back in the chair behind the counter and pulled the petals one by one from a Shasta daisy. The door chime tinkled merrily and she quickly brushed the mess she'd made into the wicker garbage basket.

"Jessica, you'll never believe what happened!" a bouncy voice greeted her.

"Hi Rochelle. What's going on?"

Rochelle, who was every bit as bouncy as her voice, leaned across the counter top. "The museum agreed to lend us the swords we wanted."

Jessica blinked at her. "What?"

"I've just come from the museum. They've agreed to loan us three swords from their collection."

"Why would we need swords from their collection?"

"The play, dummy, remember?" Rochelle tossed

her blond curls impatiently. "You better not have forgotten the dress rehearsal we have tonight. Seven o'clock sharp at the old theatre."

Jessica hadn't forgotten. "I thought we already had swords."

"But not *real* swords," Rochelle said smugly.

Given the amount of damage being done with the wooden prop swords, Jessica had to ask, "Won't using real swords be a little dangerous?"

"You'll just have to be careful. In fact, I'll put you in charge of safety. " Rochelle bounced away from the counter. "Gotta run. Places to go, people to see . . ."

The door tinkled shut behind her and Jessica sighed. She wondered if it was too late for second thoughts. Checking the clock, she closed up shop and headed for home.

* * * * *

"As I recall," said Ellen over supper. "Your exact words were: 'It might be fun.' That was, of course, before you found out that the real reason they wanted you for the lead was because you took fencing in high school."

"The three musketeers as women," Jessica said, with a sigh. "I can't believe I'm a part of it. I love Alexandre Dumas's books."

"Don't worry," Ellen assured her. "I've seen the

costumes. And I promise you, they're hot."

* * * * *

Jessica had to agree with Ellen as she looked in the full length mirror at the theatre. She especially liked the boots - thigh high black suede that slid easily over the black satin, tight fitting breeches.

The shirt was some sort of silky material, white and billowy with enormous sleeves. A black satin musketeer's jacket went over top and a large black hat complete with a poofy white plume finished the costume.

"Who paid for all this?" Jessica asked Rochelle, who was practically falling out of a blue satin period dress.

"They're rented. Well, actually, Jennifer's boyfriend's brother runs this costume place and he's letting us use them for free as long as we make sure we advertise his store on the posters."

"Here." Peter, one of the stage hands, handed Jessica a sword belt. "This isn't the real sword, it's the one that goes with the costume. Jennifer didn't want anyone accidentally slicing up a costume until opening night."

"It looks pretty real," Jessica said, unsheathing the sword. "Maybe we should just stick to these. A real sword could damage more than just a costume."

"No," said Rochelle impatiently. "We have to use

the real ones. The museum is counting on us for free advertising." She went off in search of Jennifer, readjusting the bodice of her dress as she went.

"Now that I've seen some of these costumes, I'm thinking this production might not be so bad after all," Peter said with a cheeky grin.

"That's what all you guys are saying."

Peter laughed and went back to work. Jessica admired herself in the mirror some more and tried to figure out what to do with her hair.

"Rochelle wants our hair loose," said a voice behind her.

Jessica caught a glimpse of a similarly dressed musketeer behind her. This one had long blond curls.

"That's ridiculous! How can you fight with hair in your face?"

Tammy shrugged, "I already pointed that out to Rochelle but she wanted to make sure everyone knows we're women."

Jessica giggled, "As if anyone could miss that little piece of information with Vikki around."

"Did I hear my name being taken in vain?"

A third musketeer came over to join them in front of the mirror. She was short and dark-haired, but what she lacked in height she made up for in chest size.

"Look at this thing," Vikki complained. "This jacket doesn't even come close to closing."

"Could be worse," Tammy assured her. "You

could have my problem." She overlapped the front of her jacket to show just how much room she had.

"God, all this satin and feathers, we look like we're going to a pimp's convention," Jessica said.

They moved away from the mirror as they heard raised voices coming from the wings. Rochelle and Jennifer were arguing vociferously, as they did almost every rehearsal. Jessica moved a few steps closer to hear what it was about this time.

It appeared the two women were having a difference of opinion over which swords should be used. Rochelle wanted the real swords to be used at all times, while Jennifer thought the fake ones were realistic enough. When she threatened to take back the costumes, lest they be damaged during rehearsals, Rochelle threatened to cancel the play altogether. They finally compromised. Fake swords would be used for rehearsals and real ones for the play itself.

After that rehearsal went off without a hitch. Everyone knew their lines and Jessica and her fellow musketeers wielded their fake swords with aplomb.

"Jessica, could you come here for a minute?" Peter asked.

Jessica, still in her costume, followed him to a store room.

"Rochelle wanted you to have a look at these. She's worried they might be too heavy."

Jessica picked up one of the swords from the museum. "They're heavier than they look," she admitted.

"Here," he handed her the sword belt. "See how much the whole thing weighs you down."

She removed the costume sword belt and strapped the real one around her waist.

"It weighs about the same like this," she said. "The length might be awkward during the chase scenes, though. I'd better let Rochelle see this."

Jessica had no luck finding Rochelle. She checked the stage, the wings and even went back to the storage room. By this time Peter had locked up and gone home, so she headed back to the dressing room to change.

Unfortunately, the door to the room she'd left her street clothes in was locked, as were all the others she tried.

"Damn!"

As much as she didn't want to wear the costume home, there didn't seem to be anything she could do about it. There weren't any other clothes lying around other than extra costumes hanging from a rack. And none of them were an improvement on what she was already wearing.

"And what am I supposed to do with this sword?" Rochelle would kill her if anything happened to it.

After searching the theatre one more time, she admitted she had no choice. As ridiculous as she'd look, she'd have to wear the costume home. The sword was easier left on the belt, but she carried the hat in her hand.

It wasn't until she was out on the street that she remembered that though her purse, with her cell phone in it, was locked away, there was a phone backstage. Jessica tried to catch the door before it shut but she was too late. She heard the ominous click as it automatically locked.

Jessica leaned her head against the door, "This just isn't my night."

"Oh, double damn!" she said, looking at her watch. She was supposed to meet Howard at her place at eleven, it was almost that now. There was nothing to do but start walking.

"If I had any money on me," she muttered to herself, "I'd buy a lottery ticket on the way home. I've had such rotten luck tonight that I'm due for something good to happen."

It could be worse, she reminded herself. The play could have been one that required a slinky costume. At least the jacket was warm, if not a tad on the flamboyant side. But she was stuck with the sword and the hat as well, which made it impossible for her to go unnoticed.

A car horn honked behind her. Jessica studiously ignored it. Jerks blowing car horns were the least of her problems tonight.

"Jessica? Hey, Jessica!"

She turned around, delighted to see Howard waving to her from the open window of an ancient Volkswagen Beetle, rust spots showing through the bright yellow paint. "Howard? You have no idea how glad I am to see you. You would not believe the night I've been having. I—"

"Come on," he said, reaching over and opening the passenger door for her. "When you didn't show up at home I thought maybe you'd missed the bus," he said once she was sitting beside him.

"You're a life saver, Howard. Hey, where are we going?"

"We don't have much time," he answered. "We can't be late for the spell."

"I can't go dressed like this!"

"It's dark, nobody'll notice," he glanced over at her. "Well, they won't really care if they do notice."

"But . . . ah, damn," she slumped down in the seat. "Where are we going, anyway?"

"Spirit Rock."

"That figures."

Spirit Rock was the site of a series of ritualistic murders in the early 1900s. To this day there were reported sightings of ghostly figures and mysterious lights appearing around the rock.

"Jess," he glanced over at her again. "I really want to thank you for helping me."

"No problem. What else are friends for?"

"No, I mean it. No one but you has ever believed in me. It's really meant a lot, especially this last couple of years."

She looked over at him, surprised to see how tense he was as he watched the road. Part of her hoped that something *would* happen tonight, just enough to prove to the others that he was right.

"Even when we were kids you could do some pretty amazing things," she told him. "You were the smartest person I knew then and you still are. If you believe so strongly in this, who's to say you're not right?"

"Thanks, Jess," he said again.

"Enough already. Tell me, what's my part in this test of yours? I refuse to disclose whether or not I'm a suitable candidate for virgin sacrifice."

"Nothing that drastic," he assured her. "I'm going the use the power the coven raises in an attempt to teleport you. All you need to do is just stand there."

"I don't suppose you could teleport me all the way home, could you? I'm dying for a bath."

"I'll be lucky if I teleport you two feet, let alone twenty miles," he said. "Oh, by the way, here," he took one hand off the steering wheel long enough to reach into his pocket and hand her back her medallion.

"I was able to reset it so you could have the half without the symbol back. If you don't mind, I'd like to keep the other piece for awhile longer."

"Take all the time you need."

"I didn't get anywhere with my research on its origins," he told her. "But I have a friend who's a geologist and he swears it's made out of moonstone."

"Moonstone?"

"It's semi-precious. Not particularly valuable, but
—"

"So it's more or less just costume jewelry."

"No," Howard said slowly, "I wouldn't say that. Like I said before, it has a very strong magical aura. I think that the symbol has something to do with luck or good fortune."

Jessica held the disk in her hand for a minute before placing it around her neck. "I could have used its luck earlier," she told him glumly. "I haven't made much more headway with mom's diary, either. A lot of the pages are faded, or stuck together."

Howard glanced at her, "Are you still worried about the possibility of being adopted?"

She bit her lip and stared out at the night rolling by. "I found a passage that said: 'I don't know where he came from or where he went, but I thank the Lord he found me worthy of his gift.'"

"What gift?"

"That, my friend, is the million dollar question."

The gate was open and the small parking lot at Spirit Rock Conservation Area was about half full. It was on the tip of Jessica's tongue to ask if they had permission to be here, but then she decided she'd be better off not knowing. Maybe one of the coven members had other talents besides magic. Howard parked and led her to where a group of about fifteen people waited.

Jessica was surprised that everyone looked so normal, not a long black robe or a broomstick in sight. The ages ranged from late teens to senior citizens. They were dressed mostly in jeans and t-shirts, a couple of women in long broomstick skirts, and one older gentleman looked like he'd just come off the golf course.

"Okay, Howard," a tired-looking woman in an *I'm on Debt Row* t-shirt said, "Let's get this over with."

Jessica was a little irritated at her attitude. Couldn't she see how much this meant to him?

"This way," was all Howard said.

He led the way along the trail to Spirit Rock. Several people carried flashlights, although with the full moon extra light wasn't needed. Crickets chirped, a cow lowed in the distance and the water could be heard lapping at the nearby shore. A slight breeze rustled the leaves of the trees. It was a beautiful night.

Howard had Jessica stand with her back to the rock and placed everyone else in a circle around her. He took up the position directly opposite her, also just inside the circle.

"I want everyone to link hands," he said. "Just focus on drawing the night's energy to you. When I start the spell you should feel a slight charge building. Whatever you do, don't let go until I'm done."

Jessica shifted impatiently. The dew from the grass had leaked right though the suede of her boots and her feet were cold and damp. She hoped she could have the boots cleaned before Jennifer saw them.

"Jessica, hold still. If the spell works, you should end up in the parking lot."

"What if it doesn't?" someone from the group snickered.

Howard ignored the heckler and raised his hands. The air around them went still. He began a rhythmic chanting. It was almost too quiet to hear at first, but it slowly grew in volume until Jessica could clearly make out the words, although she couldn't understand them.

He stopped on a high note and began again - the same incantation, only slightly higher in pitch. As he started for the third time, he began weaving his hands in an intricate pattern almost like sign language.

Jessica sucked in a breath as she was suddenly surrounded by a tingling sensation. Judging by the gasps she heard from the circle she wasn't the only one feeling it. *My God*, she thought. *This might actually work.*

The tingling sensation intensified. Jessica couldn't move, couldn't speak. It was like she was frozen in place even though there was a sensation of movement all around her. Her vision swam. Howard's chanting filled the night. She could feel the power of his voice.

Jessica was reminded suddenly of her nightmare and a nameless fear filled her. She would have screamed if she could. The stars spun above her. There was a terrible wrenching sensation, then nothing at all.

Chapter Six

I t was the endless pounding of the surf that woke her. Jessica tried to roll over and groaned as she came up against something hard and unyielding. Every muscle complained of misuse. She felt sick and her head hurt; sitting up didn't help at all.

Cradling her head in her hands, she tried to remember what had happened the night before. It had been dark and there'd been a bunch of people. Had she been at a party? Drinking too much would certainly account for the headache.

No, she remembered now. Jessica struggled to her feet.

"Holy Saint Christopher!" Her aches and pains were temporarily forgotten. Mouth open, all she could do was stare. "I can't believe he actually did it," she whispered.

She closed her eyes and tried to will the park to

reappear, unable to believe Howard had succeeded in teleporting her. It didn't work. In front of her was a wide expanse of shimmering water while behind her rose towering cliffs of dark, grey stone. The sun was shining directly over head.

"Where the hell am I?"

The rocky shoreline was not unusual for the Georgian Bay area of Lake Heron, but there was an unfamiliar tang in the air and the water was a startling turquoise, not the more familiar angry grey of late August. And it was probably her imagination, but the sun was just a little too bright, a little too big.

She shivered as a bird screeched harshly over-head, a lonely sound over the noise of the water. There was not so much as a hydro tower in sight to indicate some kind of civilization, just miles of desolate shoreline, arcing away in a wide bay. There wasn't even any traffic on the water.

"Now what do I do?" Tears of frustration welled up in her eyes.

It was probably going to be a while before Howard recovered enough to start looking for her. How long had it taken for him to recover from the violet incident, a couple of days? It could be weeks before he recovered from this! Would Howard even know where he'd sent her?

Looking around, she shivered again. She certainly didn't want to be caught out in this wilderness when night fell. The cliffs were too sheer for climbing. That left only one option – walking.

Jessica stumbled on the rocks and suddenly realized what she was wearing. "Oh, damn! Jennifer is going to kill me!"

She was still dressed in her costume from the play, from plumed hat right down to suede boots. Just what every woman stranded on the beach should be wearing, she thought. She cursed Howard under her breath as she picked her way along the shore.

"He just couldn't wait for me to change my clothes, could he? If anything happens to this outfit, I'm going to kill him. After he pays for the replacement."

An hour later found her perched on one of the boulders ranged along the base of the cliffs. She had the jacket over her arm and was fanning herself with the hat.

"This is ridiculous," she muttered. "It hasn't been this hot all summer." She'd kill for an ice cold beer right about now. "I wonder how sick I'd get from drinking that water?"

She'd still seen no sign of civilization, not even any boats out on the water. The bay looked so wet and inviting, not an oil slick in sight. Jessica frowned. Was it her imagination, or had the shoreline shrunk over the last hour? It seemed strange that the waves were so high when there was hardly a breeze.

Shrugging, she slid off the rock. Probably just her mind playing tricks on her. Now, how was she going to get a drink without getting wet?

Another fifteen minutes of walking brought her to a section of shore where large flat slabs lay like giant stepping stones. The water ebbed and flowed between them. It seemed clean enough.

Jessica knelt down as close as she dared to one of the little channels and used her hands as a cup. She coughed and sputtered and couldn't spit the water out again fast enough.

"Salt!" she choked. "It's not the lake, it's a coast! There are no seacoasts around here!"

She stayed crouched where she was as her mind tried to come to terms with what she should have realized earlier. The cliffs were too high, the water too blue, and the resemblance to Georgian Bay was only fleeting. This was someplace entirely different.

Her head started to ache in earnest. The water glittered in the sunlight, aggravating her thirst. The plume from her hat dipped in front of her face. Jessica counted to ten.

"I am going to kill Howard."

She'd be impressed with his magical skills later. Right now she needed a sense of purpose to keep her going and killing Howard suited her just fine. She started walking again. It seemed pointless, but it was better than doing nothing at all. She tried not to dwell on the fact that she could be hundreds of miles from civilization, days away from rescue.

"Damn." She kicked at a stone and stubbed her

toe. "I could be anywhere, like a piece of flotsam washed up by the tide."

The beach was definitely getting narrower. Jessica hesitated. What if she ran out of beach on the other side of the point she was walking towards? She looked back the way she'd come and felt a cold chill of fear. The beach wasn't just tapering inwards, the whole thing was shrinking.

"Oh my God, tide! The tide's coming in!"

She stared up at the cliffs. The tideline was there, well above her head. She stumbled along the shore, seeking some possible way of climbing the cliff.

"Come on, Jessica. Don't panic. Panic will kill you quicker than anything else. If you can climb the escarpment you can climb this cliff." But rock climbing on the Niagara Escarpment was nothing like this. It was set in the woods, with natural hand holds and trees to help climbers. This cliff was smooth and unrelenting.

By the time she'd followed the shore to the point jutting out into the bay the beach had shrunk to less than three feet wide. The far side of the point showed nothing encouraging. Jessica stared up at the cliff and swallowed hard. She could do it, she just had to have confidence in herself. It was only the first handhold that was hard.

She took off her boots and rolled them up in the jacket, tying them in place with the sleeves. There was just enough give left in the sleeves to tie the whole thing to the back of her belt. It was an unwieldy mess, but it would make for easier climbing. The hat would just have to fend for itself, she decided, and left it on her head.

A pile of boulders nestled in the curve of the point seemed like a good place to start. The cliffs were in shade now, but far from being a relief it made it harder for Jessica to see. Pressing herself against the rock she reached up, feeling with her finger tips.

She made a mental note to thank Ellen for insisting on pooling their money on a rowing machine instead of a stationary bike. The bike wouldn't have built up any muscle in her arms the way the rowing machine had. She had the feeling that before this was over, she'd need every ounce of muscle she could muster.

As she inched her way upwards, she tried to look neither up nor down, concentrating on the next finger and toe hold. Why was it taking so long? How much further could it be? She risked a quick glance downwards and swallowed hard. The beach had all but disappeared. She shut her eyes against a wave of dizziness and took several long, deep breaths.

Down seemed like a very long way away. She ventured a quick look upwards and was dismayed to realize she was only about halfway there. Every fingernail was broken and a couple of her toes felt like they were bleeding. She refused to look to confirm it.

Her muscles throbbed, even the ones she didn't

know she had. About two thirds of the way up she got a break in the form of a small ledge. If she was careful, she could sit and rest for a bit.

Closing her eyes she leaned back so she wouldn't be tempted to look downwards again. Just staying on the ledge seemed like a reasonable option at that moment. She was hot and sweaty. Everything hurt and even if she got to the top of the cliff, what then?

"Jessica, you've got to stop this negative thinking," she told herself. "You're more than halfway there. You can do this."

Carefully, she got to her feet and started upwards again. Her progress was even slower than before; doubts of her ability began crowding her thoughts. The wind picked up, forcing her to pull the brim of her hat down.

Her arms and legs were quivering with the strain. Twice she slipped. Her heart pounded with fear as she hung on. A pattern to her climbing emerged. An inch or two of progress, then rest and breathe – another inch, another breath. The sweat soaked shirt clung to her back, although the voluminous sleeves flapped distractingly in the breeze.

As she neared the top, Jessica was certain she heard voices.

"That's it," she said. "I'm hallucinating. I'm a goner."

"There is someone below!" a voice wafted downwards.

"Do not be a fool," a second voice answered.

"I tell thee, my lord," the first voice insisted, closer, "I heard a voice."

Jessica clung to the cliff, dazed, as two shadowy figures appeared above her.

"Who are you and what do you there?" the second voice called down to her.

"Stupid damn question," Jessica muttered under her breath. And what was with the hokey accents? "You'll never find out if you don't lend a hand," she yelled back.

There was a momentary consultation before one of the figures ducked out of view and quickly returned. A coarse rope snaked down to meet her. Jessica caught it and with the last of her strength wrapped it around herself and hung on. The two figures at the other end began hauling and in no time at all she reached the cliff top and rolled over the edge in an ungraceful heap.

She lay for a few moments in the grass, breathing deeply. One of the voices began to speak but she cut them off with a wave of her hand. "Gimme a minute."

When her breathing eased and she thought she could move without throwing up, she maneuvered herself into a sitting position.

"Thanks," she said finally. "It's lucky for me you guys were up here." Her breath came easier and she was starting to feel better. Pulling the hat off she wiped the sweat from her brow. "For awhile there I wasn't sure I was going to make it."

She untied the bundle from her belt and unwrapped her boots.

"But, but . . ." voice number one stuttered. "Thou art a woman!"

Jessica glanced up at the voice. The sun was behind the two figures rendering them indistinct shadows. "Nothing gets by you, does it?"

Now that she could see the damage she'd done to her toes they began to throb with pain. She eased her socks over them and carefully pulled her boots back on. "Look, I'm grateful for your help and all, and I'd be more than happy to thank you properly later, but I've had a truly horrendous day and I just want to get home and climb into a nice hot tub. Could you tell me where the nearest phone is?"

"We . . . ah . . . phone? What is a phone?"

Jessica pushed her hair out of her eyes and squinted up at the two shadows in front of her. "Cut the kidding. Which coast am I on, east or west?"

"This be the northern coast," voice number two answered.

"North?" Jessica ignored the pain in her toes as she scrambled to her feet. "What do you mean, north?"

The two men in front of her glanced at each other. "We stand upon Death's Head, northern most point of the kingdom of Ghren." The taller of the two men spoke slowly, as though to a particularly dense child.

"Now look, I'm sure you both find this very funny, but I —" Jessica stopped abruptly and stared. She pivoted slowly, eyes widening.

The landscape in front of her was wilder and greener, more breathtakingly beautiful than anything she'd ever seen outside of a National Geographic magazine. Out on the water a three masted sailing ship was coming around another point of the bay. Beyond the two men, in the distance, were the tents of a camp and beyond that the barely discernible outline of a castle.

"Are you guys filming a movie, or what?"

Before either man could answer a shadow passed overhead. Jessica glanced upwards and screamed as a huge raptor dove towards her. Its talons raked her upraised arm, cutting the billowing sleeve to ribbons and leaving a trail of bloody furrows.

Jessica sank to her knees, pain lancing through her arm. She watched, dazed, as the two men beat off the bird's attack with swords. Swords?

With a final scream of defiance the bird soared off into the sky.

"How severe is thine injury?" the elder of the two men asked, kneeling beside her.

"What . . . was. . . that?" she gasped out as he examined her arm.

"A gerishawk. Thy wound is not deep, but the

fowl's talons carry poison. Canst thee walk?"

With his help Jessica got to her feet. She swayed as her vision blurred. He made a worried sound and scooped her up effortlessly in his arms. Jessica's eyes closed.

"Lord Ewan, who is she?" asked the first, younger voice.

"She is one of Power. That is enough. Perhaps the gods sent her to us in our time of need," Ewan replied. "And the gods help our healers if she dies."

That doesn't sound very reassuring, Jessica thought, and then passed out with Ewan's words echoing through her mind.

Chapter Seven

T his time it was the sound of voices that woke Jessica up.

"She is very fair."

"Gareth, you should not be in here," a woman's voice scolded.

"I was sent by His Highness. How fares the lady?"

"He seems over anxious concerning this stranger." It was more question than comment.

"He believes her to be one of Power," Gareth whispered. "'Tis his hope she can be persuaded to aid our cause."

"For truth?"

"Aye. She came upon us as we stood upon Death's Head. Her wounds are from the attack of a gerishawk. There is much that is strange about her, her manner, her dress . . ."

There was a rustle of cloth as someone moved around.

"Come," the woman said. "I would tell His Majesty myself how fares his guest."

Jessica waited until she was sure they were gone before she opened her eyes.

"Damn," she said, but not too loudly. She'd been hoping the whole stranded-on-the-beach, cliff-climbing episode had been nothing more than a Very Bad Dream. Unfortunately, she recognized the voice of Gareth as the younger of the two men who'd helped her over the cliff-top.

Gingerly she levered herself up into a sitting position. From the amount of canvas surrounding her, she deduced she was in one of the tents she'd seen in the distance. However, the bed she was in was no mere camp cot. It had a wooden frame and a mattress that, if she was not mistaken, was filled with straw.

The sheets were nicer than anything she'd ever owned, and over them was a dark green coverlet embroidered with silver thread. A quick look under the covers determined that someone had dressed her in a nightgown of some soft, white material. Her arm was wrapped in cloth bandages from wrist to elbow.

"That bird . . ." she said with a shudder, remembering. She had a strong urge to just curl up and close her eyes until everything was back to normal. She was hallucinating; someone had slipped her some bad drugs. All she needed was a good night's sleep and everything would be okay.

"Jessica . . ."

Jessica stifled a yelp at the sound of the disembodied voice. She glanced around wildly trying to pinpoint the source.

"Jessie? Are you there?"

"Howard? Is that you?"

"Jessie, I–"

"Howard? Where are you? Never mind," she said quickly. "Just get me out of here."

"I can't, Jess."

"What?" Her voice rose to a shriek.

"Calm down and just listen for a minute. Something went wrong with my spell –"

"So I noticed. Jeez, Howard. When you screw up, you screw up big time."

"– something powerful enough to yank you out of our time continuum interfered."

"What are you talking about?"

"You're trapped in a parallel universe."

"A what? What do you mean, trapped?"

"Will you stop interrupting me!"

She had never heard Howard speak so forcibly.

Jessica shut up.

"That pendant of your mother's . . . I told you I sensed something powerful about it. I think that it belongs in the universe you're in and it somehow pulled you in with it. It's also the reason I'm able to communicate with you. I still have the other half – it acts as some kind of magical link. Whatever you do, don't lose that pendant."

"Howard —" Her hands clutched at the bed linens as she tried to calm herself down.

"Look, Jess. I know this is a lot to throw at you all at once but you're just going to have to hang on until I can bring you back."

"When's that going to be?" Jessica asked in a small voice.

"I don't know, Jess. I'm working on it. Now, there are a few things you should know about your situation —"

"Only a few? Do you know what I've been through so far?" She was getting angry again. "I just about drowned in the ocean you dropped me beside, I climbed a goddamned mountain, I was attacked by a bird with poisonous claws and now I'm being held prisoner by two sword-waving lunatics who think I can help them in some kind of who-knows-what crusade!"

"Jessie, remember all those sword and sorcery movies you used to make me watch with you? Well, brace yourself. Your fantasy of living in that kind of age is about to come true. The dimension you're in is similar to our middle ages, with one major difference. Magic is very real where you are. And I'm not talking about the kinds of spells I've been struggling with. I'm talking about wizards and dragons and unicorns. The whole sheebang."

"Are you serious? Howard –"

"Jessie? The link is weakening. Don't worry, I'll be back later. Just be careful, you've got . . ."

"Howard? I've got what? Damn!"

Jessica lay back on her pillows feeling utterly drained. This whole thing was just so impossible.

Moments later the tent flap lifted to admit one of the most gorgeous men Jessica had ever seen. He looked like he belonged on the cover of one of the historical romance novels Ellen was so fond of.

He was tall and tanned with golden hair that curled down to his shoulders. His eyes were blue and the teeth he flashed as he smiled were perfect.

"My personal healer believes thee free of the poison," he told her, dropping down onto a small stool at her bedside. "How fares thy arm?"

Jessica flexed her hand. "Mostly numb."

"It will pass," he assured her. "I am Ewan, Commander of the Narrows Outpost, Keeper of the Royal Seal, and heir to the throne of Ghren."

"I'm Jessica," she said, too bemused to think of a suitable, if not fictitious, title.

He bowed from the waist, an elegant gesture even done sitting down. "Thou art welcome amongst us, Lady Jessica, for however long thou hast need."

"I, uh, thank you." Jessica struggled to sit up again. He reached behind her and deftly arranged the pillows to make her more comfortable.

"How long was I out?"

"Out?"

"Uh, unconscious."

"Ah. It has been three days and two nights since the attack of the gerishawk at Death's Head."

"I've never seen anything like that bird before," Jessica said with a shudder. "Are they common here?"

Ewan shook his head. "The gerishawk is very rare in our land, but drawn to those of Power."

The other man, Gareth, had mentioned something about power too but somehow Jessica thought it more prudent *not* to ask about it.

"What's Death's Head?" she asked instead, pretty sure she already knew the answer.

"Death's Head is the point of land my squire and I met with thee upon."

"Death's Head," Jessica repeated with a shudder. "Good name."

"Aye, that it is. Hast thou need for aught? A drink perhaps, some victuals?"

"I . . . ah . . . thank you. If it's not too much trouble I could stand something to eat."

He arose gracefully. "I will return with a feast," he promised.

Jessica stared at the tent flap as it closed behind him. A grin spread across her face. Maybe being stuck in this dimension wasn't going to be so bad after all.

* * * * *

A mote of blue witch light danced around the massive wooden bed high in the north tower of the castle, chasing the dust motes that appeared in the beam of late afternoon sun shining through the narrow window. The man in the bed stirred. The mote paused and then zipped over to hover above his face. The man muttered something unintelligible and stirred again; there was rapid movement beneath his eyelids, as though he was struggling to awaken. The mote hummed happily and then vanished with a quiet popping sound.

By the time the old wizard finished climbing the twisting staircase to the tower room, the man was awake and sitting up in the bed. "What time is it?"

"Don't you mean, 'what day is it?'" the old wizard asked, puffing slightly. He lowered himself into an armchair near the bed.

"What day? It's been days?" The man swung his legs over the edge of the bed. "What—"

"What did you expect, casting your spell so close to a Well?" the wizard asked angrily. "What were you thinking?" Then, as though he couldn't help himself, "Did it work?"

"I—I can't be sure," the man answered slowly. "Kiran—"

"Do not use that name!" the man said furiously. "Kiranthus has been dead for twenty-five years."

"Fine, *Thackery*, when you're feeling up to it, you

may join me in the scrying chamber." The wizard struggled to his feet and then vanished.

Thackery sat on the edge of his bed, head resting in his hands, waiting for the spinning to subside. He knew Paranithel had a hard time understanding why he did not return to his original name, but when he left his old life behind he wanted every vestige of it gone, including his name. Kiranthus was the young wizard who'd lived happily with his beautiful wife Farenalyssia. Thackery was angry and cynical, and apparently reckless.

The pain in his head was finally starting to subside. He supposed it served him right. One of the first things they taught the budding magic-users who flocked to the school was to draw on the Well for power, but only as much as necessary.

The magical Wells of Power were useful for replenishing one's energy, but even the most advanced wizard used extreme caution around them. Kiranthus would never have cast his spell so close to the Well of course, but Thackery had been impatient.

With a heartfelt sigh, he managed to get to his feet and made his way slowly to the window. Instead of the lush fields and vast forests of his homeland, he looked out over the harsh beauty of the desert. He could see the Well in the distance, shimmering through the waves of heat.

If he focused his mage-sight he could see the lines of energy running from the Well to the castle, fueling the spell of coolness Paran had set in the rocks. It was a small spell really, but it allowed the northern wizards to endure the desert heat.

With another sigh he turned from the window and left the room. Paran would be getting impatient and to be honest he was more than a little impatient himself to know the results of his spell.

Where the scrying chamber in Paranithel's keep had been in the dungeon, the one in this castle was in the south tower. Paran had chosen the location himself, claiming that the higher altitude was more conducive to the energy needed for proper scrying. Thackery was out of breath by the time he reached the top of the tower.

"You're out of shape," Paran said. He stood by his favorite scrying bowl on its stand in the centre of the room. It was large and shallow, made of thin, black marble.

Thackery raised an eyebrow. "And from the way you disappeared from my room, you used magic instead of climbing all those stairs. What would your students say?"

Paran snorted. "My students know better than to question my comings and goings. Are you ready?"

Mouth suddenly gone dry, Thackery nodded. Without needing to be asked, he went over to the cabinet that was filled with crystal balls, stacks of bowls, and bottles and jars of various liquids, and returned with a large urn. His hand trembled slightly as he poured the pale yellow oil from the urn into the bowl. Setting the urn down again, he joined Paran and they stood side by side, hands resting lightly on the edge of the bowl. Paranithel began chanting.

The oil shivered and then started to swirl in the bowl. Faster and faster it spun until a small whirlpool formed. The whirlpool expanded, wider and wider, leaving a clear space in the centre of the oil. The two men leaned forward.

Images flowed across the oil, moving too fast to make any sense of. There was a blinding flash. The men lost their hold on the bowl as they reeled backwards in shock, and the spell was broken.

"This is what comes of using wild magic," Paran said, shaking his head to clear the spots in front of his eyes.

"It was the only way to keep Anakaron from detecting the spell," Thackery snapped. "The images were going too fast for me to tell. Did it work? Was my retrieval successful?"

"I believe so," Paran said slowly, "But there was something else . . . Fetch me the essence of pedrian."

Thackery went back to the cabinet and returned with a small silver vial. Paran added three drops of a blue liquid from the vial to the oil and then motioned for Thackery to join him. This time he waved his hands over the bowl while chanting. The oil boiled and frothed and then cleared again. A picture formed and they both leaned over it.

"It's the northern continent," Paran said, after a few minutes. "I'm not sure what part, however."

"It looks familiar," Thackery said. "I think I've— no!" His eyes widened. "It's Ghren. I'd stake my life on it."

"Ghren," Paran mused. "Didn't you hold the position of Royal Tutor there at one time? I remember you writing about your student, Dominic. He was quite promising, I recall. Perhaps we could contact him and—"

Thackery was already shaking his head. "Dominic disappeared right before I did. It's one of the reasons I'm no longer welcome there."

"This is not good, my boy. You retrieved your daughter, but you overshot your mark. She's there, a continent away in Ghren."

Chapter Eight

J essica ground her teeth together in frustration. At the rate she was going the enamel would be worn away completely by the time Howard found a way to rescue her. It had been three days since she'd awakened from the bird attack and Ewan's healers, not his personal one but three of her underlings, were driving her insane.

One of them, a tall, thin, nervous man with a scraggly beard, thought she should be restricted to bed for at least a fortnight, whatever that was. It sounded like a long time to be stuck in a tent. Fortunately, he was voted down by the other two.

The second healer was a motherly-type woman, who got very little respect from her colleagues. Jessica might have got on well with her if it wasn't for the fact she kept trying to force noxious potions down her throat. The third healer, a short, round man who was so old Jessica wondered if he'd been pulled out of retirement, said that she'd be fine in a day or so, but in the meantime she should be bled.

She wasn't quite sure what he meant by that, but it didn't sound good. The worst part was, they seemed to think one of them should be with her at all times, giving her very little opportunity for an un-chaperoned visit with Ewan. He visited her as often as he could, but his princely duties seemed to take up a great deal of his time.

Dealing with them one at a time was bad enough, but today they descended on her in a group, only to start arguing immediately about her treatment.

"Maybe you should discuss this outside," she said, raising her voice.

All three of them turned to stare at her.

"It's just about time for my dinner and I'm sure all this arguing can't be good for my digestion." She tried to look as though her stomach pained her.

The female healer brightened immediately. "I know just the potion for that. Gentian root with a touch of ginger. I'll make a tea of them."

"No no no!" the skinny one said. "Angelica is the answer, with peppermint and turmeric." He hurried after her.

"Potions aren't the answer. A full meal followed by a proper bloodletting. I think I know where . . ." the rest of what the oldest healer was saying was lost as he followed his colleagues out of the tent.

Jessica breathed a heartfelt sigh of relief. She was just getting comfortable when a page stuck his head through the tent flap. Seeing she was alone, he came the rest of the way in.

"My lady, His Royal Majesty, Prince Ewan, would visit with thee."

"You may tell his Highness that I would be most pleased by his company." Jessica had to suppress a giggle at her formal answer. It sounded so elegant coming from Ewan and so cheesy coming from her. She smiled at the page and he grinned shyly in return before disappearing.

A few minutes later two pages held the flaps of the tent wide for Ewan himself. He was followed by a tall, lanky man with blond hair and brown eyes. The newcomer was dressed in a homespun white shirt and buff coloured trousers, with the high, cuffed boots that everyone seemed to wear, and was carrying what looked like a pregnant guitar.

"My lady," Ewan said, taking her hand to kiss the back of it. Jessica blushed. "How dost thee fare?"

"I'm good, I'm fine." Jessica wished she knew more about the middle ages so she could at least pretend to speak the way Ewan did. She wondered what she sounded like to him.

"I fear I have been a poor host. Too often my duty takes me from thy side."

"It's all right. I understand that you must be busy."

"Nay," he shook his head. "'Tis no excuse for my neglect. Thy confinement must be tedious beyond bearing."

"I have to admit I've never been one to just lie around in bed," she told him. In fact, that was the one good thing about the visits from the healers. They kept her from going stir crazy.

"It is as I suspected. But fear not, my lady. I have found what I pray to be a satisfactory solution." Ewan gestured toward the man standing just inside the entrance to the tent. "I would introduce to thee the minstrel, Sebastian Descarte."

The minstrel took a step closer. "My lady," he said, bowing deeply.

"The lady Jessica is our most honored guest. We would take it amiss should anything displease her."

"I've never met a minstrel before." Jessica wasn't sure what to make of Ewan's introduction. Sebastian didn't seem bothered by the thinly veiled threat. In fact, there might have been just a hint of humour in those brown eyes.

"It is my hope that he can ease the burden of thy convalescence," Ewan continued. "And should thee need aught, my squire shall be at thy disposal."

It took Jessica a moment to decipher his meaning. "Thank you, your highness. You are most kind."

"'Tis my pleasure," he assured her. "Alas, I cannot stay. Duty beckons. I must take my leave of thee and pray I may return forthwith."

He was gone before Jessica could formulate a reply.

"Please, have a seat," Jessica told Sebastian, motioning to the chair Ewan normally occupied.

He sat down, resting the base of his instrument on the ground and leaning the neck against the side of the chair. "Do you have a favorite song you'd like me to play?"

"No, I . . . I'm sorry, I'm not really familiar with your kind of music. Look, I know Prince Ewan has kind of forced you into this. If there's someplace else you'd rather be, it's okay."

Sebastian studied her for a moment. "To be honest, there hasn't been a lot for me to do since we made camp here. The soldiers would rather get drunk and sing camp songs, not the sort of thing that requires accompaniment. And I'm not good for much else."

"You don't talk like Prince Ewan," she said suddenly.

He grinned. "Not many do. The so-called high court dialect is fashionable in the Eastern courts. Ewan likes to be fashionable."

"Hmm. You don't—"

The tent flap opened and the older healer entered carrying a large bowl. "Oh, good. I beat the other two here. Now, if you'll just lie back I can start putting these leeches on you."

Jessica blanched. "Leeches?"

Sebastian leaned over. "You know, you don't have to do what they tell you. Ewan said you were an honoured guest. That means it's their job to make you happy."

"Leeches would most definitely *not* make me happy." Jessica eyed the healer who was looking for a place to set down his bowl. "Listen up. You are not putting those things anywhere near me."

"But—"

"Furthermore, you and your cohorts can take your potions and your teas and . . . well, dump them. I'm not being your lab rat any more. I'm fine and as long as you three stay away from me I'll continue to be fine. So get out and stay out, and take those slimy things with you."

His mouth opened to argue, but she kept going. "If you don't, I'll have to speak to the prince."

His mouth snapped shut again. Without another word he picked up his bowl of leeches and scurried from the tent.

"Well done!" Sebastian said with a grin.

"So," Jessica said, making herself comfortable against the pillows. "Tell me, Sebastian. What else is an honoured guest entitled to?"

* * * * *

"Jessie . . ."

Jessica stirred in her sleep but ignored the intrusive sound.

"Jessica . . ."

The voice was louder this time, but the bed was really soft and warm and comfortable. Jessica ignored the voice and burrowed further into the pile of quilts she was under.

"Jessica!" The voice was distinctly impatient.

"Just five more minutes, Ellen."

"Jessica, wake up!"

"Howard?" That didn't make sense. What would Howard be doing in her bedroom? Memory of where she was came flooding back and she sat up in bed. "What time is it? Why can't I see anything? Oh my God! Am I blind? Is this some kind of delayed reaction to one of those potions those crazy healers gave me? I knew I shouldn't trust them, I—"

"JESSICA! You aren't blind!"

"Did you just yell at me?" she asked with a sniffle. "You never yell."

There was a heartfelt, disembodied sigh. "You are not blind," Howard told her, enunciating each word with care.

"Then why can't I see?"

"You can't see because there's probably no light in your damned tent so it's even darker than it is outside. And before you ask," he continued as she took a breath to interrupt, "The reason I woke you in the middle of the night is because I didn't think it would be wise for anyone to catch you talking to a disembodied voice and this is the first time you haven't had someone in the tent with you."

"Oh. I-I-I'm sorry I overreacted. But . . . wait a minute. How did you know I'm alone?"

"Remember I told you before that your pendant was powerful?"

"Yeah . . ."

"It's filled with some kind of magical energy. When I hold it and concentrate I-I don't know how to explain it." He sounded a little frustrated. "It's not really *seeing* things, it's more like *knowing* things. Like knowing when you're alone. I know all kinds of things about the world you're in now."

"Well isn't that just wonderful?" Her voice turned angry. "I want to go home! This is nothing like the movies. They don't have doctors here, they have healers. With leeches! And there are no bathrooms! I have to use a chamber pot. A chamber pot! I haven't had a bath since I got here and—"

"Will you be quiet?" Howard demanded. "I don't know how long the link allowing us to communicate will last so we need to make the most of it. Now, while you been lying around getting waited on hand and foot, I've been working my ass off doing research —"

"I haven't been getting waited on hand and foot!" she said in a hurt tone of voice. "Okay, well maybe I have, but I've been through a lot. I need some con-valescence time."

Howard made a rude noise. "Convalescence my ass. You're being an attention whore. Now listen, there are a couple of things you need to know."

"I am not an attention whore," she muttered.

"Are you listening to me?"

"Go ahead, I'm listening." She pushed the pillows into a pile behind her so she could sit up more comfortably. "Have you figured out how to get me home?"

There was no answer to that. Jessica found the silence a little ominous. "Howard? Are you still there?"

"Yeah, sorry Jess. I'm here. And no, I haven't figured out how to bring you back yet, but I'm working on it."

"I know you are Howard."

"I—how are you doing, Jess? Are they treating you all right?"

"I'm an honoured guest," she said, smiling in the dark. "When Ewan can't be with me he's arranged for his squire to be at my beck and call. And he even loaned me his minstrel to keep me entertained."

"You need to be careful, Jess. Remember I told you magic is real in your universe?"

"Yeah, I remember. But I haven't seen anything magical so far." Truth be told, she hadn't seen much outside of her tent.

"Trust me, it's out there. It just might be hidden."

"Hidden? Why?"

"There are a lot of different kingdoms in the

world you're on—"

"Cut to the chase, Howard." Damn she hated the way he liked to beat around the bush.

"Not all the kingdoms are welcoming to users of magic. In fact, some of them are downright nasty."

That certainly got her attention. "How nasty?"

"Think the Salem witch trials and the Spanish Inquisition."

Jessica shivered. "Okay, that is nasty. But why do I have to be careful?"

"You have magical abilities."

"I what?" She couldn't possibly have heard him right.

"It's probably something you've had all along, it just took being sent to this other world to trigger it."

"I what?" Jessica repeated.

"I'm not sure how powerful you are, that's probably going to take some experimentation, but—"

"Are you insane? I do *not* have magic powers and the only thing you're going to experiment with is getting me home!"

"I know it's scary, Jess, but you'll be all right. I'll help you learn to control your power—"

"Howard—"

"Jessica? The link is weakening again. I'll be back as soon as I can. It'd help if you could arrange to be alone once in awhile. In the meantime, be careful."

"No! Don't go!" Jessica felt her throat constrict. "Howard?"

But he was already gone, leaving her alone in the dark. She lay back down but it was a long time before she went back to sleep.

Chapter Nine

"You have got to be kidding!" Jessica looked at the clothing laid out on the bed.

After her pre-dawn chat, Jessica decided maybe Howard was right. Maybe she was enjoying the attention of her invalid status a little too much. So this morning, after having breakfast with Ewan, she requested her clothing so she could get up and maybe even have a look outside her tent.

"Is something wrong, my lady?" Somehow the voice of the lady's maid lacked the sincerity of Ewan's on the word *lady*.

The dress laid out on the bed was lovely, as were the silk undergarments, but Jessica was not in the mood to play dress up.

"When I asked for clothing I meant my own."

"Forgive me, my lady," the maid said. "But these

were the clothes I was told to bring you. I am sorry if they are not up to your standards, but they are the best I could do in such trying times."

Jessica sighed heavily. Time to soothe some ruffled feathers. "I didn't mean to sound ungrateful," she said. "I just—what is your name?"

"Eleanor, my lady."

"I didn't mean to sound ungrateful, Eleanor, it's just that I'd be more comfortable in my own clothes."

"I do not know what was done with them. Shall I help you dress now?"

"Help me dress?" Jessica echoed. What was she, five years old? She took a closer look at the dress lying on the bed, noting the elaborate lacing, the yards of material, and the complicated layers. Maybe she was going to need to suck it up, just this once. It's not as though she could go searching for her own clothes in the voluminous nightgown she was currently wearing.

"Thank you," she said, with as much dignity as she could muster. "I believe I will take that help."

Although the dress wasn't as uncomfortable as it looked, Jessica was mortified at having to have help getting into it and she just couldn't muster up the appreciation for it that Eleanor thought it deserved. It was a deep green colour, made out of some heavy material that probably cost a small fortune, with an under-dress of silver. It had long, pointed sleeves and laced up both the front and back. It was much heavier than it looked and she felt stifled in it.

"Is it supposed to drag on the ground like this?" she asked, twisting to look at the train flowing behind her.

" 'Tis the fashion, my lady," Eleanor told her.

Jessica eyed the bundle of material the maid was bringing closer. "Is that what I think it is?"

Eleanor stopped in her tracks. "My lady?"

"I am so not wearing that thing on my head!"

"But . . . my lady!"

"No! I draw the line at that ridiculous headgear." The flowing veil was bad enough, but it was supposed to be held in place by a weirdly shaped, padded device.

She was saved from a heated argument with the maid by the gentle chime of the bell affixed just outside the tent.

"Come in," Jessica called, still eyeing the headdress with distaste.

Gareth entered, followed closely by Sebastian. Jessica couldn't help preening a bit as their eyes lit with admiration. Eleanor sniffed in annoyance.

"If there's nothing else, my lady?"

Jessica fought the urge to roll her eyes. "You may go, Eleanor."

Cradling the headdress in her arms like it was a baby, Eleanor gave another sniff and left the tent.

"His Highness sends his regrets but he will be unable to join you until this evening," Gareth told her.

"Might I add, my lady, you look most beautiful." He blushed as he said this and dropped his gaze.

"Indeed, you look quite fetching," Sebastian agreed. "It's too bad it's wasted on just the two of us." At her inquiring look he added, "His Highness has requested that you allow him the pleasure of escorting you on a tour of the camp this evening."

Jessica frowned. "In other words, he wants me to stay in my tent."

"I fear so," Sebastian admitted.

"And what if I don't want to stay in my tent?"

There was a slight hesitation as the two men shared a look. "It would not be . . . wise to go against the prince's wishes."

"I see," she said thoughtfully. "Am I a prisoner?"

"Nay, my lady!" Gareth was quick to protest. "Thou art an honoured guest! 'Tis only for thine own safety the prince wishes thee to remain."

Jessica sighed. She'd been looking forward to finally getting some fresh air, but on the other hand she was dependent on the prince's good will and didn't want to do anything to jeopardize it.

"I guess we might as well sit down then," she said, a little ungraciously. She wasn't normally the type to pout, but she felt like she could use a good pout right about now.

"Gareth," she asked. "Do you know what happened to the clothes I was wearing when that bird attacked me?"

"Y-yes, my lady," he said. He tensed up and wouldn't meet her eyes.

"Well?"

"I—I believe there was no saving them, my lady."

Jessica felt the blood drain from her face. "They're gone?" she whispered. Jennifer was going to kill her. "Even the boots?" She'd really loved those boots.

"Nay, I believe the boots still remain, as does thy sword. Would thou have me fetch them?"

"I would be very grateful if you could," Jessica said sincerely.

Gareth all but leaped to his feet, glad to be of use. "I shall return with all speed."

She watched him leave with something akin to relief. At least the museum's sword was safe. Thank God for small favours. She sighed a gusty sigh of relief.

"You seem to be much attached to your clothing, milady," Sebastian ventured.

"Jessica."

"I beg pardon?"

"My name is Jessica. And the clothes weren't mine," she said without thinking. "They were borrowed for a play. I just happened to be wearing them when I arrived on the beach. Jennifer's going to have a cow when I tell her they're gone. But at least the museum's sword is safe."

"Indeed," he said, a note of surprise in his voice.

"Is this having of cows a common occurrence where you are from?"

Jessica sat bolt upright in her chair as she suddenly realized what she'd said. "I mean – that is – I –"

"I think there is a most interesting story to your journey here," Sebastian said slowly, watching her carefully.

She paled slightly, panic churning in her stomach. Damn it, she'd known she wouldn't be able to keep up the pretense. Now Sebastian was going to tell Ewan what a fraud she was and they'd put her in the stocks or something much worse. They didn't use the guillotine in the Middle Ages . . . did they?

"Tell me, Jessica, who sent you here? What plot is being hatched?"

"What? No one, no plot! You have to believe me, my being here was a total accident!" Jessica jumped to her feet and paced back and forth, muttering. "Damn it, Howard, if I ever see you again I am so going to make you pay for that costume. And then I'll beat you to death with your Merlin walking stick!" She whirled to face Sebastian again. "I swear to you, my being here is a total accident. It was all a mistake."

"A mistake?" Sebastian repeated doubtfully.

Jessica took a step closer. "Yes, a big, fat, stupid mistake, made by my ex best friend Howard."

"I see."

"Are you going to tell Prince Ewan?" she asked in a small voice.

"No."

"Because if you are, I'll deny everything and—what did you say?"

"I said no, I will not tell the prince."

Jessica's legs gave out and she sat down abruptly on the bed. "You won't?"

Sebastian shook his head. "Nay. In fact, I am at your disposal should you require assistance to perpetuate your deception."

"You are?" she asked hopefully. "Why? I mean, not that I'm not grateful – I can use all the help I can get – but why would you help me?"

"Let's just say I have my reasons," he said evasively. "Besides," he continued with a grin. "I think you're in dire need of a friend, and truth be told I could use one too."

"You?" Jessica said, relaxing. "You probably have tons of friends. You're a musician – women are always all over the musicians."

The animation left his face and Jessica wondered what she'd said wrong.

"Things aren't always what they seem," Sebastian said quietly. "Especially in the Kingdom of Ghren."

Gareth chose that moment to return, breaking the uncomfortable silence. Jessica could have kissed him.

"Your sword, my lady," he said, bowing low and offering it with a flourish.

"Thank you!" Jessica said, taking from him. "I would have been so screwed if I'd lost this! Oh!" she

looked at his confused face, then darted a look towards Sebastian. "I mean, I would have been most
distressed to have lost it. It's, um, it's a family heir-
loom."

Gareth nodded cautiously.

" 'Tis a beautiful weapon," Sebastian said. "May
I?"

"Of course." Jessica passed the sword over to
him.

"Most unusual workmanship; it's from the South,
I believe, is it not?" He stared pointedly at her.

"Um, yes, yes it is," she agreed quickly.

"'Tis most unusual for a lady to carry such a
weapon," Gareth said.

"Yes, well. Um, I—"

"How good are you with it?" Sebastian asked suddenly, distracting Gareth again. Jessica shot him a
grateful look.

"I used to think I was pretty good, until I saw
Prince Ewan and Gareth fight off that bird."

Gareth blushed and ducked his head.

"Maybe Gareth here could give you some pointers," Sebastian suggested. "He is the squire to the
prince."

Jessica's face lit up. "That would be wonderful!"

"I—but—I . . . I would need permission from the
prince."

"I think the Prince has enough to worry about
without having to see to his honoured guest's train-

ing. We wouldn't want to unduly worry him when this is something we could take care of ourselves, would we?"

"I . . . nay, we would not."

"On the other hand, we would want Lady Jessica to be able to defend herself should she be attacked by ruffians, wouldn't we?"

It was all Jessica could do to hold back her laughter as Sebastian worked his logic on the poor squire, his face a picture of innocence.

"I . . . aye. You speak the truth."

"Then I think just giving her a few pointers, without bothering the Prince about it, would be an admirable thing, would it not?"

Gareth looked from one to the other. When Jessica gave him an hopeful smile, he caved. "I—I—believe so, yes."

"Then it's settled!" Sebastian said, beaming. "Starting tomorrow, we'll find time each day for a little swordplay."

"You're very good at this," Jessica muttered to him.

"I know," Sebastian whispered back. "I've had lots of practice."

Gareth shifted from one foot to the other. "I could not help but notice . . . I mean no disrespect . . ."

Jessica and Sebastian both looked at him curiously.

"Thy sword is need of polishing. T'would be my pleasure to see to it," he blurted out, ducking his head and blushing.

"That'd be great," Jessica told him. The least she could do for the museum's sword was to make sure it was well taken care of.

"I'll see to it at once."

"Oh, but—"

He picked up the sword and was gone before she could stop him.

"He didn't need to do it right this second," she said to an amused Sebastian.

"I think our young friend is somewhat besotted," he told her with a chuckle.

"He's what?" Jessica had to think about that for a moment. "Oh. Oh!" That's all she needed, a teenaged squire with a crush on her. "What am I going do about it?"

Sebastian gave a shrug. "Why do anything? There's no harm in it."

"If you say so," she said dubiously. "Sebastian . . ." she plucked at invisible threads on the coverlet she was sitting on. "You said you'd be willing to help me . . ."

"Yes, I did. And I meant it. What do you need?"

"The thing is . . . Look, I'm sure you've guessed that things are different where I come from."

"And you require my help with more than just sword play?" he guessed.

She turned to look at him and couldn't help the faint note of pleading that crept into her voice. "I just don't want to say or do the wrong thing in front of the prince."

He nodded. "I can understand that. Have you had no dealings with the nobility where you are from?"

"There *is* no nobility where I'm from. Well, over in Europe there is, but it's really not like it is here. Where I'm from we're all pretty much equals."

"Truly I would love to hear more about your land," he told her, raising his hand when she would have interrupted him. "But that can wait until another time. For now, why don't I start with the expectations and duties of a lady of the court."

Chapter Ten

While on the one hand Jessica was grateful for Sebastian's tutelage in the finer points of the nobility of Ghren, she despaired of keeping everything straight in her mind.

Sebastian didn't seem too worried about it though. "If anyone questions anything you do, just tell them that's the way it's done in the South."

"And what if I run into someone from the South?"

He shrugged. "Then tell them you were raised by one of the nomadic tribes and that's how it was done with them."

"You have an answer for everything, don't you?"

"Of course I do, I'm a bard," he said with a grin.

"Really? I thought you were just a minstrel?"

"A slip of the tongue," he said quickly. "Now let's try that curtsy one more time."

He stood in front of her and bowed, and she returned the courtesy by sinking down into a perfect half-curtsy.

"Remember, only direct a full curtsy to someone who's higher in rank, which in your case would be the prince or his father."

"Got it." Jessica nodded.

A page tinkled the bell at the door to her tent to announce the imminent arrival of Prince Ewan.

Jessica felt a faint stirring of panic. "I don't know if I'm ready for this. I mean, having Ewan visit me while I'm confined to my bed recuperating is one thing, but this . . ."

"You'll be fine," Sebastian assured her. "Let him do most of the talking, it shouldn't be too hard," he added with a grin.

"Thank you, Sebastian," she said, placing a hand on his arm.

The bell outside her tent tinkled merrily as the flap opened and Ewan entered. His eyes narrowed briefly as he took in how close Jessica and Sebastian were standing to each other.

"Were it anyone but you, Sebastian . . ." he said, voice cold. "You are dismissed."

While Jessica looked on in surprise, Sebastian executed a perfect bow. "Milord, milady." He was gone before she could say a word.

"Ah, my lady Jessica. Thou art most resplendent. My colours suit thee well, as I knew they would."

"Your colours?" Jessica asked, still a little disturbed by his treatment of Sebastian.

"Aye, silver for the purity of the royal line of Ghren, green for the fertile lands. But come, let me showest thou the encampment that thee might know the might of Ghren."

Pushing her misgivings aside, Jessica allowed Ewan to lead her from the tent. The sun was beginning to set, which made it easier for her eyes to adjust to the natural light. The encampment was much larger than she'd expected. Her tent was situated on a rise in the land, allowing her to look down over the sea of plain white tents, cook fires, people, and animals that extended throughout the entire valley.

"Magnificent, is it not?"

Jessica nodded in agreement. Bemused, she turned in a circle, taking as much of it in as she could. Her tent was one of several on this particular rise, all sporting flags that were green with a silver snake and lion on it. Standing outside the largest tent, there were several guards in green and silver livery who stood at attention and saluted as Ewan passed by. According them the faintest of nods, he tucked Jessica's hand in the crook of his arm and led her down into the encampment.

The tents closest to the hillside appeared to be living quarters for the officers and their families. Children dressed in homespun clothing darted in and out of the shadows, laughing and chasing each other. Several times they passed groups of woman seated under the broad branches of a large tree, doing needlework and gossiping. These groups inevitably fell silent when they caught sight of the prince.

Beyond this area was a make-shift market where vendors were hawking an astonishing variety of wares. They didn't enter the market but paused so Jessica could have a look at it. She'd been to a renaissance fair once but it had been nothing like this.

They passed by the smithies, where large, heavily muscled men were pounding glowing metal into horseshoes, knifes, and swords. Despite the heat coming from the forges, Jessica would have liked to have lingered, but Ewan drew her onwards.

There seemed to be a section for each craft – weavers and spinners, leather workers, basket weavers, potters, and, well away from the rest of the encampment, the tanners. Jessica's favourite were the scribes, where for a price, young men in monks robes would read or write messages.

The light was growing dim by the time they returned, and Jessica was exhausted. Maybe she wasn't as fully recovered as she thought, but there was no way she was going to admit it to Ewan. He'd probably sick his army of healers on her again.

"Now that thou hast been seen in my company, 'tis safe for thee to pass through the encampment at will."

"It is?" Jessica asked.

"Aye, my lady. All now know thee as my guest, and one who is not to be trifled with. Indeed, should they try they will face my wrath. "

Jessica didn't know what to say to this so she stayed quiet.

"And now, alas, I must return to my duties." Ewan bent over her hand and kissed it. "I shall see thee at dinner."

"I look forward to it," Jessica said, stifling her yawn until he departed.

One of the pages held the flap of her tent open for her, and she smiled her thanks, then sank down on her bed with a sigh once she was inside.

"Dorothy, you're definitely not in Kansas any-more," she muttered under her breath. "For one thing, I'm pretty sure Kansas never smelled so bad."

Up here on the hill, inside her tent, the smell wasn't noticeable, but it hung over the low-lying areas like a mantle, growing worse where families were clustered together and even more so in the areas where the soldiers seemed to gather. Ewan, she'd noticed, often dabbed at his nose with a lace-edged handkerchief. At the time she thought he had a cold or allergy, but now she wondered if the cloth had been perfumed. Hadn't she read somewhere about people holding perfumed cloths to their noses to combat the stench of poor sanitation?

She hadn't seen any laundry facilities or bathing areas, but one thing she had definitely noticed was that very few of the women were dressed in dresses as elaborate as hers. It made Jessica feel out of place, although probably they just had more sense than to traipse around the camp in their good clothes. Maybe being thought of as a noblewoman wasn't all it was cracked up to be.

* * * * *

Thackery heard the sound of Paran's laboured breathing long before the peak of the wizard's hat he insisted on wearing crested the stairs. The hat made Paran look foolish, although he didn't seem to care. He paused by the doorway to catch his breath before moving closer.

"When you are not up here trying to stare a hole through my best scrying bowl you are pacing back and forth wearing a rut in my good carpet. You need to find a new hobby."

"I can't help myself," Thackery said, shrugging helplessly. "She has not left my thoughts in all the years we were apart and now, to have her so close . . ."

"She looks so much like her mother," Paran said, peering into the bowl. "Who is that with her?"

"That is Prince Ewan." The words came out short and sharp. "He was a nasty sort as a lad and he doesn't seem much improved with age. I do not like the attention he is paying to her."

They watched in silence for a few moments.

"This is so hard, Paran. She has no idea she belongs on this world, no clue as to who she really is."

"Has she shown any magical abilities?"

"None that I've seen. They may be latent, or perhaps she has none."

The old man snorted. "With you as her father? I would say it is more a matter of her lacking the knowledge to tap into them." He stroked his long, white beard thoughtfully. "Perhaps it is just as well."

Thackery looked at him in surprise. "What do you mean?"

"Think of it. Anakaron is drawn to power. Were she to display the power that you, or even her mother, had at that age he would be drawn as a moth to a flame."

"Perhaps you are right. But I would be happier if I knew she had a way to protect herself."

"Have you thought of a way to draw her to us?"

"No." Thackery waved a hand over the bowl and the image of Jessica disappeared. "I need to go after her."

"No, it is far too dangerous! You are fortunate the power surge you created bringing her to this world did not attract undue attention as it is. The ruse of making it appear as though that fledgling wizard sent her here by mistake was a good one."

"That was your doing, not mine. My only thought was to bring my daughter back to her home."

"And so you have. But you must let her come to you. You cannot take the chance of being caught on the northern continent."

"So much time has passed, perhaps Anakaron has forgotten—"

"Do you really think that even after all these years Anakaron will have forgotten you?"

Thackery turned away with a sigh. "No. No more than I could forget about him."

"And what about Jesseminathus? You, above all people, know what Anakaron was capable of when it came to his desire to possess Farenalyssia. What do you think he'd do if he knew she had a daughter?"

Chapter Eleven

After her tour of the encampment the day before, her dress had to be cleaned. Eleanor offered her a selection of other dresses to choose from in its place, but Jessica wanted something a little more comfortable, and a lot less elaborate. Eleanor was so thoroughly scandalized by her request for trousers that Jessica was ready to give up. She dismissed the maid and then flopped down on her bed with a sigh.

It was at this point Gareth and Sebastian paid her a visit. Jessica sat up and eyed the squire up and down, which made him blush and Sebastian cock an eyebrow.

"Gareth," she said in her most cajoling tone of voice. "Do you think you could find me some men's clothing in my size?"

She smiled sweetly and gave him the puppy dog

eyes that always worked when she asked Howard for a favour.

Gareth gulped and stuttered, and then nodded. "I will do my best, milady."

"Shame on you," Sebastian said as the tent flap closed behind the squire. "Playing on the poor boy's affection like that."

Jessica shot him a guilty look. "I know, but desperate times call for desperate measures."

Gareth returned more quickly than she expected with an assortment of hose, trousers, tabards, tunics, shirts, and a beautiful velvet coat, much like the one she'd been wearing for the play. She shooed him and Sebastian out of the tent so she could change into dark, close-fitting, homespun trousers, a white shirt, and a short sleeved leather jerkin over top. Sighing with relief, she called them back in for a viewing.

"Thou art most beautiful!" Gareth said, then immediately blushed and ducked his head.

Sebastian looked her up and down with a serious look on his face. "Are you sure this is a good idea?"

"Maybe not, but it's more what I'm used to and besides," she said, giving a final tug on the belt. "It's so much more comfortable and practical."

"Ghren is a somewhat . . . conservative kingdom. I would caution you that few women ever go about attired thusly. The prince may not like it."

"Well the prince doesn't have to like, only I do." she said stubbornly. "I'll just make sure I'm wearing a dress whenever I'm with him."

"Then I must say I agree with Gareth. You are beautiful indeed, my lady Jessica."

With her hair in a simple braid and dressed in more familiar, if not more comfortable, clothing, Jessica enjoyed herself far more with Sebastian and Gareth than she had with Ewan. The people she met were definitely friendlier, not standoffish as they had been when she was the prince. She didn't dwell on why that might be.

The next morning Jessica snuck out of her tent before Eleanor arrived. She met Gareth and Sebastian in a grove just far enough from the camp so they wouldn't be noticed, but close enough for protection if they needed it. She was a little disappointed that she wasn't able to show off the museum's sword, but Gareth insisted they use wooden practice swords. He took his role as her instructor very seriously.

"First I will need to determine how much you know of swordplay."

He passed her one of the practice swords and had Sebastian stand facing her with the other. Jessica opened her mouth to protest, then shrugged instead. She stood in front of Sebastian and held her sword in guard position.

"Begin," Gareth said.

Thirty seconds later, Jessica was lying on her back in the dirt. "Ow," she said, shaking out her smarting fingers. Her practice sword lay several feet away.

Sebastian offered his free hand to help her up, but not before she caught the look that passed between him and the squire.

"I wasn't ready," she grumbled. "You surprised me is all."

It was to their credit that neither man pointed out an enemy wouldn't wait until she was ready.

"My apologies," Sebastian said.

Gareth gave her what she thought was supposed to be a reassuring smile. That only made it worse.

"Again," he said.

Five times she and Sebastian crossed swords and five times Jessica ended up on her butt in the dirt. It was Sebastian who thought to ask when the last time she'd had to defend herself was.

"With a sword? Never! Using a sword is just for fun, uh, where I come from."

Sebastian made a kind of choking noise while Gareth just kind of moaned. And that ended her lesson for the day.

"Perhaps," Gareth suggested as they made their way back to camp, "Thee might consider setting aside the sword and carrying a dagger instead?"

"In close quarters a well honed dagger can be far more effective than a sword," Sebastian pointed out.

"No way," Jessica shook her head. "Where I go, the sword goes."

Gareth sighed. "Then we must meet earlier upon the morrow."

"And perhaps again in the afternoon," Sebastian suggested.

"Aye."

Jessica glared at the two men as she trailed after them. She hadn't done that badly . . . had she?

* * * * *

After her third day of clandestine meetings with Sebastian and Gareth, Jessica's muscles were finally starting to loosen up a bit. As much as she'd give for a hot tub or a hot oil massage, even getting clean again would be a blessing.

"Eleanor," she said as the woman entered the tent, "I can't stand feeling so grubby any more. Is there some way I could get a bath?"

"A bath, my Lady?" Eleanor seemed a little repulsed by the idea. Jessica vaguely remembered that in medieval times a lot of people had an aversion to bathing.

"A bath," Jessica repeated firmly.

"Well, my Lady," Eleanor hesitated. "I might be able to borrow a horse's trough. It could be scrubbed out and water heated . . ."

"Sounds like a lot of work." Jessica had visions of coming out of that bath smelling like a horse. "Any other ideas?"

"Personally, I'd use the river," Sebastian spoke up from the corner where he was softly strumming his mandolin. "In fact, I do, on a regular basis."

"It certainly sounds cleaner than a horse's trough. How private is it?"

"What few ladies might be tempted to go there are resting at this time of day, and the men are at arms practice."

"Sounds perfect. Eleanor, soap and towels if you please."

Eleanor curtsied and left, looking as though she'd just sucked a lemon.

"What was with the face?" Jessica asked, staring after her in surprise. "It's not like I'm asking for her first born."

"You do realize that a lady would expect her maid to join her, if for no other reason than to scrub her back," Sebastian told her.

"Good thing I'm not a lady then," Jessica said with a grin. "And I'm more than capable of washing my own back, thank you very much. Unless of course you'd care to join me?"

Jessica was growing fond of Sebastian. He reminded her a lot of Howard.

"Thank you, no," he grinned back at her. "You are a personal guest of the prince, and I quite enjoy my head being attached to my body."

Her eyes widened, "He wouldn't really, would he?"

"Do not underestimate the Prince Ewan," he said gravely. "Things are not always what they seem."

Jessica had the feeling he was about to say more but Eleanor chose that moment to return. A few minutes later, laden with everything she needed for her bath, including fresh clothes, she was following the path to the river. She grinned, thinking about the look of relief on Eleanor's face when she realized she wasn't expected to come too.

The river, though small as rivers go, was everything Sebastian promised. She hesitated at first, not really trusting his assurance of privacy. However, the deep, clear pool beckoned and she shed her inhibitions along with her clothes.

The water was surprisingly warm from the sun, and deep enough for swimming. Jessica resisted the temptation to just laze about in the water. Someone else might come along with the same idea she had.

The soap lathered up easily, without any of the greasiness she expected. She'd read somewhere that soap was made from fat in the middle ages. Just another of the many differences she'd discovered so far. She soaped up her hair, and then ducked her head under water to rinse it. It felt so good to be clean again!

She hated to leave the water, but the longer she stayed the more fearful she was of discovery. She couldn't shake the feeling she was being watched. Quickly, she rubbed herself dry with the rough towel, then put on the clean shirt she'd brought with her.

Once covered by the shirt she didn't feel so exposed and was able to relax. Yawning, she stretched out in the sun on the bank of the river to let her hair dry. She was just teetering on the edge of sleep when she was interrupted.

"Jessica . . ."

"Go away, Howard, I'm sleeping."

"You're not sleeping and we need to talk."

"I don't think I'm talking to you yet. Besides, I haven't felt this good since I got here."

"Tough. I'm tired of you wallowing in self-pity. You've got things you have to start dealing with, as soon as possible."

Jessica sat up quickly. "I am not wallowing!"

"And you're not sleeping any more, either." There was a hint of smugness in his voice.

"Creep," Jessica muttered as she pulled on the rest of her clothes.

"First of all, I wasn't kidding about the magic . . ."

She raised a hand that he couldn't see, "I believe you, really I do, but I haven't seen any signs of it myself."

"I'm serious Jess, you have magical abilities. Just how much I'm not sure, but definitely some. You need to learn your potential and how to control it before it gets you into trouble."

"Trouble? How much more trouble could I be in?"

"Well, I—"

"Never mind, I don't think I want to know. So now what? I mean, I have this magic in me, how do I get it out?"

"The first step is helping you touch the magic. Close your eyes." He paused, giving her time. "Now, center yourself, like you do in your Tai Chi exercises. Bring your awareness to the surface."

Jessica did what he told her. The sensation of inner peace was slow in coming, her thoughts kept spinning. She began slow breathing exercises. The sound of the river and the sun on her face combined to relax her.

"Good," said Howard, just like he was with her. "Now, reach deeper inside of yourself, and tell me what you feel. Really push."

She reached, and could almost feel something but it stayed just out of her reach. Again and again she tried, each time falling just short of her goal. It was tiring work, and very frustrating. The harder she tried the longer it took with the next try.

"This isn't working, Howard."

"Relax, Jessie. You're making it more difficult than it needs to be. Stop trying so hard. This isn't something that can be forced, it needs to be felt. Now, try again."

With a sigh, Jessica did what she was told, and failed yet again. Keeping her eyes closed, she rested for a bit. She listened to the birds in the trees and the water passing in the river. She felt the sun's warmth permeating her.

Suddenly, her eyes snapped open. "Oh! What

was that?"

Jessica looked around with wonder filled eyes, expecting everything to have changed somehow. She was a little surprised it hadn't. "It's like . . . I don't have the words to describe it. It's like a brilliant iridescent pulsing flame, hot and at the same time cold to both extremes. Is that, is it. . .?"

"That's it!" Howard exclaimed. "You've touched the magic within. That's exactly what I felt the first time, only mine's more of a spark. And now that you've found it, it will always be there for you."

"I can't believe it," Jessica said. "And you think I've always had that in me?"

She looked up into the trees, trying to see them in a more magical light. It was a little disappointing that all she saw were trees.

"I think so, it just took the transfer to bring it to where you could sense it."

"But what do I do with it?"

"With the right training, anything you want. We'll start with something simple," decided Howard. "How would you like to learn to make fire?"

"I don't know, Howard. It sounds kinda dangerous." Having magic was one thing. Using it was something else altogether.

"Not really," he assured her. "With your first few attempts you'll be lucky if you can make a spark, let alone a flame."

"Do I have to wave my hands around, chanting

like you did?" As cool as it would be to work a magic spell, there were limits to how far she'd embarrass herself.

"Probably not. From what I can tell, you have what's known as intuitive magic. It's more a matter of focusing and then directing the magic to take the form you want it to."

"Focus and direct. I can do that. So . . . now what?"

"Maybe you should move to someplace with a little more concealment. The last thing you need is for someone from the camp to see you."

"You mean they could see me bathing from the camp?" Her voice rose as glanced around her, appalled. "No wonder it felt like there were eyes on me. Why didn't you warn me? Oh, jeez, this is so embarrassing!"

"Jessica!" Howard's voice rose as well so he could be heard over her tirade. "I didn't mean to imply someone could have been watching you from the camp. It's just that having someone catch you attempting magic might turn out to be more than just a bit embarrassing. And magic can be more noticeable than a naked woman."

"Well, maybe magic's more noticeable to *you* than a naked woman . . ."

Jessica felt, rather than heard, his mental sigh of exasperation. She could picture him running a hand through his hair making it messier than ever. She grinned at the image in her mind.

"Jessica, could you try working with me here?"

"Okay, okay, don't get your panties in a twist."

She moved a little deeper into the woods lining the river and found a large, flat rock in a bit of a cleared area. It was surrounded on three sides by trees; the fourth was open towards the river.

"I suppose you want me to collect some firewood now."

"Just a few twigs and some dried grass. Let's not make it too hard."

Jessica gathered up a respectable pile of tinder and as a precaution, surrounded it with a small ring of stones. Better to be safe than sorry.

"Okay, now what?"

"Stand back a bit to give yourself some room. Feel the magic within you, then think of flame, or fire. You can point to where you want the fire to go, if you like. Sometimes it helps to give the magic a direction."

Jessica stood back a few paces from her tiny fireplace. She reached for the magic within, and for a few seconds just revelled in the sensation. It would be so easy to become lost in the feeling it evoked.

She felt the magic pulse as it responded to her. Raising her right hand, she pointed at the tinder and thought of fire.

The resulting explosion of flame threw her backwards.

Chapter Twelve

J essica saw stars when her head hit the ground. By the time she recovered her wits and was sitting upright again, the flames had burned themselves out.

"Jess! Are you all right?"

"What happened?"

Howard's voice was as shaky as she felt. "I don't know, Jess. I – through our connection with the amulet I could feel the magic explode right out of you. I'm going to have to study this. Just don't try using magic on your own until I figure out what happened. You must have a lot more power stored inside you than I counted on."

She opened her mouth to reply, then heard the noise of someone approaching. Several someones, by the sound of it. Howard went silent before she could tell him to put a rush on those studies of his.

"My Lady Jessica," exclaimed Ewan as he rushed into the small clearing. "What has occurred? Hast thee been set upon?" He was carrying his bared sword and leading several guardsmen, also with swords in hand.

"I'm sorry," Jessica said. She could feel her face heat in embarrassment. "It was just a little accident."

The guardsmen behind Ewan muttered nervously. Jessica couldn't blame them, she couldn't quite believe it herself. The grass of the clearing was scorched, as were the nearest overhanging trees. Even Ewan looked a little nonplussed, but he at least sheathed his sword.

"Whatever were thee doing here?"

Discretion being the better part of valor, she decided it would probably be better if she didn't confess that she'd been bathing in the river and then practicing magic. "I . . . um . . . I was out for a walk along the river."

She wasn't sure if he believed her or not, but all he said was, "Thee should not wander from the camp without a proper escort."

"I see that now," she said, keeping her eyes down in what she hoped looked like an expression of contrition.

"May we escort thee back to the camp?"

Jessica meekly took his proffered arm, and walked beside him with as much dignity as she could muster.

The guardsmen followed, still muttering amongst themselves, swords in hand.

* * * * *

"I was curious about something," Jessica said as she and Ewan dined that evening.

Ever since he'd escorted her around the encampment, Ewan insisted they have dinner together each night in a civilized fashion. A small corner of her tent had been cleared and a table for two set up. A steady stream of pages served them their multi-course meal, and two more pages stood ready to refill wine goblets or offer a fine linen napkin. Jessica did her part for civilization by making sure she wore a dress.

"Thou hast only to ask and I will make haste to alleviate thy curiosity," he said promptly.

Jessica toyed with the food on her plate while she chose her words with care. "I understand this is your land, and this appears to be an armed camp, but I have to wonder who, exactly, you're fighting with."

"Ah," Ewan speared a piece of what Jessica thought might be chicken. The bland food tasted pretty much the same each night. A line creased his brow as he frowned and she itched to reach over and smooth it away. "Be assured, as a stranger and guest amongst us thy safety is in no peril."

"I wasn't worried about my safety." But she *was* becoming increasingly curious.

"I would not needlessly trouble thee."

"My people have a saying, a trouble shared is a trouble halved."

"A most interesting adage." Ewan toyed with the stem of his goblet and sighed. "It is a not unusual tale, but one most unflattering to our royal judgment." He straightened in his seat and squared his shoulders.

"My father took into his employ a wizard of middling power, as is custom for a king of his stature. The wizard was not as he seemed and an argument ensued with my father casting the varlet out." He took a sip of his wine. His blue eyes darkened with anger. "Through trickery and treachery the wizard came into possession of our castle and now sits yonder in comfort while we are kept at bay by his army of demons and monsters."

Jessica was listening wide-eyed, not even pretending to eat. "A whole army?"

"Aye. He was more cunning than he appeared and turned to the black arts for his petty revenge. We took him in on good faith and thus he repays our generosity." Ewan threw down his fork with a clatter.

Jessica started.

"Forgive me, my lady," he said, instantly contrite. " 'Twas not my intent for thee to be exposed to my ill humour."

"It's all right. I don't blame you for being angry over this whole situation."

"My Lord?" the voice came from outside of the

tent.

A look of intense anger flashed across Ewan's face at the interruption, gone so quickly that Jessica wondered if she really saw it.

"Apologies, my lady. It seems I must cut our time together short."

"I understand," Jessica said.

She stared thoughtfully at the tent flap after it closed behind him. Finishing her meal, she dismissed the pages and went over to sit on her bed. When she was sure she was alone she pulled out the pendant.

"Howard? Are you there?"

This was the first time she'd tried to initiate contact and she breathed a quiet sigh of relief when he answered.

"I'm here, Jessica."

"Did you hear what Ewan and I were talking about?"

"I heard you questioning him about this fight they seem to be having."

"Well, what do you think?" Jessica reclined against the pillows and closed her eyes.

"I don't know, Jess," Howard hesitated. "It almost sounded to me like. . ."

"Like what?"

"Never mind. It's a shame you were interrupted."

"When I first woke up I overheard Gareth talking to someone and he said they thought I might be able to help them. Could I?"

"Jessica, you tried to call up a fire and just about blew yourself up. I don't think getting involved at this stage of the game is a very good idea."

She could almost hear the frown in his voice.

"But if there's something I could do, shouldn't I do it? I mean, I do sort of owe them for taking care of me."

"What happened to good old, 'I don't get involved in other people's problems' Jessie?"

She blushed, even though there was no one to see her. "Nothing, I just think I should try and help if I can."

"This wouldn't have anything to do with tall, blond and studly, would it?"

"No! I - well, maybe, just a little."

There was a moment of silence through which Jessica could picture Howard smirking at her. She supposed it served her right for describing Ewan in such glowing terms.

"You don't think I have that Swedish thing going on, do you?" Jessica asked, sitting up suddenly.

"Swedish thing . . . Do you mean Stockholm Syndrome?"

"Same diff."

Howard sighed loudly. "Jessica, you do not have Stockholm Syndrome. You're suffering from it being too long since you've had a boyfriend. So am I, but I'm not feeling the urge to go do something that could get me killed."

"But—"

"Listen, we're going to have to talk about this later, I'm having a hard time hearing you, this amulet must have a time limit. Just promise me you won't try any magic on your own."

"But—"

"Promise me!"

"I promise," she said, pouting slightly. "Jeez Howard, you sure know how to suck the fun out of things."

"Just be careful, Jess," Howard replied, voice fading.

* * * * *

"So guys," Jessica said while she was having the noon-day meal with Gareth and Sebastian. What was it they called it, luncheon? Nuncheon? Ewan was off doing whatever it was that princes did during the day; she usually only saw him in the evenings. "Tell me about this monster army that chased everybody out of the castle."

Gareth choked on the drink he was taking. Sebastian merely raised an eyebrow. "What would you like to know?"

"Well, for starters, how come everyone's camped out in this valley instead of in the castle? I mean, when you saw the monster army coming, why didn't you just batten down the hatches and hold them off from inside the castle? Isn't that how a siege works?

"An interesting question," Sebastian said. "I was not present when the attack occurred. I arrived after the fact. Gareth?"

Gareth swallowed hard. "It was ghosts that drove us forth. Fearsome ghosts. At first it was only the nobles being haunted – specters and nightmares being visited upon them in the dark of night. Little sleep was had and tempers grew ever short. Then the phantoms began to appear after the sun had arisen. We knew not from whence they came. So fearsome were they we fled, with barely what we could carry, 'til we arrived hither."

"So the wizard conjured up an army of ghosts to drive everyone out of the castle, and now he keeps you out with his army of monsters," Jessica mused. "What does he want?"

"Your pardon?"

"Has he made any demands? Sent a representative to negotiate for anything?"

"I . . . nay, he has done none of these things."

"So he's just sitting there, all by himself in the castle while his monsters keep everyone else out," Jessica said thoughtfully. There was something fishy about this whole set-up. She couldn't understand why no one seemed to see it except her.

They finished their meal in silence, and when they were done Jessica pulled on her boots and strapped on her sword.

"Okay guys, let's go."

Gareth and Sebastian exchanged confused glances. "Go where?" Sebastian asked cautiously.

"To the battlefield of course. I want to see this monster army for myself."

"Nay!" Gareth exclaimed. "'Tis madness!"

"If I'm to help you," Jessica explained patiently, "I'll need to see what I'm up against."

"There are places from which to see battleground without putting ourselves at too much risk," Sebastian admitted. "It should be safe enough."

"The prince will be most displeased," said Gareth.

"Then we just won't tell him," Jessica said sweetly.

* * * * *

"I don't see anything unusual," Jessica said, glancing around.

They were concealed in a copse on a hill overlooking the so-called battlefield. The field was rutted and churned up in places, but other than that it looked pretty harmless. It certainly didn't look as though terrible battles had been taking place on it.

In the distance the castle stood on a rise, squat and formidable looking. Jessica was disappointed there was no moat surrounding it – what was a castle without a moat? There was a flag waving from the tallest tower, but it was too far away to make out the crest on it.

"The monsters be there," Gareth said in a whisper. "They just be hidden."

A horn sounded to the left of them.

"What's that?" Jessica asked.

"It's the call to battle," Sebastian told her. "It looks like we're in for a skirmish."

They watched as a small detachment from the army formed a double line along the edge of the field. Ewan — Jessica could tell it was him from the way he carried himself and from the green and silver he wore — rode a magnificent white horse up and down the line. She imagined he was offering last minute instructions and encouragement. There was no movement from the field until the horn sounded once more and Ewan led the charge.

From out of nowhere, the monsters appeared. Jessica stared open-mouthed at the sheer size and variety of them. Some had fur, most had scales, and a very few had both. Their teeth went from large and dripping with venom to huge and terrifying. A few had wings and had risen in the air to make strafing runs on the incoming soldiers.

Ewan's army was not doing well. They were clawed and bitten and overwhelmed by sheer numbers, while they managed to do very little damage to the monsters. In fact, it appeared as though they weren't even leaving a mark on the monsters.

The horn sounded again and this time it was a call

to retreat. Ewan's soldiers left the battlefield and made their way slowly back to camp, taking their wounded with them. As the last soldier left the battlefield, the monsters went back to wherever it was they came from.

"I beseech you," Gareth begged. "May we not return to the camp?"

Jessica nodded. "I think I've seen everything I need to see here," she said.

She'd seen enough, and more. In fact, she'd seen right through the monsters. Ewan's men were fighting an army of illusions.

Chapter Thirteen

After their trip to the battlefield, Gareth excused himself to attend to the prince. Sebastian suggested he and Jessica visit the marketplace on the north side of the camp and she agreed absently, mind still on what she'd witnessed on the battlefield. She couldn't wait to see what Howard had to say about it.

Though she tried to focus on the wares the vendors had on display, she was too preoccupied to pay them the attention they deserved. Finally, Sebastian suggested they stop for a drink at one of the open-air taverns.

"I'm sorry," Jessica said, once they were seated. "I haven't been very good company."

"I understand your distraction," he said, as the bar maid set two wooden mugs of mead in front of them. "The demon army is an awe inspiring sight."

"Ewan said this whole thing started because of an argument the king had with a wizard. Do you know any of the details?"

Sebastian took a sip of his drink. "Gareth's story of how everyone was driven from the castle is essentially what most people agree on. What caused the argument between King Randolph and the wizard, however . . . I've only had rumours to go on, but I think I've been able to piece together the truth."

Jessica took a sip of her mead. The sweet honey flavor burst over her tongue leaving behind only the mildest of burns as it made its way to her stomach. "Hey!" she said in surprise. "This is pretty good!"

Sebastian grinned at her and she blushed. "Sorry, go on with your story."

"As is the case with so many conflicts, this one had to do with money. The wizard performed a service for the king and then either tried to extort more money for it, or the king decided the service wasn't worth as much as he promised."

"Okay, I'm with you so far. Why didn't the wizard just use his magic to steal the money he was owed, or thought he was owed?"

"It might have been some wizard's code, but I believe the reality is that Randolph keeps the treasury in a magic proof vault. He's never been comfortable around magic workers."

"It seems odd that the wizard hasn't simply held the castle for ransom until he gets what he wants. I wonder if there's something else going on here."

"If there is, I know nothing about it." Sebastian paused for a sip of his mead before continuing. "I hope you realize that you are under no obligation to help the king . . . or the king's son."

Jessica blushed. "I know, it's just . . . I like to feel useful."

"An admirable quality, when used wisely, but foolish when one becomes embroiled in a difficult, and dangerous, situation."

"Jeez, you sound just like Howard," Jessica muttered.

"Howard?"

"Oh, he's my best friend. Back where I came from, that is."

"He sounds like a very wise man. I would very much like to meet him some day."

"I'm sure he'd like that too," she said, grinning suddenly at the mental image of Howard meeting the handsome bard. Suddenly, several things clicked into place. Ewan's snide comments, the way Sebastian didn't have a harem of women fawning over him . . . "Does the fact that you're gay have anything to do with the reason Ewan trusts you around me?"

A frown furrowed his brow. "I do not believe I am any happier than the next man, nor does it matter to Prince Ewan."

"That's not what I mean. I mean gay, as in homo-sexual, a lover of men, not women."

Sebastian's face cleared of all expression. "Forgive me, my lady. I did not realize you did not know of my preferences. I will not trouble you further." He rose as if to leave.

"Wait a minute!" Jessica sputtered, confused at his sudden coldness. "What just happened here? Where are you going?"

It was his turn to look confused. "I—I assumed you would no longer wish to associate with me, that knowing the truth you find me offensive now."

"Sit down," she told him. "I take it this has happened to you before? That friends have turned on you because of your sexual preference?"

"I have no friends in Ghren," Sebastian said softly, in a voice that broke her heart. He sat back down. "I had one true friend, but he has disappeared. That's why I came back – to find out what happened to him."

"I'm sorry," Jessica said, reaching across the table to lay her hand on his. "If there's anything I can do to help, just let me know."

"I thank you, my Lady Jessica. And I apologize for jumping to conclusions."

"It's all right. I understand, really I do. My friend Howard is a lover of men too."

"Truly?" he asked in surprise.

"Truly," she assured him.

"He is a very lucky man, to have you as a friend," he said with a smile.

She grinned back at him. "Damn right he is."

* * * * *

Jessica was enjoying her time with Sebastian so much that it was with surprise she saw one of the servers threading his way through the crowd, lighting thick candles on the tables and torches set on stakes around the perimeter of the tavern.

"I didn't realize it was getting so late," she said. "I guess we should be getting back. Ewan's probably wondering where I've wandered off to."

They were both a little tipsy from the amount of mead they consumed, but made it back to Jessica's tent without tripping over anything – or anyone.

Ewan was pacing back and forth in front of her tent. He stopped when he spotted them and stood waiting with his arms folded across his chest. Jessica thought he looked like a parent waiting for a pair of teenagers who'd stayed out too late

"Uh, oh. Looks like we're in trouble," Jessica said with a tiny giggle.

"Mayhap thee art not what thee pretends minstrel. Should there be aught to have me believe otherwise, I will with all haste finish what the king began ten years ago," he said in a clipped tone to Sebastian.

Something flashed in Sebastian' eyes. "Your pardon, my lord, I—"

Jessica stepped in between the two men. "It was

my fault. I've heard of mead before, but I've never had the chance to try it. I gotta say, it really packs a punch, know what I mean?"

Ewan looked over her head at Sebastian. "You are dismissed, minstrel."

Without looking at Jessica, Sebastian bowed and made a hasty retreat.

"Hey!" Jessica smacked Ewan on the chest. "That was downright rude!" She didn't like the way he was glaring at Sebastian either.

Ewan gave himself a little shake, and the look he gave her was one of complete contrition. He took her hands in his and sank to one knee. "Please forgive me, my lady. I was but overcome with fear for thy safety. 'Tis perilous times we abide in."

"I guess I could have let someone know where I was," she said, just a little grudgingly. "Or at least paid better attention to the passing time. I'm sorry for worrying you."

"Then let us speak no more of it," he said, rising to his feet again. "We shall dine and make merry, and our cares will be no more."

Jessica would rather have spoken more about the way he treated Sebastian, but Ewan was already leading her into the tent and summoning his pages. Maybe it was just the mead, but he didn't seem quite as princely as he had before.

As if he sensed something of her mood, Ewan put himself out to be more charming than ever that evening. He plied her with wine and flattery and fine food until Jessica forgot she was annoyed with him and he was once again her shining hero. He didn't even seem to mind she hadn't changed into a dress for him.

At the end of the evening he paused by the flap of her tent and for a heart-stopping moment Jessica thought he was about to kiss her. However he only kissed her hand, as usual. She tried not to appear disappointed.

"My lady, it would give me great joy if thou wouldst consent to accompany me for a ride on the morrow."

"That would be wonderful," she said dreamily.

"I shall sleep and dream of thee," he said.

He kissed her hand again and closed the tent flap behind him. Jessica sighed, a sappy smile on her face as she turned away to get ready for bed. While she put up with Eleanor helping her with the elaborate dresses, she refused to have help getting her nightgown on.

"Did I just hear you agree to go for a ride tomorrow?" Howard's voice broke into her haze of happiness.

"Yes you did. A ride with a prince."

"You do know that a ride means horses, don't you?"

Jessica frowned as she started unlacing her jerkin. "So?"

"Have you ever been on a horse?"

"Sure I have!" she said defensively.

"The pony ride in Harrison Park when you were ten doesn't count," Howard said dryly.

"I've watched plenty of Westerns, how hard could it be?" Her voice was slightly muffled as she pulled a voluminous nightgown over her head.

"I don't even know where to start with that one," he said with a sigh.

"Listen, Howard, there's something else. I got Gareth and Sebastian to show me the battlefield—"

"You what?" His voice rose an octave.

"Chill! We were perfectly safe. Anyway, it was really weird . . ."

"How so?"

"Well, this monster army everyone's so worked up about? I watched Ewan lead a charge against them – they just appeared out of nowhere and cut his army up bad before he finally retreated again. But the really weird part? I could see right through them."

"What do you mean, see through them?"

"Exactly what I said. It's like they were projections, or ghosts, or—"

"Or illusions," Howard said thoughtfully.

"Yeah. But the thing is, no one else seemed to realize it." Jessica pulled down the covers on the bed and removed the warming pan. Damn, she could get used to this.

"Are you sure about that?"

"Yes, I'm sure. But how come I can see through these things and no one else can?"

"Probably because of your magical abilities."

"Really? So you think I'd be, like, immune to these things? I mean, I can see right through them so they can't hurt me, right?"

"I don't know Jess, I'll look into it and see what I can find out. Promise me you'll stay away from them until I do."

"Sure thing, Howard." She yawned and climbed into bed. "Maybe we can use this as a way to help Ewan get his castle back."

"I don't know about that, Jess. But I'll look into it."

Chapter Fourteen

J essica drew herself up to her full height of five feet, six inches and stood with her legs braced apart, her hands fisted on her hips. She was prepared to do battle.

"You can't be serious!"

"To wear anything else would be scandalous, my lady," Eleanor said emphatically.

"It's a freaking dress!"

"'Tis a riding habit, my lady. 'Tis what the other ladies will be wearing, though I daresay none will be so fine."

"Other ladies?" Jessica said weakly.

"Aye, my lady. Tis a royal procession."

Crap! That sounded really . . . official. Ewan wasn't just some random hot guy, he was a prince, and people looked up to him. Could she really afford to embarrass him by showing up in pants? Maybe she needed to give in just this once.

"How can wearing a dress be less scandalous than wearing pants for riding?" she asked, a little desperately.

"What else wouldst thee wear when riding side saddle?"

"Side saddle?" Jessica blanched.

"How else would a lady ride?"

In a daze, Jessica allowed herself to be dressed in what amounted to an elaborate costume in heavy dark green cloth with silver trim. Compromising on her hair, she allowed Eleanor to braid it and then coil the braid over her head, pinning it in place.

"Thank you, Eleanor," she said. "Now, would you be so kind as to tell his majesty I'll just be another few minutes? I have something I must attend to . . . alone."

Sniffing her disapproval at foreigners and their high handed manner of keeping royalty waiting, Eleanor did as she was told. The second she was out of sight, Jessica pulled out her pendent.

"Howard?" She shook the pendent as though that would wake him up. "Howard, are you there?"

"I'm here, I'm here," he said, sounding irritable. "You just interrupted me in the middle of—"

"I don't give a tiny rat's ass what I interrupted you in the middle of, I'm in serious trouble here!"

"Oh for the love of . . . what did you do this time?"

"I didn't do anything! I just need you to tell me everything you know about riding side saddle."

There was a pregnant pause.

"Did you say side saddle?"

"Yes I said side saddle! I don't have much time, so could you please hurry up?"

There was a snorting noise that sounded suspiciously like laughter before Howard got himself under control. "Well, if you're lucky, they'll use one of the earlier versions which were pretty much just a padded seat with a foot-rest and your horse will be led by another rider."

"That doesn't sound so bad. What if I'm not lucky?"

"Then you'll end up in one of the more normal looking saddles where you hook your right leg around the pommel. There'll be a horn as well for stability. And instead of a foot-rest, there'll be a covered stirrup to put your left foot in. Oh, and you'll be the one in charge of steering the horse."

"This is starting to sound way too complicated," Jessica moaned. "Maybe I should just pretend I'm sick."

"You'll do fine. Just remember to keep your back straight and to hold the reins evenly."

"Okay, here goes nothing. Thanks Howard."

"You're welcome, Jess. Good luck."

And to think she'd once laughed at him for majoring in Medieval Studies in college. She owed him a bottle of scotch. Or at least an apology. Jessica took a deep breath and exited the tent. Ewan and Gareth were waiting patiently just a few paces away, pages holding the bridles of three horses.

"I'm sorry I kept you waiting," she said, eyeing the horses with trepidation.

"Nay, 'tis we who are early," Ewan said, dismissing her apology with a wave of his hand. "Thou art most becoming in thy riding habit."

She almost asked becoming what before stopping herself. Instead she smiled and said simply, "Thank you."

Ewan led her over to the horses. Her heart sank as she saw one of them was saddled in the second version of side saddle Howard had described.

"I pray thee forgive our barbaric ways, my lady. There is no mounting block. If I may be so bold as to offer my services?"

Jessica had no idea what he was talking about, but nodded anyway. She let out a small gasp as he picked her up easily and placed her in the saddle. Hooking her right knee over the pommel, she searched out the stirrup with her left foot.

"Allow me, my lady," said Gareth, coming to her rescue. He held out the covered stirrup and she slipped her foot inside, smiling her thanks at him.

Settling in the saddle with the minimum of squirming, she took the reins from the page holding them out to her. Ewan and Gareth mounted their horses with a grace she'd be incapable of even if she had been wearing pants.

"Shall we join the others?" Ewan asked.

She nodded, mouth suddenly gone dry. This was it, she was going to ride this horse if it killed her. And if the horse didn't kill her, the stifling riding habit probably would.

* * * * *

"One of these days I expect to climb this staircase and find your skeleton draped over that scrying bowl," Paran said, setting the tray he was carrying down on a nearby table. Pointing his staff at the bowl he chanted under his breath.

Thackery jerked upwards. "What do you think you're doing?"

"What I should have done much sooner. You've hardly eaten or slept in days. This has got to stop."

"Restore the image!"

"Not until you eat something!"

Energy crackled through the room. The two men glared at each other. The tension ratcheted up a notch and objects on the shelves began to rattle.

"Enough!" Paran rapped his staff sharply on the floor. The energy dissipated. "You will do your daughter no good if you bring the castle down upon us both. Now eat!"

Grudgingly, Thackery moved over to the table

and sat down. As he started to eat, Paran joined him, pouring them each a goblet of wine.

"How fares the child?" Paran asked.

Thackery shook his head. "She is no child, but a woman grown. And every bit as headstrong as her mother was."

"Has she shown any signs of her power?"

"Aye," Thackery said with a sigh. "It appears that what you predicted is true, her power appeared in a quite explosive manner." He went on, between bites of his meal, to explain about the explosion she caused when trying to light a fire.

"This is not good, my friend. This is not good at all."

"Fortunately she listens to the advice of the young man who helped send her here. And he has advised her not to attempt any more magic for now."

"So just how impressive was her fire?" Paran asked, trying to sound casual.

"Larger than my first attempt, and more controlled. The blast hit the wood and went straight up instead of in all directions. She did very little damage."

They shared a smile of pride, and then Thackery's slowly faded. "But that dog Ewan is still sniffing around, wining and dining her. I do not know what he wants from her, but he wants something."

"Has he made advances on her?"

"No, but that is not surprising. He's of the old school who believe a witch's power is only as strong as her virginity."

Paran snorted. "Just as well. At least this way he'll leave her alone."

* * * * *

For the first half hour of the outing, Jessica thought she might actually enjoy riding side saddle. But then she developed a cramp in her leg. She tried shifting her bottom, but not only did it not help the cramp, it made the horse shy as well. Surreptitiously, she glanced at the other women in the riding party and was relieved to see a couple of them looked just as uncomfortable. The other three were sitting in their saddles with ease, chatting with the knights riding beside them.

The group consisted of six ladies including Jessica, Prince Ewan, three lords, whose names she promptly forgot as soon as she was introduced to them, ten knights, six squires, and a bevy of pages. Fortunately, with so large a group they kept to a sedate walk. Jessica's horse was docile enough that pretty much all she had to worry about was keeping her seat.

Ewan seemed to be in a particularly good mood. He kept up a steady banter with the knights nearest to them and pointed out things of interest to Jessica as they rode. When she admired a low-hanging tree covered in blooms, he used a knife to cut her a small sprig. She held it to her nose to breathe in its fragrance.

"This is beautiful," she said, inhaling again.

"Aye, 'tis most beauteous indeed," Ewan agreed. But he was not looking at the flowers.

Jessica blushed and ducked her head, almost missing his small smile of satisfaction. She worked the flowers into the braid on her head so she wouldn't lose them. Disney could definitely have modeled Prince Charming after Ewan.

"Where are we going?" she asked, to distract herself.

"Ah, 'tis a surprise," Ewan said.

No matter how much she cajoled, he remained firm in wanting to keep their destination a surprise. They continued riding and eventually Jessica's cramp eased. The scenery was beautiful and the day warm without being too hot. Just over the next rise was their destination.

"Oh, it's beautiful!" Jessica exclaimed.

The woods gave way to a flower-filled meadow with a rippling brook meandering its way nearby. The pages and squires had gone on ahead and set up a picnic lunch amidst the blossoms. When the pages saw the riders, they abandoned their posts around the food and hurried forward to take the horses reins.

Jessica's horse stopped when everyone else's did, for which she was eternally grateful, and Ewan helped her from the saddle. If Ewan's hands lingered on her waist a trifle longer than necessary, then she was not about to complain. She looked up at him and smiled.

"Thank you, your highness."

"'Tis my pleasure, my lady," he replied, tucking her hand under his arm and leading her towards the pristine white cloths laid out on the ground. There were cushions for the ladies and the lords to sit on. The knights, being in full armor, preferred to stand, while the squires and pages were busy serving.

The meal was every bit as elaborate as she'd come to expect when dining with Ewan. There were multiple courses and way too many choices. Jessica felt stuffed long before the feast was done. Fortunately, after everyone was finished it was decided they'd rest before returning to the camp.

"What's that up there?" Jessica asked, pointing to a rise in the distance. There looked to be some kind of ruins there, or maybe some standing stones, like a miniature Stonehenge.

Ewan gave her an inscrutable look. "That, my lady, is a Well of Power."

Jessica squinted at the standing stones on top of the hill in the distance. "A Well of Power?" She turned and caught the look on Ewan's face. It was gone before she could put a name to it – anger? disappointment? annoyance? Maybe it was a combination of all three.

"Surely thou hast them in thy land? 'Tis whence the power of magic resides."

It took a moment for Jessica to figure out what he

was telling her. If she understood correctly, the power of the well was magical in nature, which explained the look Ewan had been giving her. If she was a magic worker, like he assumed, she'd know this. While the subject had never really come up between them, she had the feeling that her position in his camp was dependent on his assumption that she had magical powers. So she did what any sane person in her place would - she lied through her teeth.

"Oh, I see. Yes, of course we have them where I come from; we just call them by a different name."

"Indeed."

He didn't quite look like he believed her. Jessica smiled her most sincere smile and crossed her fingers behind her back. His eyes narrowed a fraction.

"Mayhap thee might wish to venture closer?"

"Yes, of course," Jessica replied, hoping that was the right answer. Evidently it was. His face cleared and he offered her his arm. She was starting to enjoy the gallantry of this lifestyle, it was so romantic.

Four of the knights accompanied them, presumably to guard the prince in case of an attack, so the stroll to the hill was not as romantic as it could have been. Jessica was not quite ready to give up the hope that Ewan was interested in her as a woman, which made her a little disgruntled at having four chaperones.

There was no path, but Ewan guided her around to the side where the slope was gentler. Fortunately, her riding habit did not come with a train, so it was much easier to walk in than a gown would have been. Still, Jessica wished she was wearing something a little more suited to hiking, like jeans and a tee-shirt.

She slanted a look at Ewan. He may be hot, and a prince, but he really needed to loosen up a bit when it came to women's fashion. Whenever he saw her in her pants and jerkin, he got this pinched look on his face, as though he just got a whiff of something really smelly. She stifled a giggle as a vision flashed in her head of the super short green dress she'd worn when she and Ellen went out drinking. Ewan would probably have a coronary if he ever saw that dress.

At last they reached the top of the hill. It was higher than it looked; she was a little out of breath. The only resemblance between Stonehenge and this place was the fact they were both made of stone, and they were both set in a circle. The ancient stone circle in front of her was much smaller than Stonehenge, and the stones weren't nearly as high. Nor were they connected by capstones.

There were actually three circles of stone on top of the hill. The outer circle was made of tall, dark grey monoliths, standing like silent sentinels. Two of them were leaning slightly, one was only kept upright by leaning on its neighbour. They were weathered with age, moss growing on them although the vines that grew in abundance in the surrounding trees left the stones alone. In fact, once past this ring there was nothing growing at all.

There had been a faint hum in the air as they started up the hill. It grew in volume as they climbed and by the time they reached the top of the hill Jessica realized that it was not a sound she was hearing, but a vibration she was feeling. Now, standing within the first ring of stones, she could feel the hum crawling over her skin.

The next ring was low to the ground, only rising about a foot in height. The stones were placed tightly together – not even moss could have grown in the cracks between them. They were an earthy brown in colour, almost like wide, flat bricks. There was writing carved into them, a beautiful, cursive text that Jessica wished she could read. She almost asked Ewan what they said, but then thought better of it. If she was expected to know about the Well, then she was probably expected to know what the writing was.

The knights had stopped at the outer ring, spreading themselves out to keep vigil in all four directions. She was aware of Ewan still beside her, though her focus was on the ring in the centre. The hum had risen in pitch, making her whole psyche vibrate.

Jessica reached out a hand and could feel an almost physical barrier rising from the earthen ring. Leaving Ewan behind, she stepped over the low ring, pushing through the barrier with ease. In front of her was the third, and final, ring.

The final ring was made of what looked like crystal – she could make herself believe it was made of diamonds, but that's what it looked like at first glance. It, too, rose about a foot in height, but the stones were sharp and jagged, more like shards than stones. Within this circle was a layer of pristine, white sand that glowed like diamond dust.

Closing her eyes, Jessica straightened up her back and inhaled. It was like inhaling a cold fire. She could feel the power burn its way down and fuel the spark of magic inside her. It was a heady feeling. The pull of the magic was almost irresistible and without conscious thought she took a step forward, stepping over the shard-like ring.

Too late she realized her mistake.

Her eyes snapped open. "Oh, crap!"

Everything dissolved into white fire.

Chapter Fifteen

I t was the pain in her head that woke Jessica. She groaned and stirred, not quite ready to open her eyes yet.

"Here," a soothing masculine voice told her. "Drink this. It will help with the pain."

"Sebastian?"

"'Tis quite safe to open your eyes," he said, amusement lacing his voice. "We are the only ones here."

Jessica thought about it for a minute, then cautiously cracked open her eyes. To her relief, she was back in her tent and the only light came from a fat white candle on the small table beside her bed.

Sebastian helped her raise her head enough to drink from the wooden mug he held for her.

"What happened?" She felt like she'd been run over by a herd of buffalo followed by a troop of dancers wearing soccer cleats tap dancing on her head. "And how did I get back here?

"You were brought from the Well on a litter. You're suffering from a magical backlash," Sebastian told her gravely.

"A magical what?" Jessica blinked rapidly to try and clear her vision, but the minstrel kept wavering in and out of focus.

"Backlash. You drew in too much power too fast at the Well."

"The Well," she mused. "I remember Ewan showing me the Well. It didn't look like any well I've ever seen, more like a Zen garden with all those rocks and sand." Her voice faded away as she remembered the way it made her feel, the irresistible pull of the magic.

"What is it?" Sebastian asked.

"It was such an incredible feeling," she said. "The power was like nothing I've ever felt before. I just wanted to drink it down."

"It appears to me that's exactly what you did, only I'd say you over-indulged."

"I guess that's where the old saying "getting drunk on power" came from," she said with a giggle that turned into a wince. "This has got to be the world's worst hangover ever."

"Try some more of this," Sebastian suggested. He helped her raise her head again and she obediently took another drink.

"This doesn't taste half bad – which one of the healers came up with it?"

"None of them, I fear," he admitted. "'Tis my own remedy."

"Really? I'm surprised they'd let you get away with it. You'd think with me being unconscious they'd jump at the chance to start messing with me again."

Sebastian looked away and feigned an interest in the carvings on the mug he was holding.

"What is it?" she asked. When a reply was not immediately forthcoming, she tried again. "Sebastian, why aren't there any healers in my tent?"

He sighed heavily. "It's because they're afraid."

"Afraid? Afraid of what?" she asked in surprise.

"It's your power they fear," he admitted reluctantly.

"My power? But I don't even . . ." her voice trailed off.

"Don't even know how to use your power?" he asked shrewdly.

"Well, now that you mention it, yes."

"One more sip and I'll let you rest again," he said.

She obediently raised her head again and took another large drink.

"Ghren has never been a land to tolerate magic well," Sebastian told her. "In fact, until the wizard currently occupying the castle, there has only been one other wizard in the king's employ, and that was almost ten years ago."

"What happened to him?" Jessica asked.

Sebastian shrugged. "No one knows. He disappeared about the same time as the king's oldest son."

"Oldest son? You mean Ewan has a brother?" In all their time talking together, Ewan had never once mentioned having a brother.

"He did have. It is rumoured the prince ran off with the wizard to become his apprentice. Of course it is also rumoured he was used by the wizard as a sacrifice in a dark magic spell."

"But surely the king tried to find him?" Whatever Sebastian had given her was starting to work and she managed to sit up a little straighter in the bed.

"A token search was made, of course, but although he was first born, he was not the favourite son. In time his name was stricken from the family tree and soon it became forbidden to even mention his name."

"That's terrible!"

"That is the way of the monarchy. Their word is law, never forget this. They own the land and everything and everyone on it. They can do whatever they please and none dare gainsay them."

There was a bitter tone to his voice that made Jessica wonder just what had been done to Sebastian in the past. One look at his face made her decide not to ask.

"I grew up in the court of Ghren," he continued. "I left a year before the prince disappeared – it was my time of journeying towards becoming a bard."

"Not that I'm not glad you're here now," Jessica said, "But if Ghren is so terrible, why did you come back?"

"Because growing up I had one friend to whom I owe not only my loyalty, but my life. I cannot rest easy until I have determined what happened to him."

"The king's oldest son," Jessica guessed.

"Aye."

Jessica was beginning to have very mixed feelings about this whole being stuck in another dimension business.

"So just how big a deal is it, what happened at the Well?" she asked Sebastian. "I mean, should I brace myself for a mob bursting in at any second to drag me off to be burned at the stake?"

"Why ever would they do that?"

She took comfort in the fact that he looked genuinely puzzled by her question. "Isn't that usually what superstitious peasants do to witches?"

He shook his head at her. "Nay. While they may fear those of power, they would never attack without provocation. You have harmed no one, and you are under the prince's protection."

"Well that's a relief." She settled back down in the bed, ready to doze off again, when a sudden thought struck her. "How much do you know about magic?"

"Very little," he admitted. "Though I was tutored alongside the princes, magic was forbidden to us."

"Damn. Oh, well. I guess I'll just have to figure it out on my own."

"Figure what out?"

"How to get past those monsters surrounding the castle to talk to the wizard inside." The more she thought about it, the more it became plain to her that to get rid of the army of illusions, she needed to go right to the source. And then once she helped Ewan get his castle back, she could concentrate on getting home.

"Are you mad?" He looked appalled at the idea. "If you place one foot on that battlefield you will be torn apart. Countless others have tried and failed."

"Ah, but were the others as powerful as I am? Jessica O'Connell, wizard extraordinaire." For some reason she found this extremely funny, and started to giggle.

Sebastian frowned at her. "His Highness will never allow you to put yourself at risk like that."

"Then we just won't tell him what we're doing," she said with a yawn. "I think tomorrow you, me, and Gareth should pay another visit to the battlefield."

Sebastian didn't try to talk her out of her scheme; he could see her mind was made up. But he sent up a silent prayer to gods he no longer believed in that Ewan would never find out about it. For all their sakes.

* * * * *

In the morning, while she still had a few minutes to herself, Jessica pulled out the milk-white pendant. "Howard? Are you there?"

"I'm here, Jessica. How are you feeling?"

"Fit as a fiddle," she assured him. "Sebastian makes one hell of a hangover cure."

"I felt that power surge all the way down our link," he told her. "I've never felt anything like it. I'd give my right arm to be where you are now."

Jessica looked around with a sigh. "Trust me, I wish you were here too, Howard. This magic stuff is starting to scare the crap out of me."

"You're going to have to be very careful, Jess. Do you have any idea how much power you have stored up inside you right now?"

"What?" She sat up a little straighter where she was sitting on the bed.

"That's what those wells are used for, replenishing a mage's power. Right now you've got enough power inside you to light up a small city."

"Holy Saint Christopher! How do I get it out again?"

"The only way is through spell casting."

"Oh, jeez. That doesn't sound good at all." She got up and started pacing. "You saw what I did when I tried to create a fire, and that was before the power surge."

"Don't worry, Jess. We'll figure something out.

Now that the link between us is stronger I'm able to draw more information from your world."

"Don't call it that!" she said crossly. "This isn't my world. This is just the world I'm stuck in, temporarily."

"Sorry, Jess."

"Listen, you said before that the reason Ewan's army takes a beating any time they go near the battlefield is because they think the monsters are real, right?"

"That right."

She sat back down on the bed again. "So it would follow that if a person thought otherwise, that the monsters were just illusions, they'd be able to just walk right through them, right?"

"In theory, yes . . ."

"Good, that's what I wanted to hear."

Howard would have been very nervous if he could have seen the smug smile of satisfaction on her face.

"Jessica . . . what are you up to now?"

"Nothing dangerous. I'm just going to walk through that battlefield and right up to the castle."

"And then what? You can't hypnotize all those people into believing the monsters are illusions."

"Of course not, but I can talk to the wizard who's creating them and find out what it'll take for him to pack it up."

"Sounds a little risky to me."

"Nonsense. It's a brilliant plan."

* * * * *

"I have an idea," Paran said, leaning over the scrying bowl.

Thackery glared at him from his corner where he was sitting bound and gagged to prevent him from using his magic to go to Jessica's side. Fortunately, or unfortunately, depending on one's point of view, he was not strong in the mind-magic that would have allowed him to break his bonds with a single thought.

The surge of power from the Well was felt along the entire Well network. They'd been watching Jessica in the scrying bowl at the time, otherwise they would have never been able to pinpoint the source of the disturbance.

They'd watched in anticipation as she approached the Well, wondering how close she would get. Only the most powerful magic users were able to pass the rings. The more powerful the sorcerer, the closer to the source they were able to get. It was a source of both pride and trepidation to them that she passed so easily within the first and second rings to approach the Well itself.

"What is she doing?" Thackery asked, horrified as she stepped closer to the centre. "She has no shields, she cannot pass within the inner ring."

In shock they watched as she stepped over the final barrier, her eyes widening as she felt the raw power of the Well before she was thrown clear. It was at that point Paran realized two things. One, just how powerful his granddaughter really was, and two, Thackery would need to be restrained from going after her.

The second Jessica was thrown clear of the Well, Paran cast his own spell, but this one at Thackery, knocking him unconscious to keep him from going to her. She was Thackery's daughter, but she was also Paran's granddaughter and he, too, had to fight the impulse to rush to her side. It was too risky though. The power surge from the Well might be dismissed as one more foolish wizardling being taught a lesson, but there would be no overlooking his or Thackery's power signatures showing up at that site. They were in no way prepared to face Anakaron yet.

"I propose we make contact with her wizardling friend," he continued, still focused on the images in the scrying bowl.

There was a muffled noise in response.

"What was that?" Paran asked absently. He turned around and looked at Thackery in surprise. "Oh, I forgot." He waved his hand in Thackery's direction and the gag disappeared.

"Release me at once! What do you think you're doing? Did you really think you could keep me here while my daughter—"

"If you do not have anything useful to contribute,

I can always replace the gag." Paran said mildly. "Jessica is fine."

"I am sure you will understand if I would like to see this for myself."

Another wave of the hand and Thackery was free. He got to his feet with a groan and joined his father-in-law at the scrying bowl.

"What is she doing?"

"It appears that she's getting ready to pay a visit to Castle Ghren."

"Please tell me she knows the creatures guarding the castle are illusions."

Paran nodded. "It would appear so. I believe she seeks to find the source of these illusions."

Thackery cursed under his breath. "And you still do not see the need for me to go to her?"

"It is too dangerous." Paran was adamant.

They had this same argument almost every day, Thackery wanting to go to his daughter, Paran telling him it was too dangerous. They would probably keep having this argument until Jessica was safely with them.

"What was it you were saying about an idea?" he asked, running a hand over his face.

"Ah, yes. I don't know why I didn't think of it sooner. She and the wizardling have some kind of connection. They're able to communicate—"

"How?"

"Through Farenalyssia's amulet. The amulet was

separated into two and each retains a piece. He has been attempting to aid her in using her magic."

There was a snort from the other man. "That boy hasn't enough power to be of any use."

"And yet without him we would not have been able to draw her to this world," Paran reminded him. "One of the reasons that world was selected was its lack of magic. If he were of this world I think he would surprise you."

"All right, what has this to do with your idea?"

"It is too dangerous for us to contact Jessica, but what if we contacted her friend instead?"

"To what end?"

Paran let out an exasperated breath. "He has some knowledge of magic use and seeks to learn more of this world to help her. We could give him the information he requires."

"It is something to consider," Thackery said slowly.

Chapter Sixteen

J essica, Gareth, and Sebastian stood hidden in the trees near the edge of the battlefield. To both Sebastian and Jessica's great relief Gareth had finally fallen silent – he'd been protesting her plan the entire way to their current vantage point.

For this occasion, Jessica was dressed to please herself: close-fitting leather breeches tucked into her boots, a loose white shirt much like the one she'd been wearing when she arrived on the beach, and a leather jerkin over the shirt. The museum sword was in a plain looking sheath, belted around her waist.

She hadn't been happy as she pulled on the boots. They were starting to look a little worse for wear. Jennifer was never going to forgive her once she made it back home.

"Are you sure about this?" Sebastian asked quietly.

She looked out across the expanse between them and the castle. The land was flat and barren of trees and shrubs – probably kept that way so that an enemy couldn't sneak up on the castle – although the grass was churned up from the morning's skirmish. The castle itself sat on a rise and looked like it came from a story book, although maybe closer to something from Grimm's fairy tales than the Disney versions.

"I'm pretty sure," she said dredging up a smile for him. She *was* having second thoughts, but there was no way she could admit it now, not when she'd been so adamant in the first place. "I'm just not sure how I'm supposed to get past that wall."

There was an enormous main gate in the wall and a couple of smaller ones, but they were all shut tight.

Gareth cleared his throat, looking distinctly uncomfortable.

"What?" Jessica asked.

"There is a way," he said hesitantly. "There be the tradesmen egress on the west side. Each trade hath its own access and the weaver's gate is known to be . . . somewhat vulnerable as the weavers be lax in their vigilance."

"Oh, okay then." She studied the map she'd had Gareth draw before they set out. He'd been appalled when he realized what she wanted it for. "Which of these towers did you say was the old wizard's tower?"

There were seven towers in all. With a resigned sigh, Gareth pointed out the correct one. "'Tis unlikely the varlet will be within. The King ordered the tower sealed when the wizard Thackery was banished.

I was but a lad at the time," he added.

She smothered a smile. To her he was still just a lad. Giving her sword belt one last tug she said, "All righty then. I'll be back before you know it."

The squire and the minstrel looked on silently as she approached the edge of the battlefield. With only the slightest hesitation, she began picking her way across the churned up earth. She was no more than three feet in when the monsters began to appear.

Gareth drew his sword, ready to hurry to her aid as a pair of ogres raced towards her. Sebastian laid a restraining hand on his arm. As the ogres approached, Jessica kept up her slow, steady pace towards the castle. Gareth's jaw dropped open as he watched her make her way carefully across the field. The beasts raged around her, but she ignored them and after a few minutes they started to ignore her as well.

He made the sign of the cross as she reached the castle wall and the creatures vanished again.

"I wonder if the beasts will reappear when she returns," Sebastian said.

Gareth looked at him in shock. "After witnessing such a miracle, that is what thee wonders?"

"You speak as though you had doubts as to our lady's abilities." Sebastian tempered his teasing with a smile. It wasn't as though he hadn't had his own doubts, especially when he was watching Jessica's small form pass among all those terrible monsters.

"My fear is not only for her safety in entering the

castle," Gareth said slowly. "Such a feat serves only to show what great power she holds. My fear is for what will happen once we have retaken the castle."

"What do you mean?" Sebastian asked in surprise.

"Knowing how the king feels regarding wizards, I wonder at her welcome once she hast vanquished our foes."

"I see your point."

They watched as Jessica disappeared around the corner of the castle. All they could do now was wait for her return.

"Surely Ewan . . ." Sebastian began.

Gareth looked at him. "I have served my lord for three years now. Though I owe him my fealty I am not blind to his faults."

A moment of understanding passed between the two.

"Well then," Sebastian said. "We'll just have to be extra careful in guarding our lady."

"Aye," Gareth agreed.

* * * * *

Jessica shivered as she stood just inside the great hall of the castle. This had seemed like such a good idea when she was outside in the sunshine, surrounded by people, but now that she was actually inside the castle, all by herself . . . It was dusty and full of cobwebs. And there was a damp chill in the air that emphasized the feeling of abandonment. She needed to get this over with as quickly as possible.

Pulling out her map, she studied it carefully.

"Okay, let's see now. I'm in the great hall, so that means that the Chapel is that way," she pointed to her right, "and the kitchens would be that way. Beyond the kitchens is the midden, whatever that is, and beyond that are the stables, which I don't need to worry about 'cause they're empty. So that means the wizard's tower would be—"

"There's no need seeking out the wizard's tower, my lady. It's sealed up tighter than a nun."

Jessica shrieked and whirled around, dropping the map.

He was a little on the short side, and rather chubby, but she had no doubt he was the wizard she was looking for. He was wearing a long black robe with a matching pointed hat, and the crystal topping the staff in his hand was beginning to glow faintly.

"You scared the crap out of me!"

"I'm sorry, I didn't mean to. I don't get many visitors. In fact, you're the first visitor I've had here."

Jessica held a hand to her chest, willing her heart to stop racing, and just stared at him for a moment. "I have to say, you're nothing like I imagined you to be."

"Let me guess, you imagined someone taller, more imposing?"

"Well . . . yes."

He sighed and the light from the crystal winked

out. "I get that a lot, unfortunately."

"So, you're the one who drove everyone out of this castle and you're keeping them out with that army of monsters out there?" She was finding it harder and harder to believe. He seemed so . . . harmless.

"Well, no," he admitted. He sighed again and gestured towards the kitchens. "Maybe we could have a cup of tea while we talk?"

This was getting more bizarre by the minute. Jessica had been ready to face an angry, vengeful wizard, perhaps impress him with her awesome fire-shooting skills, but this . . . it was like being prepared for an angry attack dog and finding a fluffy puppy instead.

"I think I could use a cup of tea," she said. Truthfully, she could use something a lot stronger than tea.

He almost sagged with relief, and led the way to the kitchen. There was a fire lit in the smaller of the two hearths, giving the room a cheerier feel. A large trestle table took up the center of the room, but it was obviously a work table, there were no chairs around it. There was, however, a barrel near the end closest to the fire, and the wizard wrestled another one into place on the other side of the table.

Jessica sat down and watched with interest as he busied himself making their tea. First he swung a kettle on a hook so that it was over the fire, then found a pair of wooden mugs and tea leaves in a cupboard. In less time than she would have thought, she had a steaming mug of fragrant tea in front of her and the wizard seated on the opposite side of the table.

"So," she said, blowing gently on her tea to cool it. "Why don't you tell me your story?"

"I don't know where to start," he said, clearly unhappy.

"Why don't we start with your name?"

"My name is Wendel, of the Great Marsh Wendels."

"Okay, Wendel. You said you're not the one who's laid siege to the castle?" Now there was something she didn't get to say every day, laid siege to.

"Oh, no, no, no! That was Braxton."

"Braxton?"

"Yes!" He nodded so emphatically that his hat slipped down over his left eye.

"Why don't we start with why Braxton would want to chase everybody out of the castle?"

"He was angry with the king," Wendel said, pushing his hat up again. "They had an argument over money. Braxton thought he was owed more than he was given and the king argued that Braxton wasn't as talented as he pretended. Braxton was chased off, but he vowed he'd take his revenge."

"So why isn't he here now?"

"I don't know," Wendel said miserably. "I'm just a hedge wizard, nobody important. But Braxton said he had a job for me. I snuck in here and then cleared the way for him to hide in the wine cellar. He cast his spell to create the ghosts and banshees to chase everyone out of the castle. Once everyone but him and me were gone, he summoned the demon army to surround the castle and keep everyone out. It keeps everyone in as well."

"Where's this Braxton now?" Jessica asked with a frown.

"I don't know. I just woke up one morning and he was gone."

"So why are you still here?"

"I told you, his demon army doesn't just keep people out, it prevents me from leaving as well."

She looked at him, perplexed. Could it be that he really didn't know they were just illusions? "Obviously I was able to make it through the . . . demon army. How do you explain that?"

"You must be a very powerful sorcerer indeed," he told her, a hint of hero-worship in his voice. "I watched you from the battlements. The beasts fell back before you."

"So you have no idea how to banish the demon army?"

"No, my lady. Only Braxton can break the spell. Only him, or someone more powerful than him."

"Crap," she said.

"My lady?"

"Wendel, I'm going to need to think about this for a while."

"Yes, my lady."

"And I'll think much better with a glass or two of

wine. Do you think you could scare up a bottle?"

"Oh, yes, my lady!"

Jessica waited until Wendel vanished through the doorway leading to the wine cellar and then pulled out her amulet.

"Howard? Are you there?"

"I'm here, Jessica."

"Did you happen to catch Wendel's story?"

"Yeah, I did. Sounds to me like this Braxton set Wendel up to take a fall."

"You mean you believe his story?" Jessica took a cautious sip of her tea. Wendel had sweetened it generously with honey, but she could still taste the tangy flavour of rose hips.

"I can sense that he has very limited power. And he's right in saying that it would take a great deal of power to work a spell of this calibre."

"So what can we do about it?"

"Well, the best solution would be to have Braxton break the spell, but I suspect he's in the next kingdom by now."

"What are the chances of the spell just fading away?"

"Doubtful, with that Well of power so close," Howard told her.

"So, what can we do?"

"I have to tell you, I'm not used to magic on this scale, Jess."

Jessica sighed. "Okay, Howard. Just don't take

too long to figure this out. The sooner we can get Ewan back in his castle, the sooner we can focus on getting me home again."

By the time Wendel returned with not one but two dusty bottles of wine, Howard had gone again and Jessica had finished her tea. She'd found a pair of pewter goblets and had them sitting on the table. Together they raised a cup of the king's finest vintage.

"Outstanding!" Jessica took another sip and let the taste roll around on her tongue.

"It's been one of the few advantages of being trapped in here," Wendel admitted. "The king has a most excellent wine cellar."

"So tell me, Wendel, what kind of magic does a hedge wizard usually do?" Jessica had never heard of a hedge wizard before. Did it have something to do with gardening?

He shifted in his seat. "The usual things I suppose: love potions, wards against the evil eye, good luck charms . . . I have an amazing spell for getting rid of vermin."

Jessica shuddered. There was straw strewn about the floor of the room and she wondered what might be hiding under it. Roaches? Mice? Rats? She tried not to think about it.

"I take it you're not from around here – I know the king isn't overly fond of magic workers."

"Oh, my no. He most definitely is not. Still, there are a few of us hidden away. There are still a good many who turn to a magic worker for help."

"And what did Braxton promise you if you helped him?"

"A ten-weight of gold and the spell-books from the wizard's tower," he answered promptly. "The spell-books alone would have been worth it. The wizard Thackery was very powerful."

"He's the wizard that disappeared the same time as the king's first born son, isn't he?"

"That's him all right." Wendel nodded until his hat slipped down again. "A bad business that. Gave all us magic workers a bad name."

Jessica suddenly realized she had an opportunity to help Sebastian. "Did they ever find out what happened to Thackery or the king's son?"

"The most popular rumour is that Thackery lured the king's son away and used him in a sacrifice to work blood magic."

"And what do you believe?" she asked, making a mental note to ask Howard about blood magic, the next time she was talking to him.

The little man hesitated. "I knew Thackery," he admitted. "Nice enough fellow, something a little sad about him though. We often shared a pint at the Pig's Snout. He was very fond of the prince, thought of him almost like a son. Then one day the lad up and disappeared without a trace. Thackery knew where the blame would be laid and thought it best to make himself scarce."

"If they were that close I'm surprised Thackery didn't try to find the prince himself."

"He did. He spent two nights up in his tower casting tracking spells. The trail led to the Mythric Ocean and as you know it's very difficult to track over water."

Jessica refilled their goblets. No, she didn't know it was difficult to track over water, but there was no point in letting Wendel know it. "So why didn't he tell the king?"

Wendel snorted. "You don't tell the king things he doesn't want to hear, and the king definitely didn't want to hear that his least favourite son had run away. He put the blame on Thackery, who barely escaped with the clothes on his back. Last I heard he was headed for the southern lands."

"So I wonder what happened to the king's son . . ."

"Who knows? Wherever he is, I'm sure he's better off than he would have been had he stayed in Ghren."

"I don't understand," Jessica said. What could be better than being a prince?

She picked up her goblet but it was empty. Wendel gestured with the bottle and she hesitate slightly before nodding. She needed to pace herself. The wine was strong and she was starting to feel a little light-headed.

"He was never as mean spirited or cruel as the

king. And he wasn't arrogant or vicious like that brother of his," Wendel continued.

"You mean Ewan?"

"Aye. A true son of the king if ever there was one."

"What do you mean?" Jessica asked, ready to leap to Ewan's defense.

"There was a young lad, friends with the older prince, who had a bard-like gift of music. The younger prince couldn't carry a tune if it was in a bucket and was jealous of the lad's talent. So he starts telling the king about these choirs of lads who've had their manhood stripped away . . ."

"You mean castration, don't you?" She was starting to feel sick to her stomach.

Wendel nodded. "Next thing you know they've got the poor lad tied down and they've gelded him like a horse."

"How old was this boy?" Jessica whispered.

"About sixteen."

"Didn't they know that was too old for it to make a difference?"

He looked at her sadly. "Of course they did. But they'd run out of ways to hurt the older prince, so they hurt his friend instead."

Jessica was silent as Wendel continued to talk. It was like a dam bursting - once he got started it seemed like he was unable to stop. He had been alone in this big, spooky castle for weeks and must have been starved for companionship.

She listened with only half an ear to what he was saying. Instead she kept thinking about what he'd said about the boy being castrated. There was no way Ewan could have taken part in anything so heinous. He was a true Prince Charming, and Prince Charming would never have anything to do with such a thing.

The boy . . . it had to be Sebastian. He must have been very close to the king's other son to come back here looking for answers. Maybe they'd been lovers. Maybe when Sebastian left to go to Bardic school the unnamed brother couldn't bear to be parted and ran away to be with him. But then why hadn't they met up again?

Lifting her goblet to take a sip of wine, she realized it was empty. So were the two bottles Wendel had brought up from the wine cellar. Jessica sighed. It was time to get going.

"Wendel," she said as he paused to take a breath, "I think I can help you."

"You can?" He looked at her with worshipful eyes.

"It might take a couple of days to work out all the details, but I'm confident I will be able to banish Braxton's demon army." At least she was confident Howard would come up with a way for her to banish Braxton's army.

"In the meantime," she continued, getting carefully to her feet, "I need to go back to the camp."

"What should I do?" Wendel asked, trailing behind her as she made her way to the main doors of the castle.

"The first thing you should do is lose the robe and the hat."

He stopped in his tracks and looked at her, appalled. "But-but-but how will anyone know I'm a wizard?"

"That's my point. Think about it. Once the demon army is gone, people will be returning to the castle. What do you think they'd do if they found a wizard inside it?"

"Oh!" He shuddered. "I think once I am able to leave this castle I might try my luck in Westlawry. I hear they are far more tolerant of magic workers."

"I think that might be a good idea," she agreed. She paused at the door. "I don't know how much warning I'll be able to give you before I take on the monster army, but I won't be trying anything for at least a couple of days."

"I understand, my lady. And if I may be so bold, I would like to wish you good fortune."

"You may," Jessica said with a grin. "And good luck to you, too."

Chapter Seventeen

" Howard . . ."

Howard twitched where he sat slumped in his chair. The table in front of him held several dusty books spread across it and one lay open on his chest. He'd fallen asleep as he studied, something he was doing a lot lately.

"Howard, wake up."

The voice was louder this time and there was a catch in his breathing. One eye opened to look blearily around the room. "Is someone there?"

"Howard, go to your scrying bowl."

"My what? What's going on?"

"Please, just go to your scrying bowl."

"Is this some kind of a joke?" Howard asked, sitting upright in his chair. "Who's there?"

"This is not a jest. I am more than willing to answer your questions, but I ask that you go to your scrying bowl so that we can converse face to face."

"Seriously, who's doing this? Sam? Robert? What are you trying to pull?"

There was a heartfelt, disembodied sigh. "I told you this was a bad idea."

"Well you should have waited until he was fully awake, or entered into his dream," a second voice said.

Howard, in the meantime, was checking under his work table for hidden microphones. With some of the technology available today, the mikes could be anywhere. So could speakers and cameras. But how could anyone have gotten in without him realizing it?

"This isn't funny guys."

"No, it most certainly is not," agreed the second voice. "My name is Paranithel. I, and my son-in-law Thackery, are here to help you help your friend Jessica."

Jerking upright, Howard hit his head on the underside of the table. "How do you know about Jessica?" he demanded, rubbing his head.

"We know because we are the ones responsible for assisting you in bringing her to our world."

Howard thought about the power surge he'd felt just as he released his spell that fateful night. "Your world. You want me to believe that you're in the same dimension as Jessica?"

"Where else would we be? It is our home," the

second voice, Paranithel, said.

"This really isn't a joke?" Howard asked.

"Paran, this was a bad idea. We should just leave the poor boy in peace."

"Do you want to help your daughter or not?" Paran snapped.

"Wait a minute, daughter? One of you is Jessica's father?"

"That would be me," the first voice, Thackery, said.

"This I've got to hear," Howard said, sitting back down in his chair.

* * * * *

Jessica appreciated the fact that Gareth and Sebastian kept themselves from badgering her with questions when she rejoined them at the edge of the battlefield. She needed time to sift through everything she'd learned and she wasn't quite sure how to explain what she'd found in the castle. There was a glance shared between the two, she caught it out of the corner of her eye, but Sebastian just shrugged and they fell in step behind her.

It was a good thing the path back to camp was free of obstacles because she wasn't really paying attention to where she was going until they reached a grove of apple trees at the edge of the camp. There was a crowd of children gathered in a circle beneath one of the trees, jabbering excitedly. One voice rose above the others, obviously in pain.

"What's going on here?" Jessica demanded. It sounded like someone was being picked on and she knew all too well what that felt like. There was nothing she hated worse than bullies.

At the sound of her voice the children scattered, leaving their fallen comrade behind. Jessica knelt down beside the howling child. His leg was bent at an unnatural angle; from the looks of it he'd fallen from the tree. The apples strewn around him told them what he'd been doing up there in the first place.

"'Tis apparent they were stealing apples," Gareth said, stating the obvious. "I'll fetch the guard."

"I weren't doing nothing wrong," the boy wailed. "We was just climbing trees. You got no call to fetch the guard."

"No one's going to fetch the guard," Jessica soothed, shooting a pointed glance at Gareth. "We only want to help. Gareth, I'm sure one of the healers would be of more use than a guard. It looks like his leg is broken."

Sebastian hunkered down beside her. "Even should you be able to persuade a healer to come, they would not treat a peasant," he said quietly. "What's more, they'd report him as a thief."

"But he's just a child! And he's hurt!"

"The best thing we could do for him is take him to his kin. They'll do what they can for the pain."

"But what about his leg? Without proper treatment it won't heal properly."

"'Tis the way of things, my lady," Gareth said.

"Well it's not my way!"

Jessica couldn't believe the callous attitude of the two men. She and Ellen had taken a first aid course together, but she never imagined she'd have a reason to use what she learned. The leg needed to be set or else it would heal crooked.

"Gareth, I need you to find me two sticks. About this long," she held her hands about a foot apart, "and as straight as possible."

With a sigh, he left to do as she asked. As he left, Jessica stood up and, with her back to Sebastian and the boy, reached up under her jerkin to pull the tails of the voluminous shirt free. Taking her knife, she sliced off a wide strip. Sitting down again, she began tearing it into thinner strips.

"What's your name, sweetie?"

The boy gulped back his tears. "K-K-Kieran."

"I'm not going to lie to you, Kieran. I have to touch your leg to see how bad the break is and it's going to hurt. Are you ready?"

He nodded, eyes wide and fearful.

As gently as possible, Jessica moved the boy's leg until it was straight again. There was no sound from him and when she looked at his face his eyes were closed. He'd passed out, which was just as well.

"This is bad," she said, glancing up at Sebastian.

"I can feel at least two distinct breaks. I don't know if I can set this properly. Isn't there anyone else who could help?"

He shook his head with genuine regret. "No one cares for the fate of a peasant lad. To most lads like him are the lowest of the low."

"Well I'll just have to do my best and hope it's enough," she said grimly. "Where's Gareth with those splints? I can feel the heat of his injury through the homespun he's wearing."

Sebastian's eyes widened as he looked down at the boy's leg. "The heat is not coming from him."

Jessica looked down and her jaw dropped open. Her hands, where they rested on Kieran's leg, were glowing with a pale, green light. As she became aware of what was happening, the glow intensified and she could actually feel the energy seeking out the breaks and repairing the damage.

"Holy Saint Christopher," she whispered. The glow flared briefly, then winked out. She could see Gareth approaching with an armful of sticks.

"What do I do now?" she whispered frantically. "I can't let anyone know I can heal like this, I'll never have any peace."

"I suggest you wrap up the boy's leg as you were going to, and pretend the injury was not as severe as we'd thought."

Jessica nodded. "I can do that."

Gareth arrived with his armful of sticks, a resentful look on his face from having been sent on such an errand.

"You're just in time," she told him. "I want to get this leg wrapped up before the boy wakes up again."

He sniffed disdainfully, but watched closely as she chose four of the straightest sticks and wrapped them to the boy's injured leg.

"What are you doing?" he asked, curious in spite of himself.

"It's called a splint," she said absently. "It will hold the injured part of the leg immobile so the bone can knit back together properly."

Kieran was just beginning to stir as she finished, which was a good thing as a small crowd was converging on them. In the lead were two guardsmen, not royal guards but regular palace guards. Hurrying in their wake was a portly man and woman dressed in rough homespun, and behind them one of the pages.

"We'll take charge of the brat," one of the guards said.

"You most certainly will not," Jessica replied, rising to her feet.

"Stealing the king's apples be a hanging offence," the second guard said.

There was a gasp from the woman joining them. "He meant no harm, he's a good lad he is!"

"The law's the law." The first guard was obviously puffed up with self importance.

Jessica felt the need to take him down a peg or

two. "There was no stealing done here, the boy fell out of the tree and injured himself; we stopped to help. End of story."

"And what were he doing up there in the first place? Stealing the king's apples, I say."

"Did you never climb a tree just for the fun of it?" Jessica looked him up and down. Judging by the size of the belly hanging over his belt, probably not.

"'Tis the only reason the likes of him have for being up there," the guard said stubbornly.

While Sebastian would have loved to see Jessica best the guard verbally, he could see she was fast running out of patience and feared she might lose control of her magic along with her temper. "Perhaps, my lady, we should request my lord Ewan to intervene on the boy's behalf. Even were you not his honoured guest, I'm sure he could deny you nothing."

Jessica shot him a look. It took a moment for what he said to sink in, but when it did the guards began to babble.

"Honoured guest?"

"No, no, no. No need to bother his highness. If you say there were no crime done then we'll abide by your word, my lady."

"No need to mention this to his lordship at all."

"Fools," Gareth mutter as they hurried away. At the same time Jessica muttered, "Idiots."

They looked at each other and laughed.

"Oh, my poor babe!" the woman wailed, falling

to her knees beside Kieran. He was fully awake now and though pale didn't seem to be in pain. He was, however, in danger of being smothered as his mother clutched him to her ample bosom. The man stood clutching his hat in his hands.

"It appears the boy's injury was not as great as we'd feared," Sebastian said to them. "He'll need to stay off that leg for a few days, and keep the splint on for perhaps two weeks, but he'll be climbing trees again before you know it."

"We owes you a debt," the man said gravely. "They'd a hung him for sure, they would. You saved our boy and we won't be forgetting."

"Don't worry about it," Jessica said.

"This here be Addison," he said, drawing the page forward. "He be Kieran's older brother. If ye be needing aught in the way of help, ye can send him to fetch me. I be Reece the Tanner."

By this time Kieran was sitting up and squirming under his mother's attention. Reece gently scooped the boy up in his arms. Now that he was no longer in pain and his parents were close by, Kieran lapsed into shyness.

"Here," Gareth said suddenly, handing Kieran something that Jessica couldn't quite see. "I'd say ye earned it."

Kieran grinned, and waved at them as he was carried away.

"What did you give him?" Jessica asked.

"An apple," Gareth replied with a grin.

"There's hope for you yet," she said, patting him on the shoulder.

Gareth blushed furiously.

* * * * *

Howard ran his hands through his already dishevelled hair, ending with his head in his hands, elbows resting on his work table. It was so bizarre, utterly fantastic, but who was he to disbelieve the two disembodied voices? Part of him wished he could rewind time back to before he'd ever tried his teleportation spell, but the other part of him . . .

"Tell me again why you'd send a baby to this dimension?"

The image of Thackery in the shallow scrying bowl on the table threw up its hands in disgust and disappeared. The image of Paranithel moved to the foreground.

"I never intended to leave her alone in your world," he said sadly. "But I had not anticipated how badly the lack of magic would affect me."

"I tried to warn you." Thackery's voice was heard in the background.

"Aye, that you did. But once the woman accepted the babe as a substitute for her own, there was no reason to stay. At first I worried that her mind was not right – she believed Jesseminathus to be of her

flesh and blood, forgetting her own babe had died —
but I realized this would be to our advantage. Who
would think to question a new mother of the origins
of her child?"

"You say there's a lack of magic in this world?"
The question seemed to just pop out of Howard's
mouth on its own.

"'Tis one of the reasons I chose your world.
There are no Wells, no magical reservoirs. In time
even my inner magic dwindled to a mere spark. I
could not stay and so I left my granddaughter in the
best hands I could find."

"Jess never had a clue she was adopted," Howard
said. "I have no idea how she'll take the news now."

"You must not tell her!" Thackery shouldered
Paranithel aside. "If Anakaron were to learn of her
presence he would stop at nothing to possess her. As
it is she is in danger every time she wields her power
unwisely. He is drawn to those of great power."

"Wait a minute. Before you were saying this Anakaron wanted you all dead, including Jessica. Now
you're saying he wants to possess her? Which is it?
And what exactly do you mean by possess?"

Paranithel gently pushed Thackery to one side
again. "When she was but a babe Anakaron would
have killed her just to see her father suffer. But now
she is a woman grown, and looks very much like her
mother, the woman Anakaron desired above all others. He would stop at nothing to possess her, to make

her his and have her bear his children, whether she be willing or no."

"Okay, but if she's in so much danger in your world, why didn't you just let her stay here?"

"Because she belongs here, with her family. Or what's left of it," Paranithel said softly. "And because sooner or later she would feel the pull of her world and if she did not know how to cross over, she would be pulled apart by the force of it."

Howard sat back in his chair and digested this information for a moment. There was one question he wanted to ask that was burning a hole in his brain, but he didn't know if he truly wanted the answer to it.

"You say there's a lack of magic in this world," he said slowly, reluctantly. "Does this mean I've just been fooling myself all these years? That no matter how hard I try I'll never be able to truly work magic?"

Paranithel hesitated. "The small magicks work well on your world, but the large scale magical spells . . . no, it would not be possible."

"So that night in the park, I only imagined the power rising."

"Oh, no. That was quite real. It was very impressive, the amount of power you were able to raise using the collective energy of your group. It was most unexpected and was likely the cause of Jesseminathus over-shooting her mark when she returned to us."

"Oh." Howard felt marginally better.

"Your ability to help your friend is quite admirable," Thackery said unexpectedly. "Were you able to visit this world you would be a powerful wizard indeed."

And the chances of that ever happening were several million to one, Howard thought morosely. "Okay, let's get down to brass tacks. You know that Jess has her heart set on helping Prince Ewan?"

"Yes, we have seen this," Paranithel admitted. "I would ask that she choose another to . . . befriend, but he seems to find favour in her eyes."

"There's something not quite right about him," Howard muttered. "He's got a dark streak in his aura."

"You have *seen* this?" Thackery demanded.

"Well, yeah. Wait, you mean you guys can't see?"

"It is not our forte," Paranithel hedged. "Spirit reading is one of the most difficult arts to manage."

"He's up to no good," Howard said. "I can feel it in my gut."

"I would have to agree," Thackery said. "I know him of old, and he has not improved with age. You would do well to warn her away from him."

Howard snorted. "Jessica never takes dating advice from me. She's got it bad for this prince, and once she sets her sights on someone she's not easily discouraged."

"Much like her mother," Paranithel muttered.

"Our best bet is to help her get his castle back and hope that he shows what he's really made of. So, how are we going to do this?" Howard could hardly contain his excitement at the prospect of working with these bonefide wizards.

"I have an idea," Thackery told him.

Chapter Eighteen

J essica paced the confines of her tent. Even though she knew Gareth and Sebastian were curious about what she'd found in the castle, she put them off, claiming she was tired and needed a rest, just so she could have some time alone. She did feel drained from the healing, intentional or not, that she performed on the boy Kieran, but she was too restless to settle down. So much had happened in so short a time . . . she really needed to sort things out in her mind.

She always thought of herself as a good judge of character and she believed Wendel's story about how he came to be in the castle. He was too much like someone's jolly uncle to be in any way dangerous, and he was too kindhearted to want to make an entire castle full of people pay for the crimes of one man. The big question was, would Howard be able to come up with a plan for her to lay the illusionary army to rest? At the moment, she considered that Howard's problem, not hers. She had other things on her mind.

It was the other things Wendel had told her, the things about the royal family, that she needed to get straight in her mind. The way Ewan's older brother had been treated . . . no wonder the poor kid had run away. She hoped wherever he was he was happy. And how horrible that every trace of his existence had been erased. It must have been very hard on Ewan when his brother disappeared; she had to wonder if they'd been close, and if he missed him.

And Sebastian . . . what had been done to him horrified her. Had the king really done that just to punish his older son? She still refused to believe that Ewan had any part in it. He was too kind, too generous, he – a sudden picture flashed through her mind of how Ewan treated Sebastian. It was not a pretty picture. She kept meaning to bring it up at one of their nightly dinners, but somehow when she was actually with him it kept slipping her mind.

It was strange, really, the effect Ewan had on her. She'd hear things on her wanderings through the tent city, unsettling things about Ewan's less than princely behaviour, but as soon as she had Ewan all to herself, it would all slip her mind. She was drawn to him like a moth to a flame, it was uncanny really.

The bell attached to her tent jingled merrily.

"Come in," Jessica called.

One of the pages held the flap open for Eleanor to enter, carrying yet another elaborate dress. Jessica sighed. She and Ewan had reached a compromise – she could wear whatever she wished throughout the day, but in the evening when they dined together she would dress like the lady Ewan believed her to be.

"My lady," Eleanor began, laying the dress on the bed. "May I have a word with thee?"

"Of course," Jessica said. "What's up?"

Eleanor fussed a little longer with the dress, making sure it was laying just so, and then came over and stood in front of Jessica, clasping her hands in front of her to keep them still.

"Would you like to sit down?" Jessica asked when she didn't say anything.

"Nay, my lady." Eleanor shook her head. "I . . . thee . . . I . . ." She began twisting her fingers together and dropped her gaze, unable to look Jessica in the eye. Taking a deep breath she let it out in a sigh. "I fear I have been unjust in my judgement of thee."

"You have?"

Jessica was surprised, to say the least. Eleanor had never made any bones about the fact she resented having to serve Jessica, and Jessica respected her for it. She was uncomfortable with the idea as well, but she had to admit when it came to "dressing for dinner" she needed all the help she could get.

Eleanor squared her shoulders. "I have been petty and resentful, thinking thee unworthy of all that thou hast been given. I have erred in my judgment and I beg thy forgiveness."

"Say what?" Jessica asked in surprise. Clearing her throat, she tried again. "Uh, might I might ask what brought on this change of heart?"

"'Tis the lad, Kieran, he be my brother's youngest lad."

Again she'd taken Jessica by surprise. "I only did what anyone would have done."

"Nay, my lady." Eleanor shook her head emphatically. "There are few indeed who would have cared for the fate of a mere peasant lad."

"I'm sure that's not—"

"And there be none who would have seen to the boy's comfort, let alone his healing."

"It wasn't as bad—"

"The best young Kieran could have hoped for was a lifetime of pain as a cripple. Had the guards gotten hold of him . . ." Tears filled her eyes.

Jessica took Eleanor by the shoulders and steered her over to the bed, pushing her down into a seated position and sitting down beside her.

"I take it Kieran is a favourite," she said gently.

"Aye, my lady," Eleanor said, sniffling. She fished in a pocket of her skirt, withdrawing a pristine white handkerchief and dabbed at her eyes.

"Well I was happy to help, and I'm glad he's going to be all right. But to be honest, we both know I haven't exactly made it easy for you either."

"'Tis true," Eleanor admitted. "But thou art from a distant land, thy customs are sure to be at odds with ours."

"I have an idea," Jessica said. "Why don't we start over, as friends."

"Friends?" Eleanor looked up at that. "Oh, no, my lady. Thou art too far above me in station, I—"

"Eleanor, we both know that's not true. And quite honestly, I could use a friend more than I can use a lady's maid. So what do you say, friends?"

Eleanor looked her in the eye, as though searching for something. Finding what she sought, she smiled. "Aye, my lady. Friends."

Despite the truce between them, Jessica still found it difficult to let Eleanor help her dress and Eleanor still found it difficult to accept some of Jessica's choices when it came to said dress. They were both secretly grateful when Jessica was done with her services for the day.

During dinner that evening, even Ewan noticed that Jessica was not herself.

"Is there aught amiss, my lady?" he asked. He was wearing his dress uniform tonight, complete with his sword and the silver medallion set with emeralds he habitually wore.

Jessica mustered up a smile for him. "Forgive me, your highness, I'm just a little tired tonight."

"I thought, mayhap, 'twas the incident in the orchard that troubled thee."

"The boy falling out of the tree?" Gareth had warned her that the prince would hear of the incident and would probably bring the subject up. She shrugged. "Boys will be boys. He's not the first one to fall out of a tree and I daresay he won't be the last."

"There was a question of apples . . ."

"Was it an apple tree?" she asked innocently. "I wish I'd known, it's been a while since I've had a nice, juicy apple. And apple trees make the best climbing trees. I should know, I climbed my fair share of them when I was a kid."

"Indeed."

She took a smidgeon of satisfaction at the non-plussed look on Ewan's face. "There was something I was wondering about . . ." her voice trailed off as she tried to think.

Ewan stroked the medallion around his neck. "I am ever thy servant. Ask of me anything thou wishes."

"It was just on the tip of my tongue, but I can't seem to remember . . ." She shook her head slightly, a puzzled frown on her face.

"Perhaps it will yet come to you. But alas, I must take my leave." He rose and took her hand, placing a lingering kiss on the back of it. "Fare thee well, my lady."

"Good night, your majesty," Jessica said, absently. Whatever it was she was going to ask him had completely slipped her mind.

* * * * *

When Howard contacted her later that evening, Jessica was pacing back and forth in her tent, still trying to remember what she'd wanted to ask Ewan.

"How are you doing, Jess?"

She sat down on the bed with a heavy sigh. "To be honest Howard, I think I'm losing my freaking mind!"

"I know you've been under a lot of strain . . ."

"That's not it."

"Then what—"

"I need to talk to Ellen," Jessica blurted out.

There was a stunned silence. Then, "Ellen?" Howard repeated cautiously.

"Yes, Ellen." Jessica got up and started to pace again. "Ellen and I talk about everything. We've always been there for each other and I miss that. You have no idea how much I miss that."

"Oh, I think I have some idea." Howard had been dodging Ellen for weeks now.

After the magic experiment had gone wrong, the group at Spirit Rock retained no true memory of that night. They believed they'd been gathered together at Howard's request to perform an experiment of magic and that the experiment was successful, but that was it. They couldn't remember the details of the experiment, nor did they remember Jessica being there.

Howard, at the time, had been content with the success of his experiment. He didn't need any further validation and was sure an angry Jessica would be phoning him for a ride at any time. The night passed, and then the next day before he began to be worried about her. He almost hoped she was just lying low somewhere to pay him back for sending her to wherever it was she ended up.

The day after the experiment, Ellen was pounding on his door, wanting to know where Jessica was. Before he could even open his mouth she started in on him wanting to know about his so-called magical experiments and what part Jessica had in them. He felt a little bad lying and telling her Jessica hadn't shown up for the experiment, especially when he saw how worried she was, but there was no way he was going to tell her that he'd teleported Jessica to parts unknown. She'd think he was crazy at best, a liar at worst.

Jessica's purse and street clothes were found in the empty theatre, but police had no clues as to what happened to Jessica herself. There was no suspicion of foul play – the theatre had been locked up and there was no sign of a struggle. The theatre had apparently been the last place anyone had seen her. Police were still questioning her friends and acquaintances.

By this time Howard had made contact with Jessica and was able to feel somewhat less guilty about his part in everything until Ellen came to him two days ago.

"I have a favour to ask," she said, standing in his

doorway. "It's just . . . I . . ." she sighed heavily.

"Why don't you come in," he told her.

She sat down on the edge of his red velvet wing chair and took a deep breath. "I'm just going to come right out and say this. I've always thought all your magic crap was a crock, but is there anything you could do . . ."

"You mean like a spell?"

"All right, yes. Is there some kind of spell you could do that could help us find Jessica?"

"If there was, don't you think I'd have cast it by now? She's my friend too."

"I had to ask," she said, getting to her feet. "Thanks anyway Howard."

He'd watched her leave in silence, half-minded to call her back and come clean with the whole thing. Now he wished he had.

"All right," he said to Jessica finally. "If it's that important that you speak with Ellen, I'll see what I can do."

Chapter Nineteen

Howard rubbed his sweaty palms on the legs of his jeans as he paced back and forth in his tiny apartment. What on earth had possessed him to agree to put Jessica in touch with Ellen?

Maybe it was guilt for his part in sending her into another dimension, although apparently he was no longer to blame for that. Maybe it was the forlorn sound of her voice - even without the puppy dog eyes she used to use on him whenever she wanted a favour when they kids. Usually something to do with homework she hadn't done. Or maybe—

The sound of someone on the stairs cut him off mid-thought and he halted in his tracks. This was it. He stood frozen in the centre of the room. Ellen may look small and harmless, but there were times when she scared the crap out of him with her evil eye stare and her knowledge of the martial arts, which he'd seen her use to incapacitate a man three times her size.

There was a sharp rap on his door and even though he'd been expecting it, he gave a start of surprise. Swiping his hands one last time on his pant legs, he took a deep breath and went over to open the door.

"I got your note," Ellen said, waving the scrap of yellow paper in the air. "You wanted to see me Howard?"

"You'd better come in and sit down," he told her, standing aside.

Silently, she did so. She'd been avoiding him since the day she'd asked him about doing a magic spell, a little embarrassed at her desperation. Now she saw what she'd been too angry to notice that day and she was a little appalled.

The Howard that let her into his apartment bore no resemblance to the Howard Jessica would joke about being almost obsessively neat. This Howard wore an untucked rumpled shirt over stained jeans. His hair was uncombed and from the smell of him he hadn't showered in a while. And his apartment! For such a small space he seemed to have a lot of garbage. There were crumpled up papers and half-empty take-out containers piled up all over the tables, spilling onto the floor. A pizza box perched precariously on top of a stack of books on the floor.

"Look, Howard, if it's about the rent . . . I know I'm late, but with Jessica—"

"No, it's not the rent." Howard stopped her before she wasted her breath explaining. "Rent's the last thing on my mind. Don't worry about it." He clamped his jaw shut to keep himself from babbling and gestured towards a chair.

Ellen set the books piled on the chair onto the floor and took a seat. "So if it's not the rent, why did you want to see me?"

Howard ran a hand through his already dishevelled hair and started to pace. Ellen waited patiently while he tried to decide where to begin. At last he stopped and faced her. He opened his mouth to speak, then snapped it shut again. Spinning on his heel, he paced the length of the room again and then brushed the garbage off the coffee table so he could sit down facing her.

"I need you to keep an open mind," he began.

"Okay . . ."

"And you need to let me tell you the whole story, without interrupting."

Now he was starting to really worry her. Howard hadn't exactly been playing with a full deck since she first met him. Now that Jessica was gone he seemed to have lost a few more cards.

"I promise to keep an open mind and I'll try not to interrupt. Now tell me what's on your mind, Howard."

Howard took a deep breath and let it out slowly, then he told her everything, starting with his search for true magic and ending with Jessica now living in another dimension. To her credit, Ellen made a good audience. She didn't move, hardly even seemed to breathe. Not once did she interrupt, although a couple of times it looked like she really wanted to.

When he was finished they sat in silence. Howard kept shooting nervous looks at Ellen while Ellen stared blankly at the bookcase behind him. Finally, she gave herself a shake and focused on him.

"Howard, I may have always thought you were a little weird, but never once, until now, did I think you had a mean streak in you."

"What?" His eyes widened as he stared at her. This was the last reaction he expected.

Ellen stood so she could tower over him. "Do you really expect me to believe this crock of shit?" Her hands curled into fists and he leaned back, away from her. "Did you honestly think you could sit there and give me this cock and bull story about Jessica getting sucked into another dimension and I'd believe you? Just how insane are you, anyway?"

"But . . . it's the truth. I'm not insane!"

"Well one of us is, and it sure isn't me!" She glared down at him. "You're supposed to be her friend!"

"I am her friend! I've been her friend longer than you have."

"Fine then. If you sent Jessica into another dimension then you can just bring her back. Right now."

"It's not as simple as that," Howard said, scooting back a little further on the coffee table.

"Of course it isn't." She turned her back on him and started sifting through the papers on the end table.

"What are you looking for?" he asked, keeping a wary eye on her.

"The phone of course."

"The phone?" he repeated, puzzled. "What do you need the phone for?"

"To call the police. You've just admitted you had something to do with Jessica's disappearance. They can deal with you."

"What if I can prove I'm telling the truth?" he asked.

"How?" she asked, stopping her search and turning back to him.

"I can let you see her." At least theoretically he could. "You probably can't talk to her, not yet anyway, but you can at least see for yourself that she's all right."

"You can do that, right here and right now?" Ellen looked at him suspiciously. "How?"

He got up from the coffee table and led her into his workroom where the scrying bowl rested on his table. Thackery had taught him a simple scrying spell, he just hoped he could get it to work without the wizards' help.

"Look," he said, mustering some backbone. "I know you don't believe in magic, but your belief isn't required for what I'm about to do." He pointed to the bowl and continued. "This is just a plain, ceramic bowl, you can check it out for yourself, and I'll be using corn oil to fill it with."

He waited patiently while she picked up the bowl and examined it carefully, and when she was done he picked up a bottle of Mazola corn oil from the row of plastic bottles on the shelf beside the table. With Ellen watching his every move, he poured the oil into the bowl and then tossed the empty bottle towards the garbage can, wincing as it missed and bounced under the table.

Howard was in his element now. Ignoring Ellen glowering at him, he focused on the bowl. He repeated the spell several times in his head before waving his hands over the bowl and muttering the incantation. Ellen's gasp of surprise told him it worked before he remembered to open his eyes.

* * * * *

Ellen stared down at the large, shallow bowl filled with oil and her mouth dropped open. It was a trick, it had to be. There could be no other explanation.

"How are you doing this?" she whispered.

"Magic," Howard said smugly.

She couldn't seem to take her eyes off the picture

forming in the bowl. There was Jessica, in a tent of all things!

"Jessica? Are you all right? Jessica?"

"She can't hear you."

"Why not? What's she doing?"

"She can't hear you because my magic isn't strong enough," Howard admitted. He peered over her shoulder. "And it looks like she's getting dressed up for some special occasion."

"What special occasion? And who's that with her?" It was like watching a movie on her lap top with the sound turned off.

"That's her lady's maid, Eleanor."

"Her what?" She tore her gaze away from the bowl and pinned Howard in place with it. "What is she doing with a lady's maid? What the hell is going on here, Howard?"

"All ladies of the nobility require a lady's maid, if for nothing else than to help them dress," Howard said weakly, taking a step back. "From the looks of her dress, I'd say Ewan is finally going to introduce her to his father."

"Who's Ewan?" She glanced back down at the bowl to see the other woman, Eleanor, start fussing with Jessica's hair. She couldn't believe Jessica was putting up with this. Jess was never what you would call a girly-girl. She liked to keep her appearance low-key.

"Ewan would be the prince that, uh, seems to

have taken a liking to Jessica."

"The what?" Howard had definitely caught her attention this time.

"I didn't mention the prince?" When she simply raised an eyebrow, he continued in a hurry. "I told you how she landed on a beach and was rescued off the cliff. Well, one of her rescuers happened to be the crown prince of the land she's in and he's, uh, taken a shine to our Jess."

"Are you freaking kidding me? A prince? Leave it to Jessica to get sucked into another universe and hook up with a freaking prince!"

"It's actually a good thing really. While she's under his protection no one will dare bother her, and he's been, um, really quite . . . chivalrous."

"Wow, is that him?" Ellen asked, as Eleanor swept open the tent flap and Ewan entered. They watched as Jessica nervously swiped her hands down over her hips. Eleanor shook her head at her behind Ewan's back; Ewan didn't seem to notice. He offered his hand to her and when she took it, he kissed the back of hers before tucking her hand under his arm.

"Oh my god, look at her blushing. You'd think she was a freaking virgin!"

"Yes, I have noticed she seems somewhat tongue-tied and . . . awkward around him."

Ellen frowned. "That doesn't seem like Jessica at all. Are you sure she's okay with him?"

"Oh, absolutely. He doesn't want to take the

chance —"

When he broke off what he was going to say, Ellen glanced over at him again. "He doesn't want to take what chance?"

"There's something else you need to know about Jessica and her situation," he said. Taking a deep breath, he let it out slowly and went on to explain about how strong the magic was in that universe and how Jessica appeared to have magical powers of her own.

"Are you freaking kidding?" Ellen yelled when he was finished. "You sent her to a freaking universe where magic is freaking real? Are you insane? Do you know how much trouble she could get herself into?"

"There's no point yelling," Howard said, trying to placate her. "Getting angry isn't going to make things any better."

"Oh, yeah? It'll make me feel better! And so will this!" Drawing her arm back, she punched him, square in the face. Howard went down like a sack of cement.

In retrospect, he thought as he lay on the floor, maybe he should have mentioned the magic part sooner.

Chapter Twenty

J essica breathed a huge sigh of relief as Eleanor loosened the ties of the corset she'd been forced to put on to fit into the elaborate dress Ewan had requested she wear for lunch with his father.

"Never fear, my lady," Eleanor told her, helping her out of the dress. "Though 'tis true luncheon is not as great a tribute as dinner, it was still an honour for thee to sup with the king."

"I'm sure it was," Jessica murmured as she dressed herself in clothes that were far more to her liking.

Eleanor picked up the court dress and held it carefully. "By thy leave I'll see to the cleaning my own self. Mayhap thou will have the chance to wear this gown again."

"Mayhap you're right," Jessica agreed. "After you've seen to the dress, you can have the rest of the day off, Eleanor. I'll be able to manage fine on my own."

"Wilt thou not be dressing for dinner this eve?"

"No, Prince Ewan won't be able to make it for dinner this evening."

"As you wish, milady," Eleanor said with a curtsy. "Shall I send in the minstrel and the squire?"

"The—oh! Sebastian and Gareth. Sure. I mean, by all means, send them in." Jessica made herself comfortable, sitting cross-legged on the bed.

"Was his highness not grand?" Gareth asked, bursting into the tent.

"He certainly wasn't what I expected," Jessica admitted cautiously.

The king had, in fact, been completely unlike what she expected. She thought she'd be meeting a charming, older version of Ewan; maybe even a grandfatherly figure since he'd already been married at least twice and Ewan was his youngest son. Instead he was dark haired where Ewan was light, heavier set and more taciturn, and had none of Ewan's charm.

There was something unsettling about him, something she couldn't quite put her finger on. Ewan introduced her and, thanks to her tutoring by Gareth and Sebastian, she hadn't made a fool of herself as she curtsied. The king stared at her with his slate grey eyes like she was a bug under a microscope, then grunted and turned away. And that was the extent of their interaction.

When Ewan escorted her back to her tent later he told her how much his father had been impressed with her and then laughed at her obvious surprise.

"Verily, my lady," he'd said. "Word of thy deeds hast reached his Majesty's ear, and he was quite taken with thy beauty."

"Deeds?" Jessica had asked, slightly alarmed. "What deeds?"

"Thy championing of the peasant boy and thy skill with magic." His voice had been lowered when he mentioned the magic. "My father is not one for grand speeches, but know that thou hast garnered his favour."

For the life of her, Jessica couldn't decide whether that was a good thing or a bad thing. Before she could ask Ewan, he was called away. She almost asked Gareth, but he seemed in such high spirits over the fact she'd met the king that she didn't have the heart to burst his bubble with her paranoia.

Sebastian entered behind Gareth at a more sedate pace. "I'm sure our lady was very impressed with the king. He tends to leave a lasting impression."

Jessica glanced at him sharply, suddenly remembering what Wendel had told her. How could she have forgotten? Even if the king hadn't done the deed himself, he was responsible for Sebastian being . . . she couldn't stand to even think about it.

"I am far more interested in what went on in the castle. Gareth and I are close to being consumed by our curiosity."

Jessica hesitated, unsure of how much to tell

them. In the end she told them a much edited version of her adventure. Though she was fairly certain she could trust Sebastian, Gareth was still somewhat of a wild card and she wouldn't put it past him to hunt Wendel down afterward.

So she told them about finding the weaver's gate unlocked, just as Gareth had said it would be, and about how creepy the abandoned streets were, and how even creepier the dark and gloomy castle was.

"According to Wendel," she concluded, "The wizard who set the spell is long gone. Somehow he was able to tap into the power of the Well to fuel his spell."

"And with the power of a Well behind it, the spell will be in place indefinitely," Sebastian said. "Do you believe this Wendel's story?"

"Yes, actually. I do. He's a little naive and far too trusting, but I think he's a good person at heart."

"But someone who can do little to help break the spell," Sebastian said dryly.

"Can thee do naught about it?" Gareth asked.

"I believe I can," Jessica said slowly.

"'Tis wonderful news, my lady! I shall inform my liege."

"Hold it," Jessica said as the squire was about to dash away. "I said I believe I can. I don't think we should tell Ewan, I mean, his majesty, until I'm certain. I have a few details that need to be worked out first."

"Oh, aye." Gareth seemed to droop a little as he returned to his seat. "Prithee, what is thy plan?"

"I don't know yet," Jessica admitted.

* * * * *

After Gareth and Sebastian left, Jessica flopped down on her bed and closed her eyes, grateful for some peace and quiet. She was still rattled from her unexpected summons to have lunch with the king and needed a little recovery time.

She needed to talk with Howard. Hopefully it wouldn't take him long to figure out some way of breaking Braxton's spell. The sooner Ewan was back in his castle, the sooner she could concentrate on getting home.

"Jessica?"

"Please tell me you've figured out how to break the spell on Ewan's castle," she said without sitting up.

"I'm working on it," Howard assured her. "Meanwhile, there's someone here who wants to talk to you."

"Jessie?"

Jessica's eyes snapped open and she bolted upright. "Ellen? Is that really you?"

"It's me all right. Damn it all, what have you gotten yourself into this time?"

"Well, I did ask for a little adventure. I guess I

don't know how to do things small."

"Didn't I warn you to be careful what you wished for?" There was an audible sniff.

"Oh, Ellen. You have no idea how much I've missed you."

There was another sniff. "Yeah, it looks like you're really missing me, consorting with royalty and all."

Jessica laughed, although her own eyes were damp.

* * * * *

Howard moved away from where his half of the pendent was suspended over the work table. He could still only connect for a limited time and this time belonged to Jessica and Ellen. Once it started the spell on the amulet would run until the energy was depleted.

He'd already relayed what Jessica had told him about the castle and its spell to Thackery and Paran, and they were supposed to get back to him this evening. Thankfully, they weren't dependent on the amulet for communication.

To be honest, he wasn't in any hurry to help lift the spell from the castle. Once she helped her prince, Jessica was going to expect to find a way home. How was he supposed to break the news to her that she was already home?

While part of him understood it was in Jessica's best interest to keep her origins hidden, it still made him uncomfortable to lie to her. A lie by omission was still a lie. And even if he admitted to her that he couldn't bring her back, there was still the matter of persuading her to travel far enough south to meet her family. Why should she leave her hot, hunky prince to travel parts unknown?

"Howard," Ellen called, "something's happening."

He hurried back to the workroom and noticed the moonstone had faded to just about transparent.

"I'm sorry ladies, but you're just about out of time. Jessica, I'll try and have a plan ready for you by morning."

"Okay, Howard." Her voice grew thinner and then disappeared altogether.

Ellen started sniffling again and he silently handed her a tissue.

"I can't thank you enough, Howard."

He shrugged. "It's just a tissue."

"Not for the tissue, you nit, for sharing this with me."

"It was the least I could do for Jessica."

"I'm sorry I punched you in the face," she added, staring down at her feet.

"Well, I'm not going to agree I had it coming, but I can relate to the shock you must have felt at all this."

Ellen reached up and plucked the amulet's chain from the hook it was suspended from. "I can't believe this is your only link to Jess. What happens if you lose it? Or she loses hers?"

"Well, if I lose my half I've always got my scrying bowl. It may take some time before I figure out how to get sound as well as a picture, but I should be able to eventually. But if Jessica loses hers," he shuddered delicately. "Let's hope we never have to find out."

He surreptitiously checked his watch. It was almost time for his pre-arranged consultation with Thackery and Paranithel and Ellen showed no signs of leaving. He hadn't mentioned being contacted by the two wizards, which of course meant he hadn't mentioned what Jessica was really doing in another dimension.

"It's going to be hours before the amulet can be used again, maybe you should go home and get some rest," he suggested tentatively.

Ellen shook her head. "That's okay, Howard. I couldn't sleep if I tried." She wandered around his small living room, picking up papers and stacking them and generally tidying up.

"You really don't have to do this," he said, taking the sheaf of papers she handed him. "I can clean up my own mess."

"It's no trouble, really. I need to do something to keep me busy."

Howard sighed. "Fine. But I have some stuff to

do in my work room, and I'd rather not be disturbed."

"No problem, I'll be quiet as a mouse; I'll just finish cleaning up in here."

He stood there for another moment and then with another resigned sigh, went into his workroom and shut the door. Being slightly claustrophobic he didn't usually work with the door to the small room closed, but better the slightly uneasy feeling than being punched in the face again for withholding information.

Pulling a stool up to the table, he checked his watch again as he sat down.

"Good evening, friend Howard."

Right on time. Howard loved this. Talking with the wizards through the scrying bowl was like using a video phone. Only with magic, not technology.

"Good evening Paran, Thackery," he said as their images swam into view. "I really hope you've got a solid idea for getting Ewan his castle back. I can't help feeling that the longer Jessica is with him, the more danger she's in."

"I agree," Thackery said. "Which is why I feel the best way to handle the situation is to tap into her power and work the spell remotely, through her."

Howard's eyes widened in surprise.

"There is not enough time to teach her to do this herself, she is too new to magic. One of us could do it," Paran said, "but to forge a connection between us at this time would be dangerous to all."

"Okay, I'm listening."

"First you must—"

"Hey, Howard, do you have any furniture pol—" Ellen stopped in the door of the room.

Howard looked up guiltily from the scrying bowl as Thackery's voice broke off.

"What the hell is going on here? Are you spying on Jessica?" She took a few steps into the room and peered down at the two men in the scrying bowl.

"Howard, who is this woman? And what has she to do with my daughter?" one of them demanded.

"Daughter? What daughter?" She looked at Howard.

"Aw, crap!" Howard said, lowering his head to rest in his hands. "Paran and Thackery, meet Jessica's friend Ellen. Ellen, meet the wizards Paran and Thackery."

"Wizards? Like you?"

Howard gave a short laugh. "No, not like me. These are real wizards."

"Do not be so hard on yourself, friend Howard," Paran told him. "We would not fare much better were we to live in your world."

"Wait a minute. Daughter – someone said something about someone's daughter. What's up with that?"

Ellen was like a dog with a bone. Howard knew there would be no peace with her until she knew the whole story.

"Jesseminathus is my daughter by blood," Thackery said proudly.

"That's bullshit! Jessica's father was a cop who got killed in the line of duty right before she was born. What – did you say Jesseminathus?"

"That was the name her mother and I chose for her. Why?"

"There was a slip of paper, wedged between the two halves of the medallion. It had that name written on it."

"You're right," Howard said, raising his head. "I'd forgotten all about that."

The two wizards in the scrying bowl looked at each other. "Farenalyssia must have had a vision of what was to come."

"But why didn't she say anything to me?" Thackery demanded.

"Excuse me," Ellen said, interrupting the two wizards before they could start a full-fledged argument. "Who's Farenalyssia?"

"Farenalyssia was my daughter," the older of the two wizards told her. "And Jessica's mother."

Ellen sat down hard on another stool. "Okay, somebody better start filling me in on what's going on, or this is going to get real ugly, real fast."

Chapter Twenty-One

Once Ellen was brought up to speed, she sat there, stunned, while the wizards discussed wizardly things. She had too much else on her mind so she pretty much tuned them out while her thoughts went around in circles. Jessica was going to have a cow.

Ellen hadn't been around when Jessica's mother was alive, but she'd gotten the impression that they'd been very close. That was why it had been especially hard for her to be left in the care of her Aunt Sandra.

"How did Jessica's biological mother die?" she asked abruptly.

The three men broke off their discussion. "What?"

"Jessica's mother, how did she die? It was violent, wasn't it?"

"How could you possibly know this?" Paran asked when Thackery seemed unable to speak.

"Jessica used to have nightmares. They were starting to get progressively worse and then all of a sudden they stopped for a few years. It was right before she found that medallion that they started up again."

"I never thought . . ." Paran said, shaken. "I should have known . . ."

"What?" Howard and Ellen said at the same time.

"Our enemy lured us away and then attacked with an army of beasts," Thackery said quietly. "We found what remained of the household in the garden; Farena had only enough time to conceal our babe in the well under a spell of silence."

"I found her amulet," Paran whispered. "Torn from her body."

A shimmer passed over the image in the scrying bowl as Thackery placed a comforting hand on the older man's shoulder. "We left the amulet with Jesseminathus as a means to check in on her from time to time. We never thought . . . the violence of Farena's death . . . the amulet must have absorbed some of her dying essence."

"And every time you checked on Jessica, it triggered the memory in the stone," Howard finished for him. "It's absolutely incredible."

"We lost touch with her for a span of years," Thackery said. "You said her nightmares stopped – was she at any time separated from the amulet?"

Howard and Ellen looked at each other. "She never really had the amulet," Howard said. "She just recently found it in a box of her mother's things."

"Wait a minute," Ellen said. "Jess found the medallion in the box, but the box came from her Aunt Sandra, and before that it was stored in some old lady's attic."

"I'll bet that coincides with the time you were out of touch with her," Howard told the wizards.

"I agree," Thackery said. "She would not have to be wearing the amulet, just be within a certain range."

"Big brother is watching," Ellen muttered.

Howard shot her a glance.

"Okay, so the amulet is a magical link to Jessica," Ellen said in a louder voice. "So how does that help us help her?

"Through it Howard has been able to communicate with her and teach her to use her magic."

"Our first task is to aid her in bringing down the illusion enveloping Castle Ghren," Paran said. "Then we must entice her to the southern lands where we can finally be reunited. I suggest—"

"Do you know how crazy this all sounds?" Ellen whirled away and paced around the table. "Jessica is in no way prepared for any of this. Right now she's having a grand old time living out a ren-faire fantasy, handsome prince included. Any minute now she's going to wake up and realize she's up to her ass in alligators!"

"Alligators?" Thackery asked.

"She hasn't done too bad so far," Howard told her. "In fact, all things considered she's handling things pretty well. Granted her first attempt at magic didn't go so well . . ."

"You *know* Jessica, Howard, and these guys don't. She's been incredibly lucky so far but sooner or later that luck is going to run out."

"Which is why we must bring her to us as quickly as possible," Paran said.

"But first, the illusion," Thackery added. "I have been giving it much consideration and I believe I have come up with a way for Howard to aid Jesseminathus through the amulet."

"Me?" Howard asked in surprise.

"You will use the amulet to tap into her magic and cast a spell to take down the illusion while at the same time creating a new illusion to make it appear as though she is destroying the demon army."

"Oh, is that all?" Ellen said.

Her sarcasm was lost on the three wizards.

* * * * *

Jessica paced back and forth inside her tent. She'd just finished talking with Howard and the plan he'd come up with had so many holes in it she could use it for a golf course. All she had to do was convince Ewan to take her to the battlefield, have him call up the monster army, and then stand there facing it while Howard did all the rest. Oh, and there was the little matter of Howard having control over her body while he did so.

"It's simple, Jess. You just have to stand on a ley line near the battlefield and look all imposing, and I'll do the rest."

"What's a ley line?"

"It's an invisible line of magical energy."

"So . . . if it's invisible, how will I know if I'm standing on it?"

"Because you'll be using your magical senses to sniff it out. Now pay attention!"

He'd gone on to explain about how the ley lines were connected to the Wells of Power and with her standing on a ley line he could draw power from the well if he needed to. He seemed so enthusiastic about the whole thing . . .

Of course he was enthusiastic. He'd get to do what he'd always wanted to do – perform real magic. Only he'd be doing it using her body. To be honest, the thought of it kind of creeped her out, especially since there was no guarantee that it was going to work.

With a sigh Jessica flopped down on her bed and listened to the rain pounding down on the tent. The weather had been pretty good during her time here thus far. Kind of like late spring. The rain had started up sometime during the night and showed no signs of letting up. She didn't know what this tent was made out of but she had to give kudos to the craftsmanship. Despite the heavy rain it was snug and dry inside.

The bell outside her tent jingled.

"Come in," she called as she struggled into an upright position on the bed.

A bedraggled Sebastian entered followed by an equally bedraggled Gareth, laden down with several bundles wrapped tightly against the rain.

"What are you guys doing here?" she asked in surprise.

"We had intended to take you on a picnic today," Sebastian said, removing his wet cloak, "but the weather seems to have conspired against us. Therefore, we brought the picnic to you."

"You guys are the best!"

"It was Gareth's idea," Sebastian admitted.

"Gareth, you're such a sweetie!" She went over and hugged him; he blushed furiously. "A picnic is just the thing to brighten a gloomy day."

"'Tis what we did when I was a lad," he muttered, and quickly turned to start unwrapping the bundles.

Jessica and Sebastian grinned at each other over his head.

"Just how many people are invited to this picnic?" she asked, looking askance at the amount of food being set out.

"We weren't sure what you'd feel like having, so . . ." Sebastian shrugged and spread his hands wide.

He laid a blanket on the floor and the three of them sat down and helped themselves to the selection of meat, bread, cheese, fruit, and pastries. They washed it all down with a bottle of mead, which they passed around, having forgotten to bring cups.

They were just finishing when there was a loud clap of thunder. Gareth got to his feet.

"Pray excuse me but I must make haste to the horses. My lord's mount fears storms and I need to make sure he does not harm himself in his agitation."

He caught up his cloak and was gone before Jessica even had time to register surprise.

"He takes his job way too seriously."

"He needs to," Sebastian told her. "Should anything happen to the prince's armor or his horse, Gareth could forfeit his life."

"But he's just a kid!"

"He's a squire," Sebastian corrected. "And not only that, he's the prince's squire. As such he's doing a man's work and is therefore considered a man."

It occurred to Jessica that she really knew very little about what went on outside her tent. She vaguely recalled that the lower classes were treated pretty unfairly in the middle ages, but this wasn't *her* middle ages, this was another world. Someone needed to stand up for the little guy, but she was ashamed to admit it wasn't going to be her. She was just a guest in this time.

Sebastian opened his mouth, but whatever he was going to say was lost in another clap of thunder. The rain started pounding down even harder.

"Sebastian," she said suddenly. "What happens to the camp during the rain? I mean, we're on higher ground, so we're nice and dry, but what about the people below us? That's quite a dip the ground where the tavern's set up."

"With any luck most of them had time enough to relocate."

"And those that didn't?"

"Then I expect they and their belongings will be getting very wet." He looked at her soberly. "There's nothing to be done. They've weathered many such storms since being evicted from the castle."

Jessica sighed, wiping her mouth on a linen napkin. "Well I know at least one thing that can be done, and it's about time I did it."

"And what is that, milady?" he asked curiously.

"I can get them back into their nice, dry homes."

Jessica took a few steps towards the flap of the tent, intending to send a message requesting Ewan's presence, but suddenly stopped and turned back to Sebastian.

"Oh, Sebastian! There's something I've been meaning to tell you, but I keep forgetting."

He shrugged, unconcerned, and began packing up the remains of their picnic. "Isn't there a saying that what doesn't stay in your mind is unimportant?"

"That's just the problem, this is important. It's about your search for your friend, the other prince."

His eyebrows rose in surprise. "But what could

you possibly—"

She plunked herself down beside him. "I wasn't entirely forthcoming about what happened in the castle. I wasn't sure how much I should say in front of Gareth, so I sort of glossed over some of the facts."

"What facts?" he asked. "And what has this to do with my search?"

Without hesitation she plunged into the story of what really happened when she went into Castle Ghren, leaving out only what Wendel had told her about what had been done to Sebastian.

"Apparently, the most likely reason this Thackery person lost the trail at the Mythric Ocean is because land-based magic doesn't work so well over water." She didn't mention that the other reason could be that the prince could have died there.

"I am humbled by your trust in me," Sebastian said, after he'd taken time to digest her story. "But are you sure you can trust this wizardling?"

"I don't know if I'd let him watch over the family treasure, but I'm pretty sure his story's true. He's pretty small potatoes as far as magic is concerned, and a little too trusting when it comes to schemes that sound too good to be true."

"The Mythric Ocean is vast; I wouldn't know where to start looking," Sebastian said, stroking his chin thoughtfully.

"Is there some kind of water wizard you could

consult?" Jessica asked. "Maybe he could pick up the trail where it left off."

He sighed. "There are, but they are not common and they will not be found in the Kingdom of Ghren."

She reached out and laid her hand on top of his. "I wish I could have done more."

"You've given me a place to start looking again - that means a great deal to me. I was almost ready to give up the search."

They stared at each other for a few heartbeats.

"Are you sure you're gay?" Jessica asked.

That got a genuine laugh out of him. "Very sure. I knew even before—"

"Before what?" she asked softly when he broke off in mid-sentence. She knew, of course, what he was about to say, but he didn't know that. She hated to see the mask of indifference slide into place once more.

"It doesn't matter," he said with a shake of his head. "I've known since I was a young lad where my preferences lay."

"You've been such a good friend in such a short time . . . If you ever need to talk, I'm here for you."

"Talking will not help. What's passed is past and there's no undoing what has been done. But I thank you for the effort."

"Most eloquently said," Jessica said with a grin. "Very bard-like, one might say."

He looked at her solemnly, then said, "Truth be told, I have already achieved full Bardic status. But I have chosen not to acknowledge myself as such within Ghren's boundaries."

"Why not?" Jessica asked in surprise.

Sebastian shrugged. "Because a lowly minstrel has access to places a full Bard does not, and as you recall I am on a quest. I am also on my third year of seven years of travelling to achieve my master-bard status."

"That's a lot of travelling. Doesn't it get lonely?"

"Sometimes," he admitted. "But there's always the next town or village. I even crafted a song about it once."

"Is that part of the Bardic testing, that you write your own songs?" She was genuinely interested and hoped Howard was listening. He'd have loved being here.

"Yes it is. But alas, though the music comes easily to me, the words do not." He shook his head with a rueful grin.

"You know, it's a real shame I can't take you with me when I go. I have a friend who writes poetry. You guys would be perfect together."

"Perhaps we would, we already have one thing in common."

"What would that be?"

"Our uncommonly good taste in friends."

Chapter Twenty-Two

J essica paced to and fro in her tent, rehearsing in her mind what she was going to say to Ewan. The rain had stopped, and she waited until Sebastian had packed up the remains of their picnic before sending a message to Ewan that she'd like to see him. Now that they had a plan, such as it was, there was no reason to keep putting it off.

Although for the most part she was enjoying her time here, she missed her old life. She missed going to the movies, hanging out with her friends . . . she even missed Mr. Pressman and her job.

Oh, god, her job. Did she even have a job anymore? How long had she been here, anyway? Somehow she'd lost track of the days. Had it been days? Or had it been more like weeks?

The bell outside her tent jingled and she called out an absent-minded, "Come in."

One of the pages entered first, and held the flap open for Ewan. With his arrival, all of Jessica's worries seemed to fade away.

"My lady, I pray thee forgive my tardiness in answering thy summons," Ewan said, one hand stroking his medallion. It seemed to be a nervous habit with him.

"There's nothing to forgive," Jessica said with a wave of her hand. "I can only imagine how busy you must be."

"Prithee how may I serve thee, my lady?"

"Why don't we sit down for this," Jessica suggested, gesturing to the corner where the table and chairs had been set up. All at once she was a little nervous.

Once they were comfortable, she squared her shoulders and got right to it. "The question isn't so much how you can serve me as how I can be of service to you."

"Indeed?" He raised one eyebrow in that really cool way she'd always wished she could do.

"Indeed," Jessica said firmly. "I believe I may be able to do something about the monsters surrounding your castle, but I'll need to see the actual battlefield to make sure."

"Thou wishes to see the battlefield?" He looked rather appalled at the idea. "'Tis no place for a lady."

It was on the tip of her tongue to tell him she was no lady, but she held back. "Be that as it may, I can't tell if I can help until I see what I'm up against."

Still he hesitated.

"I promise I won't set foot on the battlefield itself."

She and Howard had been knee deep in plans when Ellen had pointed out that as far as Ewan knew, Jessica never been to the battlefield. It might look suspicious if she were to just go there and work her magical mojo. She needed to make it look good.

Howard had the nerve to agree with Ellen, and added that she needed to visit the battlefield at least once more before the actual spell-casting so he could determine where the most effective place for her to stand would be.

While on the one hand it had been nice to see her two best friends getting along so well, on the other hand it had been really annoying that they did it while ganging up on her. Jessica finally agreed to the wisdom of a pre-spell casting visit, if only to keep Ewan from guessing that Gareth and Sebastian had already taken her there. She didn't want to get her new friends in trouble.

"Very well," Ewan agreed reluctantly. "I like this not, but thy words have merit. I will make the arrangements and return."

He got up to leave, but turned at the tent flap. "I would have thee know that our continued friendship does not depend upon thy aid."

"I know," she said with a smile. "This is just something I'd like to do . . . if I can."

As soon as Ewan left her tent to make arrangements, Jessica pulled out her pendant and contacted

Howard.

"Okay, we're just about ready to go. How am I going to know if I'm close to the right place? It's not like you can tell me whether I'm getting hot or cold."

"Actually," Howard said. "That's not a bad idea. Hold on to your medallion for a second."

Jessica did as she was told. "Hey, it's getting hot!"

"What about now?"

As quickly as it started to heat up, now it was radiating cold.

"Howard, you're a genius!"

"Well, it was actually your idea," he said modestly. "Now, let's just hope there's a ley line out there strong enough for what we want to do."

"What do you mean, hope?" Jessica asked, alarmed. "Howard—" The rest of what she was about to say was cut off as the bell outside her tent jingled. Ewan was ready to take her to the site of his family's disgrace.

Jessica barely suppressed her heavy sigh as they left her tent. Why had she thought it would be just her, Ewan and maybe Gareth and a couple of guardsmen? Ewan had mustered a whole company of knights and soldiers as their escort. She felt painfully conspicuous as the group made its way through the camp and it made the walk to the battlefield seem that much longer.

It was hard to ignore the disgruntled muttering of the men over the fact there was a woman so close to the battlefield, but a quelling look from Ewan shut them up. She gathered they felt it was bad luck or something.

Jessica walked slowly along the edge of the field, which was clearly defined by the difference in the ground. Beyond the invisible border, the ground was churned up like a newly ploughed farmer's field. She held onto the milky-white stone of her pendant, looking out at the field and pretending to be all mystical while Howard searched for the optimal spell-casting spot.

"Perhaps thee should stand here," Ewan suggested, drawing her away from the edge. He gave a nod to the captain of his guards.

The man drew his sword with a flourish and spurred his horse towards the battlefield. "By the shades of my ancestors!" he cried.

Yelling variations of the same thing, the rest of the company followed. As soon as the first horse passed the invisible barrier, the monster army winked into existence. They were still transparent to Jessica's eyes, but to the warriors they were all too real.

She took a step back, feigning surprise, if not fear, and was rewarded when Ewan put a comforting arm around her.

Wow, she thought. If this was all it took to get some serious attention, she should have thought of it days ago.

Her giddiness at the prince's attention quickly devolved into unfeigned dismay as it was driven home to her that while the monsters were illusory, the men fighting were not. Nor were the wounds they were receiving. Those men out there were getting their asses kicked, all because of her.

"Please," she said, putting her hand on Ewen's arm. "Call them back. I've seen enough."

"As you wish, my lady." He nodded at Gareth who put a horn to his lips and blew a long, low note.

At the sound of the horn the soldiers disengaged and moved back to their position at the edge of the field. As the last one crossed the border, the monster army winked out again.

Jessica was silent and white faced as they made their way back to the camp. She couldn't help but feel responsible for each and every injury the soldiers accompanying them had suffered. On the one hand she knew she was being foolish because she was in no way responsible for the ghostly monsters, but on the other hand it had been her idea to visit the battlefield.

More than ever she was determined to break the spell cast over Ghren.

* * * * *

Ellen sipped from her steaming mug as she stared at the images in the scrying bowl and sighed in satisfaction. If she'd known Howard owned an espresso machine she'd have started visiting him years ago.

"Howard, what's the deal with this Ewan character?"

"Deal?" He moved to peer over her shoulder at the images in the bowl.

"It's just . . ." Her voice faded and she frowned as she concentrated on what was going on. "Is it possible Ewan has some kind of magic?"

"I suppose anything is possible," he said slowly. "He might have some kind of latent magic and not even know it. I'm not exactly sure how those things run in that universe. Why do you ask?"

"I've been watching Jessica a lot these last few days, and she acts different around him."

"She's probably just intimidated by the fact he's a prince."

Ellen shook her head. "I don't think that's it, it's something else." She took another sip of her espresso. "For one thing, he's not her type at all. Sure, he's pretty to look at, but he has a nasty streak and he's, well, a little stuck on himself. Jessica hates guys like that."

It was Howard's turn to frown. "To be honest, I had noticed that she's more subdued around him and when they've been apart for a while she seems like her old self."

"Could he have cast a spell on her?"

"Doubtful, something like that would be difficult to maintain."

"Is there some way you could check?"

"I suppose . . ."

Ellen stood back a bit to give Howard room to work. He focused on the image in the bowl and muttered something she couldn't quite catch under his breath. The image wavered for a moment, then cleared.

"He doesn't appear to have any magical abilities, but there's something not quite right about him."

"There!" Ellen pointed at the bowl. "Did you see that? He was stroking that medallion he's wearing. He does that a lot."

"It probably doesn't mean anything, it's just force of habit."

"Could you check it out anyway?"

"Ellen, I'm supposed to be—"

"Please Howard?"

Howard sighed. "Fine, but I'm supposed to be hoarding my borrowed magic to help Jessica take down the illusion spell." He took a breath and focused on the medallion Prince Ewan wore around his neck. His eyes widened. "How could I have missed this?"

"What, what is it?"

"You were right, that medallion is imbued with magic. Dark magic."

"We've got to warn her!" Ellen was ready to go to battle for her friend.

Howard put a placating hand on her arm. "We can't."

"What? Are you crazy?" She shook his hand off. "Who knows what kind of evil spell he's casting over her. Jessica could be in danger!"

"I don't think she's in any danger, at least not any more than she's already in. Like I said, Ewan doesn't have any magical abilities of his own, so the medallion isn't truly dangerous in his hands."

"Then why does he need it?"

"My guess is that Ewan uses it to make people like him." Howard could almost sympathize with him. He knew all about wanting people to like him. "Not just Jessica, but his soldiers, his subjects - that's probably why he's so popular."

"That's terrible!"

"I agree." He knew they were agreeing for different reasons.

"So Jessica doesn't really like the prince, he's just using the medallion to make her think she does."

"Oh I think her attraction is real enough. Let's face it, he is pretty hot," he said with a grin. "And he's been wining and dining her since she got there."

"Then why does he need the medallion?"

"I presume he wants to ensure she'll help them get out of their current predicament."

"So you don't think she's in any real danger?" Ellen glanced up from the bowl.

"Not per se. Right now she's very useful to him, and he's going to want to make sure she stays safe."

"What happens when she stops being so useful?"

"That is a very good question."

* * * * *

"Okay, empty your mind Jessica," Howard instructed.

"If my mind was any emptier I could stick a 'For Rent' sign on my forehead," Jessica muttered.

"Har, har. Now stop thinking so hard."

She dutifully looked at the lamp sitting on the small table in front of her and tried not to think of anything. There was a tickling sensation in her head that meant Howard was there, and then the wick of the lamp was suddenly lit.

"Great. Now let's try it again."

Jessica sighed. After visiting the battlefield with Ewan earlier, and finding a strong ley line for Howard, she was cautiously optimistic that by this time next week she'd be home in her own bed. Howard hadn't exactly agreed with her on that, but he was confident that between the two of them they could break the illusion spell over Ewan's castle.

Ewan had been overjoyed when she told him the good news. Well, maybe not overjoyed, but it had put him in a good enough mood that he'd only made a token protest when she asked that Sebastian and Gareth be allowed to come with them when she made the attempt. She figured she could use the moral support.

"You're doing it again, you're thinking too hard." Howard's voice gave her a jolt back to the task at hand.

"Howard, we've done this twelve times. I think it's time to give it a rest."

"I just don't want anything to go wrong."

"Nothing's going to go wrong, you said it yourself - it's a piece of cake."

"I just wish we had something bigger to practice on."

"Sorry, the lamp was the best I could do without looking suspicious." She went over to the bed and made herself comfortable. "If you're having second thoughts about this, you'd better tell me before I go out to the battlefield tomorrow."

"No, I haven't changed my mind, I just like to be thorough, that's all. Now, I won't be able to talk to you directly tomorrow. Are we clear on what's going to happen?"

"Yes, Howard." Jessica yawned. "I go with Ewan and his men to the battlefield and find the spot where you said the strongest ley line is. I draw my sword and step out onto the field to activate the illusion spell. Then I raise my sword above my head and give my battle cry, and the rest is up to you. Are you sure I have to give a battle cry? It seems kind of dorky to me."

"You're audience will be expecting some kind of vocal, an incantation or yell, and it'll let me know you're ready to start."

"All right," Jessica said, with another yawn. "Can I go to bed now?"

"Sorry, I didn't mean to keep you up so late."

"S'okay, Howard."

"Pleasant dreams, Jess."

* * * * *

Despite being so tired, Jessica did not sleep well that night. She tossed and turned and kept waking up from dreams of all the things that could go wrong.

Since she'd given Eleanor the day off, she dressed herself in her favourite outfit of leather pants and a billowy white shirt with a leather jerkin over top. Gareth had cleaned and buffed her boots until they looked like new. Sebastian found a plume to replace the original, now somewhat bedraggled one, on her hat. By the time she strapped the sword belt on, she was feeling quite rakish.

Ewan had agreed with her to keep what they were going to do a secret, so as not to get anyone's hopes up, so it was just him, Sebastian and Gareth, and twenty or so of Ewan's most trusted knights that went to the battle field. Jessica would have preferred to do this without the knights present, but Ewan insisted.

Jessica found herself edging along the field, trying to find the exact spot she'd found for Howard the other day. Oh, there it was. Right beside that reddish rock.

"You don't have to do this, you know," a quiet voice said right next to her ear.

She jumped. "Sebastian! You just about gave me a heart attack!"

"Sorry." He grinned, looking anything but sorry. "You were looking so serious. I just wanted to remind you that you don't have to go through with this."

"I know, but I said I would."

He hesitated a moment. "I'm sure the prince would understand —"

"I'm not doing it for him," she interrupted.

"You're not?"

"Well, not just for him. I'm doing it for all those people living in such squalor in the tent city as well."

He looked a little surprised, but all he said was, "Good."

"Wish me luck," she said, squaring her shoulders.

"Good luck," he said, stepping back.

Just as she and Howard had rehearsed, Jessica stepped onto the battlefield, drawing her sword as she did so. The army of illusions sprang to life and she held her sword over her head. She felt pretty silly. In her mind she'd been rehearsing what to say - something along the lines of "For God, the King, and his country", but what came out of her mouth instead was: "By the shade of Errol Flynn!"

Her eyes went unfocused and she felt the tell-tale

tingle that meant Howard had taken over. The sword in her hands began to glow, growing brighter as she began drawing energy from the ley line beneath her feet and feeding it to Howard. The light exploded outward, arrowing towards the illusions. As it struck, each illusion exploded into a mist of light that dissip-ated on the breeze.

Dimly, Jessica was aware of the men behind her cheering. As the last of the illusions vanished, the light enveloping her sword disappeared as well. She lowered the weapon and sank to her knees.

"What a rush!" she said in wonder. And fell flat on her face.

Chapter Twenty-Three

J essica sighed. She was lying on a cloud; it was wonderful. Stretching her arms out on either side she frowned when she didn't reach the edges. Maybe this really was a cloud. It certainly wasn't her bed. Cautiously she cracked an eye open and then quickly closed it again. There was material above her, but it was a deep green, not the white of her tent.

"Lady Jessica?" There was a rustling sound of movement. Jessica froze in place.

"Too late, I saw you move."

Keeping her eyes shut, she frowned. "Sebastian? Is that you?"

"Yes, it's me. And I must say, it's about time you woke up."

"Where am I?"

"Why don't you open your eyes and see for your-self?" he replied, his voice teasing.

She thought about it for a moment. "I don't think so." She'd been lucky the last few times she'd passed

out to wake up in more or less pleasant circumstances, but her luck was bound to run out sooner or
later.

He sighed gustily. "You're in your new quarters in
Castle Ghren."

"I'm what? You mean it worked?" Her eyes flew
open and she sat up abruptly. "Ow, my head!" She
hunched over in the big bed, clutching her head.

"Do you think you can drink this?" he asked,
holding a wooden mug out to her.

Jessica waved one arm in his direction, leaning
over as far as she could to take it from him. "Sebastian's magical hangover cure?" she asked, taking a
sip. "Oh, that's good. You should patent this stuff,"
she told him. "Actually, I don't feel quite as bad as I
did the last time this happened, but thank you."

"You are most welcome. And it's been almost a
week since you freed the castle."

The mug froze, halfway to her mouth. "A week?
Are you kidding me?"

"Kidding?" he asked, clearly confused.

"Joking, jesting, having one on."

"Nay, milady, I do not jest. You are the hero of
Ghren."

Making herself more comfortable against the pile
of pillows behind her, she thought about this while
she sipped her drink. Another frown creased her
brow. "If I'm a hero, then why aren't the healers
fighting over who gets to 'cure' me? Not that I'm

complaining," she added hastily, "it's just they seemed to be the type to try and curry favour with the prince. Is that the right expression?"

"It is," he said with a slight smile. "And you need to finish your drink before I fill you in on what has transpired since you banished the army of evil. It is best if you drink that slowly," he warned as she raised her mug.

Defiantly she took a big gulp. Her stomach gave a lurch and she took several deep breaths before the queasiness settled. "Not one word," she warned him.

He raised his hands innocently.

While she sipped, Jessica looked around her room. The walls and floor were built of dark grey stone blocks. There was a fire burning brightly in a large stone fireplace, but most of the light was from the sunshine streaming in through three tall, narrow windows. There were tapestries on the walls, but they were too far away to make out the scenes on them clearly. What furniture she could see was made of wood - the chairs had no padding or cushions and looked very uncomfortable.

There was a tall wardrobe against one wall, with a carved wooden screen beside it. The frame of the bed she was lying in was of a dark wood, which went well with the dark green canopy over her head and the green velvet bed curtains that had been tied back at each corner. Jessica had never seen a down filled mattress before, but she had no doubt that was what she was lying on now.

"Okay," she said, finishing the last sip from the mug and leaning over to hand it back to Sebastian. "What's going on?"

He made himself as comfortable as possible in the chair he'd been sitting in. "After the banishing of the evil army rendered you unconscious, his highness ordered that you be taken back to your tent to recover."

"Let me guess, you and Gareth?"

"How did you know?"

"Ewan's soldiers may be hot stuff when it comes to fighting, but they don't do so great when it comes to dealing with magic."

"Yes, well. In any case, you were most fortunate as the healers declared there was nothing they could do whilst you were unconscious, so Gareth and I were set to watch over you until you awakened. A group of knights were selected to make a foray into the castle and they returned to inform the king that all was well within."

Jessica hoped Wendel had made it out okay, or at least had the sense to hide in the pantry again.

"The king lost no time in organizing the move back into the castle, which took far less time than you would imagine. You showed no sign of waking up, but the king did not wish to delay the celebration so he had you carried into the castle with great ceremony."

"What do you mean, ceremony? What kind of ceremony could there be with me being unconscious?"

"You were placed on a pallet, draped in the royal colours, and you were there with the royal family for all to see during the king's speech."

"Seriously? That's so . . . so . . . creepy!" Jessica shuddered at the thought of all those people ogling her unconscious body.

"In any case, it was the king's decree that you be gifted with the wizard's tower, but that would have to wait until you regained your senses as only a powerful wizard would be able to break the spell that held the door shut."

"You said held, does that mean—"

"I'm getting to that," Sebastian said in a slightly annoyed tone of voice.

"Sorry."

"You were to be taken to one of the guest chambers, however as you passed the door to the wizard's tower it unsealed itself, proving once again how powerful you really are." He did not tell her that the men carrying her pallet had been so shocked they dropped her.

"It has been somewhat . . . difficult to find servants willing to staff the tower."

"I can imagine," Jessica muttered. Her hand went to her throat, automatically seeking the comfort of her medallion. She paled and her eyes widened. It wasn't there.

Sebastian looked at her intently. "If it is your amulet you seek, it lies on that table." He nodded towards the small table beside her bed. The milk-white stone lay there, chain curled neatly around it. Jessica's relief was almost palpable as she lunged across the bed, fingers closing around it.

"It was almost lost during the move," he said quietly.

Gareth had caught Ewan in the act of removing it from her. The prince had mumbled something about keeping it safe for her and sworn him to secrecy. Gareth had gone straight to Sebastian. During the preparations for the move back into the castle, Sebastian had managed to steal it back again.

"It would have been a disaster if it had been lost," Jessica said sincerely. If she lost her link to Howard she'd never get home again. The thought was terrifying.

"I was right, 'tis the source of your power, isn't it?"

She looked at him and opened her mouth to lie, then thought better of it. "Not exactly," she said, slowly.

Sebastian moved his chair closer.

"This isn't a conversation I want to have while lying in bed," Jessica said, stalling. "I'm feeling much better. Do you think I could get up and get dressed first?"

"Of course," Sebastian told her. "Do you need

help?" he asked a moment later, trying not to laugh as she struggled to make her way across the wide bed.

"No," she replied, trying in vain to keep her dignity intact. The voluminous nightgown she was wearing twisted around her legs, tangling with the sheets.

"Perhaps I could see about something to break your fast," Sebastian suggested, still struggling to keep a straight face.

"Yeah, why don't you go do that," Jessica told him. She flopped back on the pillows and waited until he'd gone before trying again. Catching her breath, she flipped the covers off and unwound the sheets and nightgown from her legs, then slid towards the edge of the bed. Even with her legs hanging over the edge it was still a drop of a foot before her feet hit the floor.

She couldn't help but grin. "Coolest bed ever!"

Going over to the wardrobe, she pulled the door open and grimaced. "You've got to be kidding!" She pulled one of the elaborate gowns out and held it up to herself. While she was sure it must have cost a small fortune, judging by the jewels studding the bodice, it had to be one of the most hideous things she'd ever seen.

Thrusting it back into the wardrobe, she pushed the other dresses aside then checked the shelf above them. "Oh, please don't tell me this is all I have to wear!"

Slamming the doors shut she turned her back to

them and looked at the rest of the room. Going over to the carved screen she checked behind it and found a covered chamber pot. She made a mental note to ask Howard about a magical spell to make a flush toilet. And maybe a shower while they were at it.

At the foot of the enormous bed was a trunk. To her great relief she opened it and found the comfortable clothes she'd collected over the last few weeks, her precious boots and the sword in its sheath lying on top.

By the time Sebastian returned with a tray filled with bread, cheese, fruit and a bottle of wine, Jessica was just pulling on her boots. He hesitated when he saw the way she was dressed.

"What?" she asked, looking up.

He set the tray on a small table near the fireplace and turned to face her. "If I may, a word of advice."

"Okay," she said cautiously, sitting down on one of the hard chairs.

"While we were in the camp your preferred way of dressing could be ignored or overlooked, but now that we are in the castle proper . . ."

"I need to start dressing more like a lady - is that what you're telling me?"

"At the very least more . . . womanly."

Jessica sighed. "I thought I was a hero now? Can't exceptions be made for heroes?"

Sebastian smiled. "Perhaps in a kingdom where magic was welcome, but this is Ghren, and it would be best if you did not flaunt your differences."

"I guess I see your point, but you've got to find me something a little less . . . ornate than the dresses in that wardrobe."

He went over to the wardrobe and looked inside, then came back to sit down opposite her.

"Those clothes are not funny," she said. He was grinning like a fool.

"The prince told your lady's maid to make a selection for someone of your stature. It appears Eleanor thinks quite highly of you."

"You can't really expect me to wear any of those! Did you see them? They're revolting!"

"Never fear, my lady. Gareth and I will see to it you are not embarrassed by what you are wearing."

"Thank you!" she said whole-heartedly.

"Now, about your amulet . . ."

Jessica hesitated. "It belonged to my mother, at least that's what I believe."

"You don't know?"

She shook her head. "I never knew my mother, at least not the woman who gave birth to me. It's a long story," she added, at the confused look on his face.

"We have plenty of time; the feast in your honour is not until tomorrow evening."

"What feast?" she asked, a little alarmed.

"The amulet first."

"Fine. In a nutshell, I found this amulet in a box of my mother's stuff and my friend Howard was trying to figure out what it was for and then he accidentally sent me to this dimension and now it's the only way we can communicate until he can figure out how to bring me back. Now what about this feast?"

"I am unfamiliar with your use of the term dimension. Is it like a spirit world?"

"Sort of. But it's not filled with spirits. It's made up of real people which are sort of like the people here, only different, and it's on another world that can't be reached by conventional means."

"And you're from this other dimension?" Sebastian's eyebrows rose. "Is such a thing possible?"

"Well it must be possible. I'm here, aren't I?"

"And your magic, if the amulet is not the source . . ."

"That's the kicker. In my home world I don't have a magical bone in my body. But here . . ."

"Here you are the most powerful wizard in the land."

"You think so?" She brightened at the thought. "I've never been the most anything before."

"After banishing the demon army, there are none who question your power."

"Yes, well . . . I, um, had a little help with that."

"Help?"

"I had the power, but Howard did all the grunt work."

"I beg your pardon?"

"I powered the spell, but my friend Howard

worked the magic for me through the amulet."

"Incredible. But with all that power, why did you simply not return home, if that is your desire."

"I don't know," she said with a sigh. "Howard's studied magic all his life, but our world has very little of it so he's not used to using it. He needs to come up with the right spell, I guess."

"This is . . . this is . . ."

"Yeah, I know what you mean. Now about this feast?"

"Tell me more of this Howard," Sebastian asked.

"You tell me more about this feast first," Jessica countered.

He shrugged. "It's just your typical celebration. Since it's in your honour you'll be seated at the royal table, most likely next to the prince. There will be food, and wine, and entertainment -"

"What kind of entertainment?"

"Music and dancing, the usual fare."

"Will you be playing?"

He didn't quite meet her eye. "I was not invited to do so."

Jessica opened her mouth, then shut it again. Clearly he didn't want to talk about it. "How dressed up am I going to have to be?" she asked instead.

"The prince's dressmakers have been working on your gown since the move back into the castle."

Jessica had the sinking feeling that any dress that took a group of dressmakers days to make was going to make the dresses in the wardrobe look like potato sacks.

Chapter Twenty-Four

S ebastian poured them each a goblet of wine. "Now tell me more of this Howard. Why did he not accompany you on your journey?"

"I guess because he was too busy casting the spell. And it was kind of an accident."

"He must be an incredibly powerful sorcerer to contrive such an accident."

"Well actually, he had the help of a coven. I'm kind of fuzzy on the details."

As though speaking about him had summoned him, Howard's disembodied voice spoke. "Jessica, are you there?"

"Howard?"

"Well who else did you think it would be?"

"But -"

"I think there's something hinky going on with —"

"Howard, I'm not alone." She shot a look towards Sebastian who sat frozen in his chair.

"What?" There was definitely a note of shock in his voice.

"It's okay," Jessica said hastily, "It's only Sebastian, it's just I thought you didn't want to communicate when anyone else was around."

"This is bad, this is very, very bad. Wherever you are the amulet's not working properly. There's some kind of magical interference."

"There are probably warding spells on the tower," Sebastian said faintly, recovering from the surprise at the sound of the ghostly voice. "Is this . . .?"

"Yes. I told you, this is how my friend Howard and I communicate."

"You *told* him about me?" There was a definite squeak to Howard's voice.

"Oh chill, Howard. Sebastian's cool."

"Actually, I'm quite warm thank you," Sebastian said, a somewhat bemused expression on his face.

"That's not - oh, never mind," Jessica said, catching herself before she launched into an explanation of what she meant. "Really, Howard, there's no reason to go all girly on me."

"It's just -" Howard sighed. "What's done is done. I just hope you can trust him. No offense, Bastian," he added.

"It's Sebastian, and none taken. If you do not dwell within the amulet, then where is your body?"

"I'm . . . where Jessica is from originally."

"Simply amazing," Sebastian said. "However,

your friend is right," he told Jessica. "It could be very dangerous should someone overhear you conversing with a non-corporeal being. People have been burned at the stake for much less."

"Are you serious?" Jessica's voice came out in a squeak.

"This is exactly why I wanted you to keep a low profile," Howard told her.

"Howard, you've got to get me out of here!"

"I'm working on it Jess, I'm working on it."

"Forgive me, but I do not understand," Sebastian said. "You have the power of the Well at your disposal, would it not be a simple matter to cast your spell?"

"Yeah, what he said," Jessica put in.

"It's not just a matter of power," Howard told them. "It's a matter of finding the right spell."

"Why can't you just use the one you used originally and reverse it or something?"

There was an ominous silence.

"Howard, what aren't you telling me?"

"The original spell is gone, Jessica. It's as though it never existed."

Sebastian nodded. "I've heard of such things happening. It must have been a master class spell, they can be used only once."

Jessica looked appalled. "But . . . how am I going to get back home?"

"I've got it all under control," Howard said hastily. "I've already started working on a new spell."

"Howard, the first spell took you years to figure out. I'm not waiting years to get back home!"

"This is a wizard's tower," Sebastian said thoughtfully.

"So?"

"I daresay there will be spell books in the wizard's work room."

It was on the tip of Jessica's tongue to ask Sebastian to lead the way to the wizard's work room but there was a knock on her door before she could make her demand.

"Someone else is here, Howard," she said. "So clam up. I'll talk to you later." She tucked the amulet under her shirt and before Sebastian could ask her to explain the expression 'clam up' she called out, "Come in."

A small face peered around the heavy oak door.

"Addison! How's your brother, Keiran?" Jessica felt a stab of guilt. She'd been meaning to ask about the boy, but then she'd gotten caught up in the whole saving the castle thing.

"He be fair to drivin' our mother to drink, what with his chafing at being kept inside 'till his leg heals." Addison grinned at her shyly. "If it pleases you, milady, His Royal Highness Prince Ewan would visit with thee."

"Of course," Jessica said.

Without another word, Addison pushed the door open the rest of the way, barely managing to avoid getting run over as Ewan swept into the room.

"Most lovely of ladies, mere words cannot express the appreciation of the entire kingdom at thy bravery."

He was several steps into the room, headed towards the bed, before realizing Jessica was sitting in front of the fireplace. Making a graceful turn, he bowed low before her, ignoring Sebastian.

"You may leave us, minstrel." It was not a request.

Jessica opened her mouth to protest as Sebastian got up without a word, but forgot what she was about to say as Ewan stroked the large emerald hanging from the chain around his neck. As the door closed Ewan pulled a chair close to Jessica's.

"My lady, it eases my mind greatly to see thee recovered from thy ordeal."

"My or—oh, that. I'm sorry if I worried you. Did everyone get moved back into the castle all right?" For some reason she couldn't quite put her finger on, Jessica felt a little uncomfortable with Ewan. There was just something a little off about him today.

"The kingdom of Ghren is as it was. Thou hast earned our undying gratitude. Should thee desire aught, thou hast only to ask."

"Um, that's very kind of you, but you've been more than generous already."

He looked with a faint air of disapproval at the way she was dressed. "Forgive me, my lady. Were not the gowns thy maid chose to thy liking?"

"The gowns are, uh, quite something. But I was going to explore the rest of this tower and I didn't want to get any of them dirty."

"Indeed. Thou hast but just risen from thy sick bed. Perhaps it would be wiser to rest for the feast in thy honour on the morrow."

"Maybe you're right," Jessica agreed, faking a yawn. She really wanted to check out the rest of the tower.

Ewan rose and bent over her hand. His lips lingered a trifle longer than usual, putting all sorts of wicked ideas into her head. Unfortunately he released her hand before she could act on any of them.

"Until the morrow, my lady."

"Tomorrow," she echoed, slightly bemused.

She shook off the feeling as he left the room, waiting a few seconds before going over to the door and easing it open. There was no one on the other side and she opened it just enough to slip through, then quietly started up the spiral staircase.

* * * * *

"He's up to something, I can smell it," Thackery muttered, staring into the scrying bowl in the tower of the wizard school.

"I wasn't aware that scents could be transmitted through a scrying bowl," Paran said mildly. "And who are you talking about?"

"That little pissant, Ewan."

"Yes." Paran came up to stand beside him. "There does seem to be more to this prince than meets the eye, does there not? Something more than the overuse of that glamour stone he wears around his neck."

"I find it interesting that he insisted Jesseminathus take possession of my tower."

"Your timing was impeccable, releasing the seal just as they were carrying her past. Although I'd like to flay those idiots who dropped her."

The man beside him was unusually quiet. Paran shot him a glance. "Kir-Thackery, what did you do?"

"I did nothing, really. Nothing of consequence."

Paran regarded him steadily.

Thackery sighed. "It was just a minor spell, well beneath Anakaron's notice."

"Fleas or lice?"

A smile twitched across Thackery's face. "Both."

The smile disappeared as they watched Jessica reach the top of the tower, passing through the warded door without any hesitation. Thackery's eyes were suspiciously bright as she wandered through the magical workroom, staring at the tapestries hanging on the walls, touching the treasures he'd collected over the years.

They saw her spy the small bookcase against one wall. She went over to it and began pulling out random books. Finding one to her liking, she carried it closer to the fireplace, sinking down onto a well padded chair.

"Now that's what I'm talking about! All chairs should be this comfortable."

For a few moments she silently leafed through the book, then closed it with a sigh. Looking up, she stared at the portrait hanging above the fireplace. It was of a woman with vivid green eyes and dark, almost black hair that cascaded over her shoulders. She was dressed in an elaborate gown of deep red, and the artist had somehow managed to give her skin a porcelain glow.

Thackery held his breath and then let it out slowly as Jessica went over and rubbed the dust off the small brass plate at the bottom of the frame. "Farenalyssia. Now there's a mouthful. She's so beautiful. I wonder who she was."

Chapter Twenty-Five

The following day, Jessica was joined by Sebastian once more for breakfast. He seemed preoccupied but he excused himself as soon as they were finished so she had no opportunity to question him. As he left he said, "Enjoy the feast tonight, you have earned it. But I pray you are careful."

Before she could call him back to explain that last remark, Eleanor appeared at the top of the stairs, cradling an elaborate gown in her arms like it was a baby. If that weren't bad enough, the lady's maid was followed closely by a pair of under maids, their arms laden with various bags and bottles and boxes.

"Eleanor, how nice to see you," Jessica said, with as much sincerity as she could muster.

"My lady, 'tis good to see thee awake. We've no time to lose if thou art to be prepared for thy feast."

"I thought the feast wasn't until this evening?" It couldn't be much more than mid morning, judging by the light that shone through the stained glass windows.

"Aye, milady. T'will be a miracle if thou are ready in time. The whole of the morning, wasted!"

Eleanor laid her burden carefully on the bed then stood back to survey the room. "You, she directed one of the under maids, "Set thy equipment there," she pointed at a small table, "then go have the men bring the tub and start carrying up water."

"I remember milady's penchant for cleanliness," she said in a conspiratorial whisper.

Jessica was a little bewildered by all the activity, but she liked the idea of a bath . . . in a real tub no less.

Eleanor eyed Jessica critically, or more specifically, what Jessica was wearing. "It was to be hoped, milady, that thy eccentricities of dress would be set aside now that thou art safe within the castle."

"Oh, I, um . . . the, uh, gowns in the wardrobe were so beautiful I thought I should save them for a special occasion."

"Indeed," Eleanor said with a sniff, not fooled at all. "Mayhap a few somewhat less elaborate gowns might be found for everyday use."

"I would appreciate it."

There was a commotion on the stairs and two burly men entered, carrying a large copper tub. It reminded Jessica of the tub she'd admired in an old western movie that Howard made her watch one time. It was oval, with high, curved sides - definitely large enough for a good, long, soak. She almost started salivating as Eleanor directed them to place it near the fire.

The two men were followed closely by a procession of somewhat less burly men, each carrying steaming buckets which they emptied into the tub. One of the maids who accompanied Eleanor sprinkled something from a blue glass bottle into the water and Jessica caught a whiff of a light, floral scent.

"This seems like so much trouble to go to," she said, feeling only slightly guilty. "Isn't there someplace . . . I don't know, lower down to do this?"

"Psht!" Eleanor waved away her concerns. "Thou cannot be expected to use the bathhouse. 'Tis for peasants and commoners!"

"Well, if you insist," Jessica said, eyes still focused on the steaming tub.

It was only a matter of minutes before the tub was filled and the men were gone. Jessica hesitated when Eleanor moved to help her undress, shooting a glance at the maids who were busy setting up what looked like a cosmetic display in one corner of the room. She'd become less body conscious around Eleanor when it came to getting dressed and undressed, but she'd never met these two women before. She glanced at the steaming tub, then back at the maids. They seemed to be ignoring her and with a mental shrug she allowed Eleanor to undress her and stepped into the tub.

"Oh, yeah," she sighed. "This is better than sex."

"My lady!" Eleanor exclaimed as the maids tittered.

"So I've heard," Jessica said quickly. "Okay, only chocolate is supposed to be better than sex, but I'm sure this comes in a close second."

"Chocolate, milady?" One of the maids asked timidly.

How to describe chocolate to these women? Jessica tried to think of a fitting metaphor. "Think of the most delicious thing you've ever tasted, and then double, no, triple the sensation. That's close to the sensation you get from eating chocolate. It's creamy and smooth, and . . . and the most decadent thing you could ever experience. It's a great delicacy where I come from."

And she really wished she hadn't brought it up because now she had a desperate craving for it. Creamy milk chocolate, heavenly dark chocolate, a big mug of hot chocolate . . . hell, she'd even settle for a chocolate chip cookie! The second she was alone she was going to contact Howard to get to work locating chocolate for her, or a spell that would let her create chocolate.

"All right, milady." Eleanor stood beside the tub holding out a large towel. "Enough lolly-gagging. Time to get out."

"But I just barely got in!" Jessica protested. "The water's still warm."

"We have much to do if thou art to be ready in time for the feast."

Much to do, Jessica thought as she reluctantly climbed out of the tub. She really didn't like the sound of that.

* * * * *

I'm in hell, Jessica thought. After she was dried off from her bath she was given a robe to wear, then seated on a stool in the center of the room. The three maids circled her like vultures, or like the three witches from Macbeth.

Eleanor picked up one of her hands to inspect and tsked before letting it drop again. "See what thou canst do," she directed one of the maids.

The maid lost no time in pulling up a chair close to Jessica and proceeded to give her the medieval equivalent of a manicure, which consisted of buffing her nails with something like a pumice stone and then rubbing a scented cream into her hands.

The other maid brought one of the small tables closer and began laying out a seemingly endless selection of cosmetics. This maid followed Eleanor's directions and began brushing and powdering Jessica's face.

"Are you sure all this is necessary?" Jessica asked.

"Quiet! Thou mustn't move thy face whilst the girl is working on it."

Jessica sighed and tried to remain stoic, but the stool was really hard and her back was starting to hurt. It seemed like forever since she'd had breakfast with Sebastian.

She wondered where he'd been off to in such a rush. It was too bad he was gone, some music would go a long way to help distract her.

"No, 'tis not right," Eleanor said with a frown.

Jessica winced as the maid used a rough cloth to begin scrubbing off the makeup she'd just finished applying. "You could try leaving a little skin behind," she suggested.

"Forgive me, milady," Eleanor said. "Thy colouring is somewhat unusual." She began applying some kind of cream that soothed the skin made sensitive by the rough cloth.

Once the maids were finished with her face and hands she thought she might get a breather, or at the very least a snack, but it was not to be. There was more torture in store in the form of getting dressed.

First there were the silky undergarments that she was seriously getting to like. Next was a floor-length under dress of some kind of silvery material with tight sleeves that went all the way down to her wrists. Over-top of that was a low cut, dark green dress that was heavily embroidered with green and silver thread, and festooned with glittering jewels. It weighed a ton.

The sleeves of this dress were wide and trailing, and lined with the same silver as her under dress.

Eleanor pulled the laces tight in the front, which emphasized Jessica's breasts but wasn't unduly uncomfortable.

"Turn around and grasp the bed post," Eleanor directed.

"What for?" Jessica asked, a little tired of being ordered around.

"Please, milady, 'tis almost time for the feast."

With a sigh Jessica did as she was told, and felt something pressing on her lower back.

"Have you got your foot in my back?" she asked in astonishment.

"'Tis the only way, milady. Now hold still." Eleanor pulled backwards and the air left Jessica's lungs.

"Too tight!" she managed to gasp out.

"But milady, 'tis the fashion!"

"Won't do me any good if I pass out from lack of air."

Eleanor made an annoyed sound, but loosened the laces in the back just a fraction. Jessica looked down at her chest.

"I don't know if you're aware of it, but my breasts are about to burst free any second now."

"Nay, milady. Trust me, thou art in no danger. All the ladies in the court will be dressed in this fashion, but none will have breasts as lovely as thine." She dusted a light powder over them.

"Uh, thanks . . . I think." She tried to surreptitiously pull the neckline of the gown a little higher and had her hand slapped away by Eleanor.

Her hair was stuffed into a net, which was se-
cured to a high, round band decorated with jewels
that matched the ones on her dress. While she really
hoped they were fake jewels she suspected that they
weren't. There was a green veil attached to the band
that draped in the back and fitted closely around her
face in the front. Unfortunately the veil was not long
enough in front to save her embarrassment should
the lacings on the bodice of the dress give way.

"Shoes . . ." Eleanor said thoughtfully. She went
to the armoire and rooted around in the bottom of it.
"Ah, ha!" she said triumphantly, and came back carrying a pair of the ugliest shoes Jessica had ever seen.
They were silver with dark green trim, had extremely
pointed toes with low, chunky heels, and they had
little cuff like embellishments that curled downwards.
They also pinched her toes when one of the under
maids stooped to put them on her feet.

"Couldn't I just wear my boots?" Jessica asked.
"No one will see what's on my feet under all this
dress."

"Nay, milday!" Eleanor exclaimed, scandalized.
"Thou cannot wear boots to a feast." She stood back
to admire her work.

"Beautiful," one of the under maids said, blushing
and ducking her head.

"Aye, thou cleans up most astonishingly well.
Thou wilt be able to hold thy head high amongst the

nobility this eve."

Jessica suddenly started feeling a little better about having to descend the winding staircase into the unknown.

* * * * *

"She's lost her freaking mind!" Howard paced from one side of the room to the other.

Ellen, who'd shown up early at his door that morning, rolled her eyes at him. He'd been ranting like this all day. She was just happy Jessica was awake and they were able to communicate again, even if they couldn't see her.

It had been hard to believe his assurances that Jessica would be fine when he hadn't been able to call up her image in the scrying bowl. Whatever was interfering with the amulet's ability to detect other people around her also seemed to block the spell to see her image.

"Will you relax Howard? I'm sure she wouldn't have let Sebastian in on her secret if she didn't trust him. And at least now we know there's nothing wrong with your scrying spell."

"She always was a sucker for a pretty face," he muttered.

She grinned at him suddenly. "You think Sebastian is pretty?" Jessica had mentioned she thought Sebastian and Howard would make a cute couple. It was just too bad they were stuck in different dimensions.

"He's drop dead gorgeous. But that's beside the point."

"The point is," Ellen interrupted, "that you were going to give the scrying spell another try so we can see if she's alone so you try and contact her again."

"Fine." He let the subject drop and started setting things up for the spell.

Ellen watched, genuinely interested in what he was doing. She had a new respect for Howard and was beginning to understand why he and Jessica were such close friends. Sneaking a look at his profile she thought it really was a shame that he was gay.

The picture in the bowl shimmered, but they were able to make out Jessica's image.

"Wow," Ellen said as they watched Eleanor put the finishing touches on Jessica's appearance. "She looks absolutely beautiful. It's too bad we can't take a screen shot of the scrying bowl."

Howard shot her a long-suffering look of disbelief.

"I'm just saying . . ." She turned back to Jessica's image. "I just hope she doesn't have a wardrobe malfunction during dinner. What?" she asked as Howard frowned at the picture.

"He's got her dressed in his colours. I'm not sure what that means, but I don't like it. He did that when they toured the camp too."

"Who did?"

"Ewan."

"The prince? But I thought you said it was a good thing if he was interested in Jess."

"Interested yes, however this is something totally different."

"Different how?"

"This isn't just letting people know she's under his protection, this is more like he's staking his claim."

Ellen's eyes suddenly widened. "You don't think he's going to ask her to marry him, do you? Oh, God, I hope not. She'd probably do something stupid like say yes."

"Or do something even stupider and say no," Howard said. "I'm sure the dungeons below the castle are full of people who've tried to say no to this guy. But I don't think that's what's going on. I get the feeling Ewan's not ready to give up Jessica's power yet."

"What do you mean by that?"

He sighed and raked a hand through his hair. "As far as I can determine, Ewan's one of those idiots who think only pure women can be magic-workers."

"Does Jessica know about this?"

"I never saw any reason to tell her."

"Are you serious?"

When he nodded, Ellen began to laugh. She laughed so hard it brought tears to her eyes.

"Care to share the joke?"

Ellen wiped her eyes and tried to get control of herself. "It's just . . . there's Jessica with this hot prince dancing attention on her, but he's not taking it any further than the hand kissing stage. It must be driving her insane, not knowing why he's treating her like a kid sister."

"I never thought of it like that before. Damn, I should have told her as soon as I figured it out."

"No, it's actually better this way."

"How so?"

"Well think about it. You know Jessica, if she got seriously romantically involved with this prince we'd never get her to leave."

He heaved a sigh. "You're right, of course. But I still wish she'd use an excuse to avoid this dinner. I can't shake the feeling she's walking into the lion's den."

"Well what can we do about it?"

"Unfortunately, all we can do is watch and wait. And if you're the praying type, maybe saying a little prayer wouldn't hurt either."

* * * * *

"I should have warned Howard that the wards on the tower would interfere with the communication spell on the amulet," Thackery said.

"No use blaming yourself," Paran told him absently. He was sitting at a table off to the side, studying a spread of cards. "It could have been worse; it could have been the prince in the room with her."

Thackery snorted. "The fool probably would have soiled himself and then tripped over his own feet in his haste to leave."

There was no answering comment from Paran and he glanced over to see what had his attention. "It's been a long time since I've seen you consult the cards," he said.

"It's been a long time since I've felt the need to use them," Paran admitted.

"And what do the cards have to tell us?"

Again there was no answer and Thackery moved to look over the older man's shoulder. "The Lovers," he said in disgust. "Don't tell me my daughter and that poor excuse for a—"

"No, that is in her distant future. And the man she will become involved with is the Knight of Swords - black hair and black eyes."

"What about this one?" he asked, pointing to The Fool.

"It's true that's a card of new beginnings and opportunities, but the position it's in . . . I'm afraid that is what we hope for her future."

"Why is The Chariot upside down?"

Paran sighed. "That's her near future - vanquishment, defeat. With The Moon right beside it, I fear she's facing deception and danger."

"This last one," Thackery pointed to the card showing lightning striking a crumbling tower. "I know this is not a good card when upright, but reversed it should be a good card, correct?"

"Not at all. Reversed, the Tower means imprison-
ment. And it's placement . . ." Here Paran paused.

"Tell me!"

"It's positioned as the final outcome."

"No!" Thackery swivelled around and stalked
over to the scrying bowl. "There has to be a way for
us to prevent this."

"Did you not see the number of major arcana
cards in the spread? It's too late. Nothing we do can
prevent what is already set in motion."

"Then I will cast the spell that will bring her to
me."

"And be reunited with her only to have Anakaran
snatch her away when he follows your power signature? Don't be such an ass."

"I cannot just sit back and let—"

"There is nothing we can do," Paran repeated,
"save for watching and waiting. She must face these
trials before we can help her on her way."

"I dislike these cards," Thackery grumbled.
"They're such a chancy thing."

"Another good reason for waiting."

Sighing heavily, Thackery waved his hand over
the scrying bowl and activated the spell to make it
show Jessica. "By the Source of all Power!" he
gasped.

"What is it?" Paran pushed back his chair and
hurried over to join him. Together they stared down

into the shallow bowl.

"She looks just like her mother," Thackery whispered.

"If she's anything like her mother, she's uncomfortable wearing all that silk," Paran said wryly. "But she is a vision, isn't she?"

They watched as Eleanor put the finishing touches on Jessica's makeup and gave a final twitch to the veil hanging from the head piece. She stood back for a last look and whatever she saw must have pleased her, for she gave a nod and then said something that was too low for them to hear.

Jessica inclined her head ever so slightly, probably afraid she was going to dislodge her head gear, and the maids swept from the room, taking their boxes and bundles with them.

"Your daughter is a vision of loveliness," Paran said. "So why is it you have a frown on your face?"

"It's the colours she's wearing. Have you noticed?"

"Aye, the dark green suits her well. And the silver is far less ostentatious than gold would have been."

"They're the prince's colours. Ewan. It's almost as though he's putting a claim on her."

It was Paran's turn to frown. "You don't think . . . marriage?"

"No, definitely not marriage. His father would never allow it. Whatever he has planned it's far worse than marriage."

Chapter Twenty-Six

J essica's courage began to flag as she waited in her room. Eleanor had wanted to wait with her, but Jessica needed a couple of minutes to herself. The maid had been adamant, before she left, that Jessica was not to sit down until she reached her seat at the table, so as not to wrinkle her gown. And she was to leave the bodice of her dress alone, else dire things might occur.

She tried to remember everything Sebastian and Gareth had tried to teach her about interacting with royalty. Her mind was a complete blank. Curtsy. At the very least she'd be expected to curtsey. Was that even possible in this dress?

Moving back to give herself more space, she took a deep breath and then immediately let it out again for fear of the bodice giving way. Keeping her back straight she bent her head slightly and held her skirt out sideways using her thumbs and first two fingers, making sure her little fingers were extended outwards.

She extended her left leg slightly behind her right one, toe touching the floor and at the same time bent her right leg slightly. Knees bending just so, she sank down into the curtsy and managed to bring herself upright again without falling over.

"Piece of cake," she muttered.

Her feet were already killing her and she was on the point of changing into her boots in spite of Eleanor's threats, when there was a knock on the door. Steeling herself, she called, "Come in."

Gareth entered, eyes widening and mouth dropping open as he saw her. "My lady, thou art beauteous!" he said, then blushed furiously.

"Thank you, Gareth," she said with more dignity than she felt. She felt almost giddy, but that could have been the glass of strong wine one of the undermaids snuck to her when Eleanor's back was turned.

"If it pleases thee, might I escort thee from thy tower?"

"Or course," she said. Unable to help herself she added, "You might want to close your mouth before you catch a fly."

His mouth snapped shut. "Oh! Thy beauty caused me to forget. His highness asked that thou accept this token of his admiration and hopes thou will honour him by wearing it this eve."

He produced a thin wooden box and opened it for her inspection. Nestled in the black, shiny lining was an exquisite emerald necklace. The delicate silver filigree was sprinkled with diamonds and emeralds, and a tear-drop shaped emerald the size of a chicken egg hung suspended from the center.

"Holy Saint Christopher!" Jessica reached out but didn't quite touch it. "It's beautiful," she said, lowering her voice. "But I couldn't possibly . . . it's much too expensive. Besides, I'm already wearing a necklace." She motioned towards her moonstone pendant.

"My lady," Gareth began, then hesitated. "My lady, 'tis not the most wise choice to refuse the gifts of royalty."

He couldn't seem to meet her eyes as he said this and Jessica realized he had a point and his point might just be more serious than he was letting on. She mustered a smile for him.

"I guess maybe it wouldn't hurt to at least try it on," she said.

His relief was palpable was she unhooked her moonstone and then carefully picked up the emerald necklace. It was the perfect accompaniment to her dress and the large emerald nestled right into the top of her cleavage. She didn't even dare to imagine how much a necklace like this was worth. The words 'king's ransom' popped into her head.

"Now, where can I leave my pendant?" she wondered out loud. She glanced around the room.

"Wouldst my lady care to leave it in this box?" Gareth suggested, having just set it down on the table.

"No, too obvious. The thing is," she said when it

looked like Gareth was going to start asking questions, "it has great sentimental value. It belonged to my mother." She looked around the room again. "I take it you'll be at the feast?"

"Yes, my lady. All squires will be present to attend to their lords."

"Figures. Let me think . . . " There were no pockets in the dress she was wearing and the thought of leaving the pendant in her room made her nervous. Anything could happen to it, despite this being a wizard's tower. She looked around the room one more time and then turned back to Gareth. "Would you be able to run me a small errand before you're needed?"

"Of course, my lady!"

"Great!" She wound the chain around the moonstone and held it out to him. "Would you be able to take this to Sebastian?"

"Aye, my lady. But —"

"Just tell him I'll get it back from him after the feast, that I'm trusting him to take care of it for me. Now, we should probably shake a leg."

Gareth glanced down at his legs and Jessica sighed. "Sorry, it's an expression where I come from. It means we'd better hurry so we're not late."

"The feast is in your honour," he said with a grin. "It cannot begin without thee."

"In that case, let's take these stairs nice and slow. It would be a shame if I fell and broke my neck after all Eleanor's hard work."

"Indeed, my lady. Eleanor would ne'er let thee hear the end of it."

It took Jessica forever to make her way down the winding staircase. Her feet were on fire and the only thing that kept her going was the knowledge that it would be even more painful going back up and that once she made it all the way down she'd get to sit down to eat. She promised herself that no matter what, she'd get rid of her damned shoes before she had to go back up there.

Ewan was waiting, none too patiently, just outside the wizard's tower. It was almost as though he was afraid to cross the threshold into the tower itself. He stopped pacing the moment he saw her. Two steps and he was invading her personal space.

"Magnificent," he said, one forefinger tracing her cleavage along the edge of the gown.

Without thinking, Jessica sucked in a breath. Something kindled in the prince's eyes but he merely stepped back and offered her his arm.

"Shall we, my lady?"

She was starting to feel like Cinderella at the ball. "We shall," she said faintly, taking his arm. Behind Ewan's back, Gareth winked at her then disappeared down a side passage. She felt like she was floating on the short walk to the great hall, the pain in her feet forgotten. A fanfare of trumpets sounded as Ewan stopped with her briefly on the threshold.

"His Royal Highness, Prince Ewan of Ghren, and

the Lady Sorceress Jessica."

They paused again just inside the room and conversation fell to a whisper, rising again behind them as they slowly made their way down the length of the hall. Jessica tried not to feel intimidated by the eyes she could feel on her and tried to focus on the music being played by the group of musicians in one corner. They weren't nearly as talented as Sebastian.

The table Ewan lead her to was raised slightly higher than the others. The king was already there, deep in conversation with the lady on his right. Jessica was suddenly very grateful for all of Eleanor's fussing. Most of the ladies present were dressed in variations of the same dress she was wearing, and many of the headdresses were even more elaborate, if not bordering on comical. If there was ever a time she wished for a camera, this would be it.

The second they were seated an army of servers streamed into the room. Jessica lost count of the number of courses, each one heralded by trumpets, but she tried to keep track of the different dishes. Howard would be expecting a full account later.

There was a salad of what looked to be watercress, violet blossoms, and cucumber, followed by another of greens and a variety of flowers. A pale, milky looking dish seemed to be a favourite of the king. It tasted much better than it looked - chicken and rice cooked in some kind of almond tasting milk. There were leeks and mushrooms in a buttery sauce, a spinach tart, and a very tender meat that she was told was pork. What impressed her the most were the pastries molded into the most amazing shapes, almost too beautiful to eat.

The tables formed a U-shape around the edge of the hall, running along two sides away from the head table. There was a large space in the center of the room and a constant array of entertainment took place there - singing, dancing, juggling, acrobats . . . Jessica found it hard to concentrate on her food there was so much to see and hear.

Occasionally Ewan or his father would snap their fingers and the squires behind them would hand over coins that they'd toss to the performers. Jessica hadn't even realized the squires were there, although Gareth had told her they would be.

Dinner seemed to go on forever and Jessica was starting to feel queasy. She'd tried taking only a little of each dish, even passed on several of them, but there was just so much food. There seemed to be only two drinks available, wine or mead. Both were rather strong and even the little she'd sipped made her sleepy.

She was also beginning to feel a little neglected. If this feast was in her honour, she had yet to see any sign of it, unless being seated at the king's table was her reward. And Ewan seemed preoccupied; he hardly said two words to her since they sat down. Idly she wondered how many rules of protocol she'd be breaking if she claimed to have a headache and asked to be excused from the table. She smiled faintly at the idea. Eleanor would have a cow.

"Something amuses thee, my lady?" Ewan asked, almost as though he suddenly realized he'd been ignoring her.

"I was just thinking how wonderful this all has been," she said smoothly, giving herself points for nonchalance.

Ewan turned the full wattage of his smile on her. "Tis wondrous indeed to have thee by my side." Turning to his father, he said, "Dost thou not think the jewels the Lady Jessica is wearing suit her well?"

The king set his cup down and turned to get a better look at Jessica. He frowned. "Is that —" He leaned forward for a better look and slammed his fist onto the table, face mottled in anger. "Nay! I will not have it! Thou cannot gift these jewels to this wench!"

At the sound of the king's fist hitting the table, the entire room went silent. Now it erupted into chaotic murmurs. Ewan and the king were on their feet, glaring at each other.

"Thou gave the betrothal gems to me to bestow on whomever I saw fit."

Betrothal gems? Jessica's hand went to the huge emerald wedged in her cleavage. This was bad. This was very, very bad. Her fairy tale was suddenly starting to unravel.

Ewan and his father stood almost nose to nose,

glaring at each other. Jessica looked from one to the other. Neither seemed like they were going to give an inch. She rose from her seat and maneuvered herself between the two men.

"C'mon guys, I'm sure this is just a big misunderstanding. First of all —"

"This is between my father and myself," Ewan told her.

"Harlot!" the king snapped at her. "This was thy plan all along. Thou wast in league with the varlet who cast the spell o'er the castle so that thou could inveigle thy way into a royal husband."

"Now wait just a damn minute!" The unfairness of it all hit Jessica like a slap in the face. King or no king, she wasn't about to be talked to that way.

Ewan pulled her away from the king. "Mayhap it would be best if thee were to wait in thy chamber."

"Did you hear what he called me? And I was the one who lifted the damn spell!"

"Aye, only because it was thee who cast it in the first place!" the king shouted.

"Gareth," Ewan called. "Escort the Lady Jessica to her rooms."

"Wait a minute," Jessica protested. "I'm not going to hide up in some tower while your father —"

"Thou art welcome in my kingdom no longer," the king stated. "Thou hast until morning to leave under thine own will, else my personal guard will escort thee to the nearest border."

Gareth was pulling at her arm, trying to direct her towards the nearest exit.

"This isn't over," Jessica said, pointing her finger at the king. "Not by a long shot."

The king gasped and clutched at his chest. As Gareth pulled her from the room she had a last glimpse of him sitting back in his chair looking pale, one hand still pressed against his chest.

"I suppose now would be a bad time to ask how the king's health is in general?" Jessica whispered as soon as they were out of earshot.

"I know not," Gareth replied unhappily, leading her towards the tower. "His temper is known far and wide, but I have never seen him like this."

"Great," Jessica said with a sigh. "Now what's the story on this necklace Ewan gave me? The king called it the betrothal gems?"

"Aye, my lady." Gareth looked shamefaced, and couldn't meet her eye. "'Tis tradition that whomsoever the heir deems fit to be his bride shall first honour him by wearing the family betrothal jewels."

"Why didn't you tell me? If I'd known that I would have refused to wear them and saved us all a pile of trouble."

"His Highness requested that I did not inform thee of the true nature of the jewels."

"Requested, eh?" More likely threatened. "Hold on a sec," she said as they reached the bottom of the stairs. She plunked down on the stone steps then fished under her skirt for her shoes. "Ah, that's better," she sighed.

"Would thou wish for me to dispose of thy shoes?" Gareth asked timidly.

"That's okay," she said, climbing to her feet again. "I think it would be more fun to pitch them from the highest window of the tower."

Gape-mouthed, he stared at her for a moment, as though not sure whether she was serious or not. By the time he'd made up his mind, she'd already started up the stairs and he hurried to catch up.

The first thing Jessica did when she reached her room was remove the emerald necklace. Placing it carefully back in its box she said, "I think it would probably be better if you took this back to Ewan for safe keeping."

"Aye, my lady," Gareth agreed unhappily.

"Oh, cheer up kid," she said, sitting in a chair in front of the fireplace to examine the damage done to her feet. "It's not the end of the world. I like Ewan and all, but he hasn't even asked me to marry him yet. I'm sure we'll get this whole mess straightened out when we talk. What?" she asked when he got a peculiar look on his face.

"Tis not the way of royalty to ask, my lady."

"I beg your pardon?"

"Tis what the betrothal jewels were created for. Thou hast only to wear them three times in public and thou wilt be handfasted to the prince."

"Holy Saint Christopher! Oh, Ewan and I are going to have a serious talk about this!" She jumped to her feet, prepared to confront him right that second.

Gareth moved quickly to block the door. "Mayhap now would not be a good time, my lady."

She stood there, fists clenched, ready to argue, then nodded abruptly as she remembered the shocked and confused faces on the guests at the feast as Gareth led her from the hall. The last thing she wanted was to be the focus of an even bigger scene than she'd already been part of. It could wait until Ewan was done with his father. Then she could really lay into him.

The sound of bells came from somewhere outside of the castle. Gareth's face drained of colour.

"What is it?" she asked. "A fire? An invasion? What?"

"Nay, my lady. 'Tis none of those things. 'Tis the king . . . he's dead."

Chapter Twenty-Seven

S ebastian contemplated the contents of his goblet solemnly. Getting drunk did little to make
up for the fact he had been denied the feast tonight. He hadn't expected to be included among the
guests, but to be unwelcome among even the musicians was a bitter pill to swallow.

He took a large drink of the wine. If he had to
swallow a pill, at least he had a very fine wine to wash
it down with. It was, in fact, one of the three bottles
he'd pilfered from Ewan's private cellar.

What had he been thinking? Had he really expected Ewan or his father to treat him any differently
now that he was a man instead of a boy? He should
never have come back to Ghren. There were too
many bitter memories.

Why was he even still here? It wasn't as though
he'd learn anything more. He wouldn't have come at
all except that the seer in Halprin had told him
Dominick was still alive and to start his search at the

beginning.

Dominick, he thought sadly, what happened to you my friend? He'd been more than a friend really, but not in the romantic sense. A brother, that's what he'd been. He'd known even before Sebastian himself where Sebastian's interests lay, and never once shunned him for it. They'd been both confidantes and sources of comfort to each other while growing up. They'd even lost their virginity together - Dominick to a dancer in a travelling troupe of entertainers, Sebastian to her brother.

So why was he still here instead of looking for his friend? A heart-shaped face with forest green eyes, surrounded by a mass of coppery hair came to mind. He was still here because his gut told him that his new friend might be in even more need of his help than his old friend.

Taking another drink, he became aware of a burning sensation coming from his shirt pocket. Frowning, he set his goblet down with exaggerated care and fished around in his shirt until his fingers closed around the amulet Gareth had brought him. Pulling it free, he stared at it somewhat blearily.

"Friend Howard, is something amiss? You appear to be trying to start a fire."

The amulet went cold with such speed he almost dropped it.

"Who is this?" Howard's voice asked in a faint whisper, after a momentary pause.

"Tis I, Sebastian Descarte, the most unwanted minstrel in the realm."

"I thought Jessica said you were really a bard? Where is Jessica anyway?"

"Yes, I am a bard, although I am not recognized as such in this kingdom. As for my lady Jessica, there is a feast in her honour tonight. The prince gifted her with other jewels to grace her lovely throat and she sent you to me for safe-keeping."

"Sebastian," Howard asked, voice laced with amusement, "Are you drunk?"

"That I am, good sir. I am drowning my sorrows, as it were."

In his own realm, Howard made himself as comfortable as he could on the stool beside his work table. Usually talking to strangers made him very self-conscious, but there was something about Sebastian that put him at ease. "Why aren't you at the feast with everyone else?" he asked.

"I was not invited." Sebastian took another swig of wine. "My presence does not find favour in the royal eyes."

"Maybe you just need to come up with a new bunch of songs," Howard suggested.

"Or maybe it is because Ghren is the most narrow-minded of kingdoms. Perhaps it is because it is so close to the Narrows."

He seemed to find this last statement extremely funny and Howard couldn't help but grin. "What's the

Narrows?"

"It's the passage ships must take inland from the Mythric Ocean to the trade routes further south."

"So that means that in effect, Ghren controls the trade routes."

"All too right," Sebastian told him.

"That must make Ghren a powerful kingdom."

"Right again, my friend. Which is why their arrogance is not to be trifled with. I-"

Sebastian broke off what he was saying as he heard the sound of bells.

"What is it?" Howard asked, catching his alarm even through the distance that separated them.

"Trouble, my friend," Sebastian told him. "Trouble of cataclysmic proportions."

* * * * *

Thackery leaned back from the scrying bowl. "Damn him to a fiery death in hell! And damn me for not realizing sooner what he was up to!"

The front legs of the chair Paran had been dozing off in hit the floor with a thump. "What's happening?"

There was no answer. Thackery was totally mesmerized by whatever was happening in the scrying bowl.

"My son, what—"

"Get another bowl to scry in, quickly," Thackery

said without turning.

"But why not just use—"

"No, I have to stay focused on what's happening in the court. You need to contact our friend Howard. He needs to get Jesseminathus out of Ghren."

"What? But why?" Paran asked, pulling his second best scrying bowl off the shelf and filling it with oil. "Tell me what's happening!"

"King Randolph is dead, poisoned it appears, slipped to him in some unseen fashion."

"And Jesseminathus being the only magic-worker in the kingdom, the blame naturally falls on her," Paran guessed.

"Oh, it's much worse than that, my friend. The jewels Ewan insisted she wear were betrothal jewels. Randolph was incensed when he saw them and an argument ensued between him and Ewan. Jesseminathus tried to bring peace between them but was unsuccessful. The king turned on her as well and harsh words were spoken before she left the hall."

Paranithel released the spell that would contact Howard.

* * * * *

"He set her up!" Howard said after talking with Paran. "That slimy bastard had this planned from the start. I knew there was a reason I didn't like him."

"There is no time to waste, my friend. Jesseminathus must be warned."

"Sebastian is already on his way to the tower."

"The minstrel? But why?"

"He's actually a bard. And as soon as he heard the bells he figured it'd mean trouble for Jess, so we thought he should go wait for her there."

"Mayhaps 'tis not a bad thing that she left the amulet in his safe-keeping," Paran said slowly.

"How so?" Howard asked.

"It has become obvious that Ewan wished to separate her from the amulet. Most likely he believes it to be her source of power."

"The idiot never did understand magic," Thackery put in.

"I would not be at all surprised if he sent someone to search her room for it while she was at the banquet," Paran continued

"But even if it was a power source he has to know he'd have to have magical abilities of his own before he could use it."

"As I said, he never really understood magic."

"He wants her weak," Paran said. "In his mind, separating her from the source of her power should do this. As for the amulet itself, I strongly doubt he would intend to use it. Instead he'd sell it - there's a market for such things and he could make a tidy profit."

"Bastard," Howard muttered under his breath.

"Indeed," Thackery agreed.

* * * * *

"The king is dead?" Jessica repeated in shock. "You don't think Ewan . . ."

"Nay milady. My prince hath a temper as well, but he wouldst not lay hand to his father."

Jessica might have had an easier time believing him if he hadn't looked so uncertain. She paced over to the narrow slit of a window but could only make out vague shapes milling around in the courtyard below; several of them were carrying torches.

"What should we do?" she asked, turning around to face Gareth again.

"I must go to my lord," he said hesitantly.

"Go," she told him. "Do what you have to do. But if you could send up one of the maids to help me get out of this dress I'd appreciate it."

Clearly torn between staying and going, Gareth hesitated on the threshold.

"Oh, and if you could maybe send Sebastian up with my medallion?"

"As you wish, my lady," Gareth said.

He was gone only a matter of seconds when he returned with Sebastian in tow.

"You need to leave, now," Sebastian told her, out of breath from rushing up the winding staircase.

"What? Why?" Jessica looked at him, genuinely confused.

"The king's death was no accident; it was poison. Ewan is making it appear as though you had a hand in it."

"If this be true, then he is right. Thou need make haste to depart at once," Gareth agreed. For once he seemed unable to defend the prince.

"I'm not going anywhere in this dress," Jessica stated firmly, not quite able to believe that Ewan would use her like this. He was a prince, for crying out loud. "One of you will have to undo it for me."

"Too late," Gareth said, standing near the door. "I can hear the guard coming."

Everyone froze as the heavy steps drew closer. Jessica couldn't believe this was happening. How had she gone from hero to villain so quickly?

"If they find thee here, they whilt take thee as well," Gareth said to Sebastian, face pale.

"Quick, under the bed," Jessica said. While she still didn't believe she was in any danger, she didn't want to take any chances with someone else being hurt because of her.

"But -" The idea of hiding while Jessica was taken prisoner didn't seem to sit well with Sebastian at all.

"Look, I'm sure this is all just some big misunderstanding. But just in case it takes a little time to sort things out, one of us should be free to get in touch with my old friend Howard." She looked pointedly at the moonstone Sebastian had taken out of his pocket to give her.

She remembered during her talk with Wendel that he'd mentioned there were special cells in the dungeon built for magic-users. If she ended up in one of them then she wouldn't be able to contact Howard. At least she'd know the amulet was safe with Sebastian, and maybe he and Howard could come up with some kind of defence for her.

"I don't like this," Sebastian told her as she pushed him towards the bed.

There was no time to argue. There was plenty of room and he slid under it easily. Jessica had just twitched the bedspread back into place when the door to her room was shoved open.

"Hey, take it easy on the door guys!" Jessica decided a brave front would probably be her best option. "And didn't anyone ever tell you it's rude to enter a lady's bedroom without knocking? I could have been getting dressed or bathing or -"

"Lady Jessica, thou art under arrest. Will thou come quietly with us?

These two were not the ordinary guards she was used to. They were big and burly and looked like their faces would shatter if they ever cracked a smile. And they didn't seem at all intimidated by the fact she was supposed to be some kind of great sorceress. Jessica wondered where Ewan had found them.

"What's the charge?" she asked.

"Regentcide."

Jessica looked at Gareth for an interpretation,

even though she was pretty sure what it meant.

"Tis the killing of the king," he whispered, pale and shivering.

"That's the most ridiculous thing I've ever heard," she told them. "The king was fine when I left the banquet. Better than fine, judging by the way he was screeching at his son. I-" Her words were cut off abruptly as one of the guards grabbed her and quickly bound her wrists together with a silver cord.

A wave of vertigo swept over her and she staggered in place, held up only by the guard's grip on her arm. "What the hell was that?"

"Tis a witch-binding, milady," Gareth told her, still unable to bring his voice above a whisper. "It prevents a magic-worker from using their magic."

It made her feel weak and disoriented, and slightly nauseous. She could only imagine how it would make a real magic worker feel. The guard pulled her, unresisting, towards the door. Gareth followed uncertainly in their wake.

* * * * *

When he was sure the room was clear, Sebastian slithered out from beneath the bed. He absent-mindedly brushed the dust off himself, unsure of what he should do next.

"Well, that complicates things a bit, doesn't it?" a disembodied voice asked.

Sebastian yelped, and jumped a foot into the air.

"Sorry," Howard said sheepishly. "I didn't mean to startle you."

"'Tis all right," Sebastian said, heart still pounding in his chest. "In truth, I'd forgotten you were with me."

"Listen, you're probably safe enough in the wizard's tower, but I suggest you move up to the work room. It's warded so that only friends of Jessica can enter."

"A wise precaution, my friend," Sebastian agreed, headed towards the door. "And then what?"

"And then we come up with a plan."

Chapter Twenty-Eight

J essica was not at all surprised to find Ewan waiting for them at the base of the tower.

"Alas, I regret the day I ever opened my heart and home to thee," he said, with great dramatic effect for the benefit of the few servants and nobility lurking about. "Had thou but trusted in me I would have made thee my queen, but thou could not wait and my poor father hast paid the price."

"Oh, cut the crap Ewan," Jessica said. "You and I both know what's really going on here and marriage wasn't even part of it."

"You see? The witch admits she never wished to marry me. She but used me for her own foul purposes."

"I used you? Now isn't that the pot calling the kettle black."

"Go, my friends, spread the word. Justice will be served."

The hall cleared and Jessica struggled in earnest in

the grip of the guards. "Justice my ass!"

Ewan took a step closer, reaching out to trace her cleavage, one finger dipping down between her breasts. "When I find a way to strip thee of thy magic, mayhap I might still find some use for thee."

"Get your filthy hands off me!" Jessica's eyes shot daggers at him and the walls around them trembled. He paled and took a step back. "Take her to the dungeon," he ordered.

* * * * *

"Nice touch," Paran said in admiration.

It had only taken a minor use of power to make the walls at the base of the tower shake.

"I was not about to stand idly by while that foul creature paws at my daughter!" Thackery's eyes blazed with the effort of holding back his rage.

Paran laid a restraining hand on his arm. "She is safe for the moment. Though to be sure a cell in the dungeon will not be comfortable, she will be in no danger. Did you not see how Ewan feared her, even bound as she was?"

Thackery watched in the scrying bowl as the guards practically carried her between them, away from the wizard's tower. The picture began to fade and he turned towards Paran. "Why have you broken the spell?"

"I have done nothing," Paran assured him. "The

witch-binding interferes, as do the guards. They give off an unnatural essence. It would take more power —"

"Well, if that's all that's needed . . ."

"Think, before you act! While a scrying spell takes little in the way of power such as Anakaron seeks, were we to draw too much it will only raise questions best left unanswered."

"Do not think to suggest I just leave her there!"

"Don't be daft! I'm suggesting nothing of the kind!" Paran retorted. "I am merely pointing out the danger of drawing attention to Jesseminathus whilst she is incarcerated. Would not our energies be better spent coming up with a plan for her escape?"

"And how do you purpose we do that without our magic?"

"First, we contact Howard . . ."

* * * * *

Jessica felt very small and helpless between the two guards as they carried her off to the dungeon. Their grip was so tight on her arms they practically lifted her off her feet. Mind numb, she paid no attention to where they were taking her.

They eventually stopped, and the knots in her stomach grew even tighter as she realized they were in a short corridor made of rough hewn rock. It was dark and damp; what little light there was came from torches set in sconces every few feet. One of the guards opened a large wooden door that was banded with iron and she had just a glimpse of a small square space before she was thrust into it.

Jessica stumbled and regained her balance, and turned just in time to have the heavy door slam in her face. The nausea and weakness she'd felt earlier were worse. Whatever was in the witch-binding must be in the walls of the cell as well. The guards hadn't bothered to remove the binding and she worried at it until her hands were free..

Holding her hands out in front of her, she stepped forward until she felt the wood of the door. Keeping one hand on the wall, she slowly shuffled her way around the perimeter. It didn't take long to make the full circuit. The room was small, maybe ten feet square. The walls were stone, as was the floor underneath her bare feet.

Something brushed her face and she shrieked before realizing it was just a fold of cloth that had worked itself loose from her headdress. She'd forgotten she was even wearing it. Chuckling at herself, she slid down the wall until she was sitting on the floor. She pulled the offensive head gear from her head and laid it down beside her, her quiet laughter turning into silent tears.

* * * * *

"Do you guys realize just how many holes this plan of yours has?" Ellen asked. She insisted on being part of the escape planning committee. "The whole drugging-the-guards scenario is fine for the movies, but this is real life we're talking about here. Jessica's life."

"I don't hear you coming up with a better solution," Howard snapped at her. He'd had almost no sleep in the last couple of days and he was worn to a frazzle.

"And the key players in this plan of yours are a couple of kids —"

"Whose family owe Jessica a huge debt! And they'll be with Sebastian."

"Just because you've got the hots for the minstrel doesn't mean he's trustworthy."

"For the last time, he's a bard not a minstrel and that's not why—"

"Enough!" Thackery's voice came through with enough force to rattle the glassware in the room. "In this Howard and I are in accord. The very fact that the min - *bard* is able to take refuge in the work room of the tower proves his trustworthiness."

"Fine!" Ellen threw up her hands and paced away from the table. Spinning on her heel she stalked back over to the scrying bowl and glared down into it. "Just saying this plan works and Sebastian gets Jessica out, then what?"

Thackery looked faintly surprised. "Then she's

free, of course. She will travel to us here in the south .
. ." His voice trailed off as he realized what she was
getting at.

"And why would she do that? As soon as she's
free she's going to expect Howard to poof her home
again. You're going to have to tell her the truth."

The two wizards in the scrying bowl looked at
each other. "No," they said in unison.

"I will tell her the truth when we are face to face.
It is far too dangerous for her to be armed with the
truth."

"Let us first secure her release," Paran said. "Perhaps then a half-truth will suffice. Howard can admit
he is unable to cast a spell to return her to her former
home, and then suggest she seek out the help of the
former wizard from the tower. Thackery, you said you
knew the bard as a lad, perhaps he remembers you as
well."

"I believe he does," Howard said, "if you're the
same Thackery that once tutored Ewan and his brother."

"It appears to be somewhat of a family tradition,
false accusations being brought against us," Thackery
said.

"I'm sure you two will have a grand old time
swapping war stories," Ellen said a little waspishly.
"Can we get on with this?"

"There is a travel pack in the workroom," Thackery told Howard. "Make sure the bard puts the two

books that Jessica," he stumbled a bit over the name, which to his mind was not nearly as fitting as the one she was born with, "left on the table into it for her to take with her. Once he has left the tower contact me and I will seal it once more."

"Okay," Howard said. "I'll get in touch with Sebastian. I hate doing this to him but it's all going to be up to him whether this succeeds or fails."

"Howard, we will await your word," Thackery said "Gods grant good fortune to us all." The vision in the bowl faded.

* * * * *

When Sebastian heard voices in the room below the wizard's work room, he had serious misgivings about his choice of hiding places. The fireplace was small, the windows narrow, and there were no empty trunks or cupboards. He froze in place when he heard footsteps on the stairs, then breathed a quiet sigh of relief as the footsteps stopped and the voices rose in anger.

It looked as though Howard had been correct, the wizard's tower was warded against intruders. Sebastian counted himself very fortunate to be included among Jessica's friends. But he couldn't stay in the wizard's tower forever - sooner or later he'd have to leave and he was getting impatient for Howard to contact him again.

Really, that was the reason he was impatient, he wanted to get out of here. It wasn't that he wanted to talk with Howard some more. Even though he enjoyed talking with Howard very much. Sebastian sighed. It was too bad Howard lived in another realm.

He made a circuit of the room, snooping through bookcases and examining some of odd objects on the tables and shelves. Standing in front of the fire place, he looked up at the portrait hanging there. Except for the colour of the hair, it could be Jessica's image he was looking at. Taking a step closer, he read the name on the brass plaque.

"Farenalyssia," he mused. "An unusual name to be sure. At least in these parts. But there is a land where names such as this are common . . . if only I could remember where."

Why was there a portrait of a woman who was obviously a close relative of Jessica's hanging in the wizard's tower? She must have been someone special to the wizard Thackery, but what?

"Sebastian, are you awake?" Howard's disembodied voice asked. There may have been just a thread of disappointment in the voice. Because of the wards on the tower he was unable to use the scrying bowl to get a visual on the bard.

"Aye," Sebastian answered. "I do not think sleep is possible in this place."

"I'm sorry you've become embroiled in our troubles," Howard said. "And I understand if you -"

"Nay, cease your apologies," the bard shook his head. "I am here of my own free will. Now tell me you have thought of a way I may be of some help releasing our friend Jessica. I would not see the lowest of creatures in Ewan's hands for long, never mind a friend."

Howard's relief was almost palpable. "Great. Because I have a plan, but a lot of it depends on you. Now, how much do you know about alchemy?"

* * * * *

Several hours later, Sebastian sat at the work table, three small stoppered bottles in front of him.

"You're sure you remember which is which?" Howard asked.

"Yes, I'm sure!" Sebastian snapped.

"I'm sorry, I'm sorry. But so much could go wrong and Jessica's not the only one I'm worried about here."

"I thank you, my friend, but your plan is a good one." He stifled a yawn.

"Okay then," Howard said. "Now I think you need to get some sleep."

"I'm fine," Sebastian insisted. "The sooner we start this the sooner it can be ended."

"By my calculations it's midday there. Not the best time to go skulking about the castle."

"Which makes it the perfect time. No one will expect-" He broke off suddenly, listening hard.

"What is it?" Howard asked, voice lowered.

"I think someone is coming."

Sebastian glanced quickly around for a weapon of some sort. All he could see was the knife he'd been using for cutting up herbs on the worktable. It was small, but sharp, and better than nothing. The footsteps on the stairs stopped and the door silently opened.

"Gareth!"

The squire looked like he'd aged overnight. His eyes were red-rimmed with dark circles under them, and his hair and clothing were dishevelled. "Now that Ewan is king he has no need for a squire. I have been dismissed. Not that I could have borne to remain in his service after what has happened."

"I am sorry, my friend," Sebastian said quietly.

"I wish to help in the rescue of Lady Jessica from the dungeon. You *are* planning on rescuing her, are you not?"

"Well, I-"

"T'would be best if we moved tonight. Ewan has sent for more of the guards that are resistant to magic as well as a priest known for his ability to strip the magic from a sorcerer. They will be arriving on the morrow."

"All right," Sebastian said, thinking fast. "The first thing we need to do is get a change of clothing to her -"

"Tis being done as we speak." Gareth almost cracked a smile at Sebastian's look of surprise. "Think you to be her only friend?"

"All right, then here's what else we need." Sebastian explained Howard's plan as best he could, taking full credit for it to preserve the anonymity of the wizards in the other realms. The former squire added a few suggestions that improved their chances for success greatly.

"Twill have to be well timed," Gareth said with a frown. "But if we wait until the Prince, I mean King, retires for the evening it will improve our chances greatly."

"Agreed. Now take these," Sebastian handed him two of the vials, "and I'll see you after the sun has set."

"You can count on me," Gareth said, and slipped out the door.

When Sebastian could no longer hear his footsteps on the stairs he pulled Jessica's amulet out of his pocket again.

"Friend Howard, are you there?"

"Still here, Sebastian. I won't ask if you can trust the kid, he wouldn't have been able to breech the wards if you couldn't, but what about the others?"

"There is a blood debt between the others and Jessica. This is not something to be taken lightly."

"Okay then. Why don't you get some sleep - maybe I will too, and we'll talk again later."

"Wait!" Sebastian held up his hand, even though Howard wasn't there to see it. "There is a portrait above the fireplace in here, a beautiful woman named Farenalyssia."

"Okay," Howard said, drawing out the word. "I'm sorry, but I can't see into the tower because of the wards. Is there something special about this portrait?"

"Only in her resemblance to Jessica. They could be sisters. Or maybe mother and daughter?"

There was a distinct pause. "It's not my story to tell," Howard said, voice laced with regret. "But I can promise you as soon as I'm able I will tell you everything."

"I will hold you to that promise, my friend."

Chapter Twenty-Nine

J essica woke with a start, unable to believe she'd actually dropped off to sleep. But how long had she slept - a few minutes, a few hours? She had no way of knowing. A dim outline of light showed where the door to her cell was, but other than that the blackness was unrelenting. If she ever got out of this it would be with a serious case of claustrophobia.

It was cold and damp in the cell, and the dress she was wearing was designed for elegance, not warmth. She was freezing, especially her feet. Whatever was used in the walls to keep her magic suppressed apparently kept vermin out as well. So while she may feel weak and nauseous, at least she didn't have to worry about rats and the like.

Again there was a noise outside her cell, muffled by the thick door. It sounded like voices raised in an argument. She scrambled to her feet at the sound of a key scraping in the lock.

"Think thee I like this any better?"

It was a woman's voice. A very familiar woman's voice.

"Eleanor?" Jessica asked, her voice raspy.

"You say this order comes from his majesty?" one of the guards was asking, a frown on his face.

"How dost *thee* think it would look were the prisoner be executed in the finery given her by his majesty? Now stand aside, ye great oaf. And hand over that torch, I'll need to see what I'm about."

The door opened a little wider to show Eleanor, torch in hand and a bundle under her arm. "T'will take no more than half a candlemark," she told the guards, who stood aside to let her in.

"Oh, my lady," Eleanor said, once the door was shut behind her. The flickering torch was more than enough to light up the small space.

Jessica could only imagine how bedraggled she was looking. "Eleanor? What are you doing here?"

Eleanor sat the torch in a sconce near the door and began untying her bundle. "We've little time, my lady. I've brought thee a change of clothing."

"To be executed in," Jessica said dully. The pleasure at seeing a familiar face dimmed in the face of what she'd heard Eleanor tell the guards.

"Nay, my lady. That was only for the guard's benefit. Ewan knows not that I am here."

"But why -"

"Turn around," Eleanor ordered. Jessica did as she was told and the maid wasted no time in loosening the lacing at the back of the dress.

"Why would you take such a stupid risk?" Jessica asked, fatigue making her more blunt than she realized. "Don't you realize what they say I've done?"

"Think thee I believe any of that foolishness? A poor maid I'd be did I not know my lady better than that. Thou had no more to do with the king's demise than I."

"Oh, Eleanor." Jessica felt tears pricking at her eyes.

The heavily embroidered bejewelled overdress fell to the floor, the silvery under dress soon following.

"I can't believe you'd risk so much to bring me a change of clothing. But thank you, you have no idea what this means to me." If she was going to die, she'd much rather do it in her own clothes.

"'Tis a small comfort I can give thee in such a place," Eleanor replied briskly, hiding her own emotion as she helped Jessica dress. "You've more friends than you realize, my lady, and all wish a part in securing your freedom."

"No, I don't want anyone putting themselves at risk for me." For the first time since she'd arrived in this world, Jessica truly appreciated having someone help her get dressed.

"Whisht, my lady. Do not fash thyself. Save thy strength."

Before Jessica could protest any further, Eleanor had her dressed in close fitting brown leather pants and a billowy white shirt, with a black leather jerkin laced over top. For her feet were . . .

"My boots!" Jessica exclaimed. "How on earth -"

"Really, my lady. The hows and whys matter not. Know only that thou will not languish here for long, but I dare not tell thee our plan."

"But -"

There was a rattle at the door and Eleanor quickly bundled up the clothing Jessica had been wearing. "Take heart, my lady," she whispered.

"Torch," one of the guards told Eleanor as she tried to sweep past them. She huffed in exasperation but obediently went back and pulled the torch from the sconce, darting an apologetic glance at Jessica.

The door slammed shut again, leaving Jessica in the dark once more. This time the darkness didn't seem so absolute. This time she had a glimmer of hope.

* * * * *

"Damn him, will he ne'er go to sleep this night?" Sebastian muttered. He, Gareth and Wendel were concealed near the new king's tower, waiting for Ewan to retire.

Wendel had been found lurking near the wizard's tower by Gareth, who brought him to Sebastian. He'd been on the road when word of the king's death, and Jessica's arrest, reached him and he turned back to see if there was some way he could help her, as she'd helped him.

"Wait, there's something happening," Wendel said.

They watched a small group approach the tower. Unlike the wizard's tower, which was tall, slender and stately, this tower was short and squat, giving it an ominous look. The group resolved itself into a pair of young women in what appeared to be their nightclothes, with a pair of guards both in front and behind them.

"'Tis the lady Margaret, and her friend lady Charity," Gareth said. "But what . . ."

He stopped mid-sentence as one of the girls made a break for it and was unceremoniously dragged back into place by one of the guards. When the small group reached the top of the stairs outside the tower, one of the lead guards rapped sharply on the door. It opened and they stood aside as the rear guards pushed the girls forward. When the door shut behind them, one pair of guards stationed themselves on either side of it, the other pair retreated to the bottom of the stairs.

"Lady Margaret is newly betrothed," Gareth said quietly. "And Lady Charity was to leave for the convent next week. I cannot believe I was in service to someone so . . . so . . ."

"Evil?" Sebastian suggested.

"For a time he seemed of better character. I

would hear things, but could not credit them when I was with him."

"It's my fault," Wendel said unhappily. "I was the one who gave him the amulet."

They both looked at him. "What amulet?"

"The amulet of Athelon. His highness may eschew magicians, but he's not above using magical tools."

"What's the amulet of Althelon?" Sebastian asked carefully. "And how did you happen to give it to Ewan?"

Wendel heaved a sigh. "When I first came to Ghren I plied my trade from a small cart. Mostly I sold amulets and such. Charms for good luck, protections against evil, that sort of thing. Harmless, really. But Prince Ewan did not see it that way. His guards overturned my cart and he was attracted to the box the amulet was in. Once he knew what it could do . . ."

"What exactly *does* the amulet do?"

"It, uh, enhances one's natural ability to make friends."

"You mean he uses it to make people like him."

"Well, yes. It doesn't work on everyone, and it tends to cloud the minds of some."

"It would take more than an amulet to convince me Ewan was a friend," Sebastian muttered. "Tell me, Wendel. Now that Gareth knows the truth, will the amulet still be effective on him?"

"Nay." Wendel shock his head vigorously. "It will no longer hold any sway over him."

"Good!" Gareth said vehemently.

"If I may be so bold," Wendel ventured. "His majesty appears to be occupied for the time being. Perhaps this would be a good time to set our plan in motion."

"Perhaps you're right," Sebastian agreed. "The sooner we're out of Ghren, the better for all of us."

* * * * *

Ellen paced back and forth in Howard's work room, pausing every so often to peer into the scrying bowl. Howard was getting a great deal better with the scrying, able to hold the image for much longer periods of time.

More than anything she wished she could catch a glimpse of Jessica. They'd been able to follow Eleanor when she brought Jessica a change of clothing, but as soon as she crossed the threshold into Jessica's cell, the image went blank.

"It's like some kind of anti-magic," Howard said with a shudder. "The whole cell is covered in it. I can only guess what it's doing to Jess."

They watched in silence as the guards took the two girls to Ewan, knowing what was in store for them.

"Jeez Louise, you really know how to pick 'em,

Jess," Ellen muttered under her breath. "Oh, look. It looks like the guys are finally going to get this show on the road."

"Good," Howard said. "I really hate this waiting."

* * * * *

"Now remember," Gareth said. "You have to make sure each of the guards gets at least a drink of the wine or a bite of food."

They decided the best way to make sure the guards received the potion Sebastian had made was through food or drink. Kieran's mother, being one of the cooks in the castle, put together a tray that would tempt even the staunchest of guards.

"Will it kill them?" Kieran asked, wide-eyed. The splint on his leg had been removed and he was dressed in one of his brother's old uniforms.

"No, nothing like that," Sebastian hastened to assure him. "Just put them to sleep for a few hours."

"Oh," the boy said in a disappointed voice.

"Too bad," his brother Addison added.

"All right, let's go."

Gareth went with the boys as far as the dungeon entrance while Sebastian waited out of sight in the alcove.

"Do you remember what else you need to do?" Gareth whispered as the two erstwhile pages prepared to go on without him.

Addison nodded. "Count the number of guards."

"Good. Off you go then."

He watched until the boys disappeared through the door at the foot of the stairs, then went back to get Sebastian.

* * * * *

The dishes on the tray Addison was carrying rattled ever so slightly as he and his brother made their way down into the dungeon.

"Halt!" a voice boomed out at them. "State your business."

There was an audible gulp from Addison, who then lost his voice altogether as a giant of a guard loomed up out of the darkness.

"We was told to bring ye food and drink," Kieran piped up. "We was sent direct from the kitchen."

"It's about time," the guard grumbled, turning and leading them to the guard room.

There were four guards in the room, three of whom were already sitting at the table.

"Ye be late," one of them snapped.

"We be sorry sir," Kieran said quickly. "Trouble in the kitchen. The spit turner was caught with the -"

"We don't care. Just serve us up and be quick about it."

"Aye, sir." Kieran set his tray down and then began unloading fragrant dishes from the tray Addison was holding.

"What's this?" one of the guards asked, taking a suspicious sniff at one of the bottles on the tray.

"Tis from His Highness," Kieran told him. "T'was his wish ye drink in his honour."

"A drink to the king, eh? Wouldn't want to defy the king. Now be off with ye."

"Beggin' your pardon sir, but we was to make sure everyone was seen to. Be this all of ye?"

"Alfrec and Stead be guardin' the prisoner. They'll eat later."

"By your leave sir, His Highness was most insistent that drinks were had."

"Fine, fine," the guard wave a hand at the hallway to the right. "Take 'em a bottle, but hurry up."

"Thank you sir!" Kieran quickly plucked up one of the bottles and a pair of goblets and hurried down the hall. He struggled with the heavy door at the end, but managed to get through it without losing his grip the things he was carrying.

His steps slowed as he neared the two guards. Unlike the other guards, these two were taller and beefier. They weren't dressed in the palace uniform, but all in black. They must be the mercenaries the new king had hired to help keep the peace.

Kieran stared at them in awe. "Is it true that magic doesn't work on you?" he asked, then blushed and quickly ducked his head.

"What do you want?"

"I-I-I brought ye refreshment. From the King. To drink in his honour."

"Huh," the guard grunted. "Fine. Hand it over."

"Begging your pardon sir, but tis my duty to serve thee."

Before the guards could protest, he passed them each a goblet and filled them with the fine wine. One of the guards sniffed it, then took a cautious sip before tossing back the whole thing. The other one followed suit. Kieran breathed a quiet sigh of relief.

"Hold on, boy." A heavy hand descended on his shoulder as he turned to leave.

Kieran froze. His heart was in his mouth, choking him until he couldn't breathe.

"Leave the bottle," the guard told him.

"Aye, sir!" he squeaked, passing him the bottle. He scuttled back down the hall to the guardroom.

"What be this one's problem," one of the guards asked, with a nod towards Addison who looked like he was about to faint.

"He be addled in the head, sir," Kieran said quickly. "He may'nt be very bright, but he's a fair hand at fetching and carrying. Be there anything else ye need?"

"Nay, off with ye," the guard waved them away.

Kieran nudged his brother and nodded at the empty trays. Addison gave a start and then picked up the trays and followed his brother out of the guard room. By the time they made it back to where Gareth was waiting for them, Addison had recovered some of his aplomb.

"Why'd you tell them I was addle-pated?" he demanded.

"It were better than telling 'em the truth, that you were like to wet yourself from fear."

Addison stopped and glared at his brother. "I was not!"

"Enough of that," Gareth told them. "Hurry up. We don't have a lot of time."

They joined Sebastian in the alcove. "Well done boys," he said. "Now off with you to your parents. Make sure the wagon's ready."

They raced away and he turned to Gareth. "I sent Wendel to watch the prince - I mean the king's quarters."

Gareth nodded. "'Tis well you did. His majesty is not one who is able to tarry at that sort of business, if you take my meaning."

Sebastian smothered a chuckle. "I do indeed. I may have to write a ballad about him some day."

They shared a grin at the thought.

"I think our friends in the guard room have had time to finish their meal. Time to rescue our lady." Sebastian pulled a dark homespun robe over his clothing, using a coarse rope as a belt. "How do I look?"

"Like someone pretending to be a monk," Gareth told him. "No monk would ever have hair of your length."

Sebastian reached into the bag at his feet and pulled out a long-tailed hood. Pulling it over his head he made a few minor adjustments before turning to Gareth again. "Is this more seemly?"

"Aye, you'd fool even the king himself, so long as the hood's pulled low."

"Right then, take this and see to the horses," Sebastian handed him the last vial, "and we'll meet at the stables."

"God speed to thee," Gareth said.

Chapter Thirty

S ebastian picked up the bag and moved in what he hoped was a priestly fashion towards the dungeon. He passed a serving man and two giggling maids along the way, but they didn't seem to question his presence. Taking a deep breath, he opened the door to the guard room.

His breath whooshed out again in a sigh of relief. The guards were slumped over the table, deep asleep. In a moment he was across the room and opening the door to the corridor where the cells treated with witch binding were. Two more guards slumped to the ground on either side of a door about halfway down the corridor.

They were mercenaries, he could tell by their clothing. And they were huge. It took considerable effort to roll them over so he could search for the keys the cell. Finally he found the key ring and began trying keys in the lock. It seemed to take forever - if he was found here there'd be two burnings at the stake.

At last the lock turned and he opened the door.

"My lady?" he said tentatively into the darkness. "Jessica?"

There was a moan from inside. There was also a moan from outside - one of the guards stirred. Sebastian cursed under his breath. This was something they hadn't counted on, that the mercenaries who were resistant to magic would also be resistant to their potion.

From the light of the torch just outside the cell he was just able to see where Jessica was slumped against the wall. The witch binding must be more powerful than they'd realized, she hardly seemed aware of his presence.

Still cursing under his breath, Sebastian picked her up and carried her into the corridor, propping her up beside the door. Then, using a strength he didn't realize he possessed, he dragged the two burly guards into the cell, closing and locking the door.

"Jessica?" He knelt beside her.

"Sebastian?"

"I'm here to rescue you," he said. "But I'm going to need your help. Do you think you can stand?"

"I can if it means getting out of here," she said. With his help she managed to get to her feet.

"Are you able to walk?"

"I think so. That cell . . . whatever it's lined with is horrible. I could feel it leeching my energy. But I'm getting better every second I'm out of there."

"That's good," Sebastian said. "I do not know how I would explain one priest carrying another."

"Priests?" She took a good look at him. "Why are you dressed like a priest?"

"'Tis my disguise. And there is one for you as well." He pulled the second robe out of his bag and helped her pull it on over her clothing. "Now, we must hurry," he told her, pulling the hood down low over her face.

"Right, this is a jail break." Jessica seemed to be having a little trouble focusing.

He led her through the door at the end of the corridor and through the guard room beyond. "Stay close," he told her, and slowed his pace to avoid drawing attention to them. He could have saved himself the trouble.

"Ho, brother," called one of the castle guards on the door to the courtyard. "Where might thee be off to so late?"

Jessica staggered slightly as Sebastian stopped suddenly. They were so close! She could smell the night air and it smelled like freedom. To be stopped now . . . Although the effects of being in the cell were wearing off, she wasn't sure how far she'd be able to run if forced to. She certainly wasn't in any shape for a fight.

"Bless you my sons," Sebastian said, pitching his voice an octave lower than normal, "for keeping such vigilant watch o'er the castle. My good brother here hath imbibed too much wine this eve and I but take him for an airing."

"A man of the cloth ought to know better."

"Aye, that he should. And rest assured he will be taken to task for his actions. Once we have him sobered up."

"I'd recommend a dunking in the river," the second guard on the door said.

"A most clever idea. Thank you, my son."

The guards stepped aside and Jessica held back her breath of relief until they were well past them.

"I think that shaved years off my life," Sebastian said.

"Mine, too." she agreed. "Now what?"

"Now we meet up with the others at the stable."

Jessica was too tired to ask questions, trusting that Sebastian had a plan to get them away from the castle. She just hoped it didn't involve her riding side saddle again. There was no way she'd be able to stay on a horse in this condition.

Just outside of the stables a large wagon piled high with household goods stood waiting, a team of oxen hitched to it.

"What's this?" Jessica whispered to Sebastian.

"This, my lady, is how we're going to get you out of here."

Before Sebastian could say anything else, the small group of people that had been waiting just inside the stable doors converged upon them. Kieran, his father Reece, his mother Meren, Eleanor, Gareth, and even Wendel, all crowded around.

Tears pricked at Jessica's eyes. "I can't believe you all came here to say goodbye."

"We're not just here to say farewell, my lady," Gareth told her. "We're helping you escape."

"No, you can't," Jessica protested, looking at each of them in turn. "It's much too dangerous. If -"

"Psht, milady," Eleanor said. "'Tis no more dangerous than remaining behind."

"But . . . all of you?"

"I suggest less talking and more moving," Sebastian said, pulling off the monk's robe. "Luck has been with us thus far. We should not press it unduly."

"I finished making the charms," Wendel said. He passed one to Eleanor, one to Gareth, and one to Meren.

Gareth made a face as he accepted his. "I like not this part of the plan."

"You're the only one the right size," Wendel told him. "The bard is too tall and I'm too stout."

With a sigh, Gareth placed the charm around his neck. The air around him shimmered and he suddenly took on the appearance of a red-headed woman dressed in men's clothing. Eleanor and Meren donned their charms as well but the only thing that changed on them was their hair colour, which also turned red.

"That's amazing!" Jessica said.

"'Tis naught but a small glamour," Wendel said, preening. "'Twill only last a handful of days."

"So . . . what's the plan?" Jessica was feeling a little overwhelmed at the thought of these people putting themselves in danger for her. They'd already risked so much just getting her out of the dungeon.

"The plan is to get you safely away from Castle Ghren. While you travel southwards with Reece and his family in the wagon, Wendel and Eleanor will be travelling west by cart," he gestured to where the wizard's cart was hidden beside the mammoth wagon, "and the lovely Gareth and I will be travelling east by horseback."

"The guards'll be lookin' for a red haired wench," Reece said, "and they'll be finding one all right, but not the right one."

"But . . . you can't uproot your entire family because of me," Jessica protested. "If you do this there'll be no coming back."

Reece spat in the dust. "Ain't nothing to be coming back to. Me and the missus has been wanting to leave for years. A good tanner is welcome 'most any place."

"Truly, my lady," Meren assured her. "I've been uneasy in Ghren since Kieran was born."

"I don't know what to say."

"Save the speeches for when we all meet up again in Vargon's Reach," Sebastian told her. "Into the wagon with you."

"Addison and me, we hollowed out a real good hidey hole for you," Kieran told her shyly. "An Gareth let us poison the stable hands and the guards."

"We didn't poison them," Gareth said irritably. "It was a sleeping potion."

Jessica grinned, overwhelmed with gratitude. "You guys are the best."

"Tis but a few hours to dawn," Sebastian said as he helped her into the wagon. There was a hollowed out center to the massive pile and she wriggled her way into the close fitting space. "We'll leave by different gates."

"Godspeed to us all," Eleanor said.

* * * * *

"The safest route would be for them to make for the Narrows Outpost and then take the channel all the way to Lake Mur. Then travel over-land from there," Thackery said.

"It's also the most obvious route," Paranithel insisted. "Ewan's men would be upon them before they even reached Kantor."

"What if they went from Vargon's Reach to Fort Meirsling, then crossed the channel to Fort Canron?" Howard suggested, studying the great map spread out in front of him. The two wizards had decided a third pair of eyes might help break the deadlock and had magicked a copy of their map to appear for him.

Thackery shook his head. "Canron is in the Kingdom of Nefron. Thieves and barbarians, the lot of
them."

Ellen sighed and took another sip of her cap-
puccino. They'd been well into arguing about possible
routes since before she arrived, and she'd been there
for two hours. Setting her mug down, she peered over
Howard's shoulder.

"If they could reach the Narrows Outpost they
could find a ship to take them south," Paran mused.

"Nay! It would take them months to reach the
south by ship. In any case they would not reach port
before storm season would be upon them."

"What if they go east around the Shadow Mountains and down through the Kingdom of Waldon?"
Ellen suggested.

"I mislike the idea of Jesseminathus being east of
the protection from the Shadow Mountains," Paran
said slowly. "But the idea has merit."

"She should be safe enough provided she works
no magic," Thackery agreed.

"Indeed, but do you think this would be possible,
or even safe? It would be only natural for her to want
to experiment with her power. And if, as I suspect,
she is able to draw power from the energy around
her, it would be more dangerous if she let it build up
inside her."

"Why can't she work magic?" Ellen wanted to
know.

The two wizards looked at each other. "When last we had word of Anakaron, he was on Raquii Island in the Siren's Sea. The Shadow Mountains provide a . . . buffer if you will."

"Okay, hold on just a minute." Ellen held up a hand. "Who the hell is Anakaron and why does there need to be a buffer between him and Jessica?"

"Well?" Her glare took in all three wizards. Howard edged away and she had the feeling she wasn't going to like what they had to say. "Somebody start talking."

"Anakaron is my greatest enemy," Thackery said quietly. "He is a blood sorcerer of immense power and was responsible for the death of Jessica's mother."

"And you think he'll be after Jessica?" she asked. She rounded on Howard. "Did you know about this?"

"I knew Thackery had an enemy," he stammered, backing away another step.

"Anakaron searches always for those of great power," Paran said. "Those he cannot subvert to his ways he destroys."

"Oh, this is just great!" Ellen paced away from the table and then back again. "It's bad enough you guys zapped her into a world she's totally unprepared for, but now you're telling me she's got some kind of evil super wizard after her?"

"Ellen -"

She cut Howard off. "You need to bring her back here, right now."

"It's not that simple," Howard started.

"Maybe not for you, but I bet it'd be real simple for them." She nodded towards the scrying bowl.

"She does not belong in your world," Thackery said stiffly. "And we are fully able to protect her."

"Yeah, once she gets to you. And how long is that going to take? I've seen the map. It's going to take months for her to reach you, no matter which route she takes." She glared down into the bowl at Thackery and he glared right back.

"Enough!" Paran said. "It is too dangerous to send Jesseminathus back to you. Anakaron has ways of knowing when excessive magic has been used. He would know instantly were we to create a portal between our worlds."

Ellen felt like hitting something. As if he could read her thoughts, Howard stayed out of her reach. She took a deep breath and let it out slowly.

"Tell me something," she said. "Let's just say that Jessica makes it all the way to your little Hogwarts in the south and you tell her who she really is and why she was raised by strangers. If she still wants to come back home, will you send her back to us?"

"Yes," said Paran. Thackery glared at him. "If that is truly her wish, then we will."

"All right. Then I suggest you guys work out the quickest route possible."

She wasn't happy about it, but she was at least willing to accept that it was too dangerous to send Jessica back at the moment.

"May I ask a question?" Paranithel asked.

Ellen nodded. "All right."

"What's a Hogwarts?"

Chapter Thirty-One

S ebastian and Gareth, riding a pair of geldings, left by the east gate at dawn. Gareth was still grumbling about having to wear the charm that made him look like a woman. An hour later, Wendel and Eleanor left by the west gate in a cart pulled by his faithful mule, Alphonse. Last to leave was the ox drawn wagon. With its heavy load of household goods and people it was the slowest moving. It left by the south gate, taking the most direct route to Vargon's Reach.

The first day out they were passed twice by guardsmen from the castle and although they would slow as they passed Meren with her charmed red hair, they continued on without comment. Late in the second day they were stopped by a squadron of guards.

"Hold the wagon," one of the guards called. Through a trick of acoustics, Jessica could hear them quite clearly from her hiding place.

"Prithee why be ye stopping an honest man and his family," Reece asked.

"Ye come from the direction of Ghren," the guard began.

"Aye. We'd be there still but for my brother. Broke his leg and can't manage the farm his own self. Nothing for it but to go Vargon's Reach t' help him out. What's this all about?"

"A dangerous criminal escaped from the castle dungeon—"

"How dangerous?" Meren squeaked. Jessica could picture her pulling the boys closer. "Why ain't ye searching for him instead of stopping ordinary folk?"

"It's a woman, mistress, not a man. And she has red hair, like yours —"

"And think ye I be this criminal?" Meren's voice rose. "Ye think I've time to be out committin' crimes with a household ta run and these two to chase after?"

"No, mistress," the guard said hastily. "We just be warning ye to keep a look out."

"We thank thee for thy warning," Reece said.

"Ye cannot mean to leave us out here alone with a dangerous criminal about!" Meren exclaimed. "Surely ye'll be escorting us to Vargon's Reach."

Jessica held her breath. What was Meren up to?

"Nay, mistress. The new king would have our hides were we to delay our search."

"But —"

"I think you have little to fear on this road. She was last seen heading east under the protection of a minstrel."

"Good hunting to ye," Reece said. "And Godspeed."

"I'll not feel safe again until we reach the town," Meren said loudly. "See if you can coax these beasties into moving a little faster."

There was a lurch as the wagon began moving again. Jessica heard the faint sound of the guards galloping off to continue their search and breathed a sigh of relief.

She was grateful when they finally stopped that night. The effects of the witch binding had completely worn off and she was starting to feel stifled in her hiding place. The next morning she broached the subject of walking alongside the wagon with the boys.

Reece thought about it for a moment. "Mayhap if we run into no one else from the castle by midday it would be safe enough," he agreed.

Her tiny crawl space was making her claustrophobic so she was very grateful when midday arrived and they were alone on the road. Meren gave up her seat on the wagon to Kieran, deciding if walking was good enough for the Lady Jessica it was good enough for her.

"If it please you, my lady," Meren said, "What be it like in your kingdom?"

Jessica had to laugh. "I don't know where to start.

It's very different from Ghren, that's for sure."

She'd already given up on trying to get the woman to just call her Jessica. The concept of a country that was ruled by something other than a monarchy was too much for Meren. Lord only knew what she'd make of technology.

Fortunately, Addison provided a distraction as he came running up with a scrape on his elbow. Meren tisked and had Reece stop the wagon. Sending Kieran off to collect a handful of white flowers from the field beside the road, she kept a firm grip on Addison's arm while she sluiced the dirt out of the scrape with some water. When Kieran returned she crushed the flowers in her hand and then rubbed them over the wound.

"There," she said. "That'll keep ye until we stop for the night."

"Ye lads both ride up here with me," Reece said. "It'll keep ye out of trouble."

Jessica chuckled at their protests as he started up the wagon again. Meren shook her head and sighed, wiping the residue from the plants on her skirt.

"I was a fair herb-wife afore I got married," she said. "'Tis something that stays with you always."

"I love plants," Jessica said. "I grow - grew - a lot of my own herbs. I've done a lot of research on herb-al remedies, but I haven't had much practical experience."

That was all the incentive Meren needed. They

spent the rest of the afternoon talking about the medicinal qualities of plants and bonding over their love of herbal medicine. There were a few similarities, but most of the plants Meren described Jessica had never heard of.

When they stopped for the night, Meren had Kieran fetch her bag of necessaries from the wagon. She searched it by feel and pulled out a slim, leather bound book.

"I started this when I first apprenticed to Old Meg, the midwife of my village." She passed it over to Jessica who opened it up and started leafing through it.

"This is beautiful!"

The pages were filled with rows of neat handwriting, along with painstakingly drawn illustrations of plants. The medicinal quality of each plant was carefully listed, along with recipes for combining them for different remedies.

"I want thee to have it," Meren said.

Jessica looked up, eyes wide. "I couldn't! This is far too valuable. And with two active boys I'm sure you'll need it yourself." She tried to pass it back but Meren refused to take it.

"I haven't opened it in years," Meren said. "All I need is up here." She tapped her head.

"I don't know what to say."

"Thank you will do nicely."

Jessica grinned. "Thank you."

For the remainder of the journey to Vargon's Reach, Meren continued to teach Jessica everything she knew of herb-craft.

"Herb-craft is a respectable trade, even for a lady," Meren insisted.

* * * * *

Vargon's Reach was a market town. Instead of walls it was surrounded by pens for livestock. Just inside this ring was one of buildings - permanent shops, inns and taverns. At the centre of the town was a giant marketplace.

Sebastian had suggested they meet at the Rusty Lion, an inn run by friends of his, and they found it with little trouble. It was still early in the day when they arrived and Reece gave Addison and Kieran each a few coins, and off they sped to the marketplace.

Jessica would have liked to check out the marketplace herself, but it was decided it would be best if she kept to her room. The fewer people who saw her, the less danger there would be.

Now she had nothing to do but wait. With any luck, this time next week she'd be safely back at home.

The Rusty Lion boasted three private dining rooms and the travellers met in one of them.

"I can't thank you enough," Jessica told her friends. "All of you. You all risked so much to help me - I can never repay you."

Standing at the back of the group, Addison winked at her. Jessica nodded her head at him, but held back her grin. Even as sick and confused as she was when Sebastian rescued her from her cell in the dungeon, she'd managed to hang onto the band from the headdress she'd worn to the fateful banquet. It had been overlooked in the dark when Eleanor had been helping her change.

The jewels in it would be more than enough to give Reece and his family a new start. Addison had caught her hiding it in the wagon and hounded her until she told him what she was doing. She was going to leave a note for his parents and he'd begged to hold it for her. He promised faithfully he'd wait until they'd been on the road for two days before giving it to them.

"Have you decided where you're going?" Sebastian asked Reece.

"Aye, we be headed east, to the mountains. Meren has kinfolk there that would welcome a tanner."

"How about you, Wendel?" Jessica asked.

"The mountain folk look much kinder on magic workers, perhaps I'll travel that way for a bit, maybe even cross the mountains."

"And you, my lady," Eleanor said with a sniffle. "Whither whilst thou go?"

"I'll be going to the nearest Well, and then home," Jessica said, with more confidence than she felt. Every time she'd asked Howard about the particulars of getting her home he'd dodged her questions.

"Then I'm thinking this be goodbye," Meren said quietly.

There was much hugging and more than a few tears shed, especially on Eleanor's part. Meren was busy dabbing at her own eyes with her apron, so Eleanor ended up crying on the hapless Wendel's shoulder. He patted her back awkwardly, looking distinctly uncomfortable.

"Remember, if thee changes thy mind, we be here for the next three days," Reece said gruffly.

Jessica thanked them all again and escaped up to her room before she started crying as well. She was going to miss them all.

There wasn't much to pack - she was wearing her beloved boots, only slightly the worse for wear, and she was carrying the sword. In the pack from the wizard's tower there were the spell books from the tower and the book of herbs from Meren. It was her hope that she'd be able to bring them with her when she crossed over.

She was just about to contact Howard when there was knock on her door and Sebastian entered.

"Gareth is seeing to the horses," he told her. He and the former squire were going to accompany her to the nearest Well.

"Good. I found out there's a Well not half a day's ride from here."

"That's one of the reason I chose Vargon's Reach as our meeting place."

"You've been such an amazing friend, Sebastian. I don't know what I would have done without you."

"Languished in prison long before the king was killed, no doubt," said a disembodied voice.

"Very funny Howard."

"I would wish I could go with you," Sebastian, "but such wishes are not for the likes of me."

"I wish I could take you with me, but I'm not even sure of the magic to get me back home, let alone to bring anyone with me. Speaking of which . . ." she paused to fish the amulet from her shirt. "Just how is this supposed to work? I just suck up power from the Well and send it to you? Or do I do some kind of spell at the same time as you? This is all pretty new to me, Howard."

"Jessica . . ." Howard stopped and then started again. "The thing is, Jess, I'm still pretty new at this too. Yeah, I've studied magic all my life, but I haven't really moved past the academic aspects of it. You know what our world is like, very little pure magic."

"But-"

"Sending you into another dimension was a fluke, something I'm not sure I could ever do again."

Jessica sat down. "Are you saying you can't bring me home?" she asked in a small voice.

"No, I'm saying I don't have the power. And before you say it," he said as though he could see her mouth open to argue, "no, you can't just send the power to me. The truth of the matter is, I don't know how I sent you there, and until I figure it out I can't bring you back."

"So I'm stuck here forever?"

"No. You're like Dorothy in the *Wizard of Oz*. You have the power to send yourself home, you just have to figure out how. You need to find someone who can teach you to use your gift. Someone on your side of the rainbow."

"Thackery," Sebastian said suddenly.

"Who?" Jessica asked, turning to him.

"The wizard who once dwelt within the tower at Ghren. I've heard he has a school of magic to the south."

"How far south?"

"He sounds perfect, Jess," Howard said. "He'd be able to teach you what I can't."

"But-"

"Don't forget, you're in the land of 'might makes right' now. And when it comes to 'might' you've got it in spades. We have no way of knowing who we can trust - someone could exploit you, or somehow steal your power."

"So what makes you think we can trust this Thackery person?"

Sebastian flashed back to the portrait hanging in the wizard's tower, but kept his mouth shut.

"I've felt his magic, Jess. You know, in the tower.

I could get a feel for the man and I believe he's trustworthy," Howard told her.

"As well he would have no love of Ghren, so you have that in common," Sebastian pointed out, when she didn't look convinced.

"All right, all right!" Jessica threw up her hands in defeat. "I'll go south to Thackery's magic school. But I don't see any yellow brick roads anywhere."

"What?" Howard and Sebastian asked in unison.

"If I'm off to see the wizard, don't I need to follow the yellow brick road?"

About the Author

Residing in Cobourg, Ontario, Carol has always had a love of reading and writing. She grew up reading Edgar Rice Burroughs and Robert E. Howard so it's no wonder her first love is fantasy, followed closely by science fiction.

She always believed she was meant to be a writer of short stories, however her stories tended to be rather long. They also tended to have a romantic thread running through them. Finally caving in to the inevitable, she embraced her genre and began writing novels of fantasy/science fiction adventure with a dash of romance thrown into the mix. She has never regretted it.

Today she writes a variety of prose: non-fiction, flash fiction, short stories, and novels – in a variety of genres: humour, horror, contemporary, romance, science fiction, and fantasy. She's also a prolific poet.

Visit Carol on her blog at: http://www.random-writerlythoughts.blogpot.com She can also be found as Carol R. Ward on Facebook and CarolRWard on Twitter.

Other Books by the Author

An Elemental Wind

An Elemental Fire